Surrounded by a legion of the dead . . .

Conan held his formidable sword in a two-handed grip, swinging it as if he were a crazed woodcutter. Its keen edge sheared through brittle shields and awkward parries, through ribs and vertebrae. Twice he was nicked from behind, and he spun as he fought. It was as if he rode upon a madman's carousel of carnage, each slash threatening to upset his tenuous balance and hurl him to the ground, where the blades of his foes would sink into his vitals and send him howling into the pits of hell.

A red mist swam in spiraling currents before his; the frenzy of battle boiled in his veins and lent fury to his every stroke. For every spine he severed, he faced anew a slew of stabbing swordpoints. He bled from a score of wounds, the crimson flow mixing with the sweat that stung every cut, bringing pain that only further stoked the fire of his rage.

A warrior's blade slashed across his lower back, and he spun with a backhand swing that shattered rib bones . . . but the swing had been too fierce—Conan's knee twisted and he fell onto the hard sand of the desert. . . .

Conan Adventures by Tor Books

CONAN

AND THE GRIM GREY GOD

—— BY ——

SEAN A. MOORE

TOR
fantasy ®

A TOM DOHERTY ASSOCIATES BOOK
NEW YORK

CONAN AND THE GRIM GREY GOD

Cover art by Doug Beckman

A Tor Book
Published by Tom Doherty Associates, Inc.
175 Fifth Avenue
New York, NY 10010

Tor Books on the World Wide Web:
http://www.tor.com

Tor® is a registered trademark of Tom Doherty Associates, Inc.

ISBN: 0-812-55267-9

First Edition: November 1996

Printed in the United States of America

0 9 8 7 6 5 4 3 2 1

To Raven, with Love—
Past, Present, and Future

*Special thanks to
Catherine C. and L. Sprague de Camp,
keepers of the flame*

Contents

Prologue:
The Jackal of Acheron

For nineteen centuries, the Holy City of Nithia had stood unconquered. Would-be assailants faced a nine-day ride through arid dunes of sun-scorched sand. On foot, the trek would have been suicidal. Only thrice in the city's history had mounted armies actually crossed the desert to reach Nithia's towering walls of white marble and stand before the massive brass gate. Always had these beleaguered invaders been forced to depart, for siege was impossible in the barren Nithian desert. Water and food lay only within the city walls, where the legendary Seven Fountains of Ibis fed bounteous gardens and nourished the city's dwellers.

Today, neither desert nor barriers of brass and stone had protected the Holy City. The gate lay mangled upon the white marble streets, crumpled like parchment in the fist of a baleful god. Nearby, Nithia's hundred elite warriors sprawled lifelessly; blood from their ghastly wounds smeared the once-pristine pavement. Tracks from the bloodied boots and hooves of Nithia's conquerors painted a crimson path from the ruined gate to the center of the city—to the greatest temple in the known world.

The gate-crashers had swept through the streets like an inescapable wave of death. Every building had been searched, every man, woman, and child butchered. Two millennia of peace and isolation had rendered the benevolent Nithians incapable of resistance. None had been able to escape the doom, for the walls that had once protected them now imprisoned them. In a morning massacre, a few hundred ruthless raiders had turned the Holy City into a grisly tomb for some nine thousand worshipers of Ibis.

By midday, the anguished cries of the last victims dwindled to silence. The only sounds were the steady booming of an immense battering ram against the temple's marble door, the grunts of the men who swung it, and the harsh commands of their leader. He sat proudly atop his steed, his crooked smile turning his face into a diabolical mask. Smeared from beard to boot with blood and gore, his red-rimmed eyes blazing with baleful fire, he looked more like a devil than a man. He raised his four-foot blade of ebon steel and shouted angrily, eager to batter down this barrier and deal more death.

The sharp bark of his cruel voice was akin to that of a jackal, and in years past, those who whispered of his deeds had dubbed him the Jackal of Acheron. None dared to utter that name in his presence—for that matter, few would speak to him at all save at his request. Indeed, only the bravest of men dared to look him in the face. The Jackal had killed men on a whim if displeased with their tone of voice or if he perceived the slightest lack of respect.

His given name was Dhurkhan Blackblade, a name that filled the hearts of men with fear and hate. His brutish biceps were thicker than a strong man's calves; his shoulders rose above a tall man's head. And Blackblade's ability to intimidate was more than physical, for he was Supreme Warlord of the Army of Acheron and brother of the dreaded Xaltotun—the necromancer whose powers exceeded those of any twenty Stygian sorcerers.

Blackblade cursed and shook a mailed fist at his men, his voice like the crack of a whip. A soldier paused to wipe his sweat-drenched brow and, in the process, threw off the rhythm of the others. An instant later, the soldier's head flew from his shoulders in a scarlet spray. It thumped down the marble steps as Blackblade ordered another to take the dead man's place. Twenty backs bent anew to the task, muscles flexing, and the exertion wrung groans and grunts from the men. A glowing, bile-green nimbus surrounded the dark iron of the battering ram's head. Xaltotun himself had imbued the metal with mighty spells that had been the bane of many portals. Sparks flew from the metal as it struck stone, and the massive door shivered in its frame.

"Solnarus!" roared Blackblade, shaking red droplets from his sword. "Thy doom is at hand, cowardly herder of Ibis's mewling flock! The Grim Grey God shall be mine!"

His diabolical laughter echoed from the stones of the dead city, and the ensorceled ram boomed again.

Beyond the weakening marble portal, seven Nithians awaited their fate in the temple's inner sanctum. Six of them knelt calmly, each facing west as they chanted slowly in low, musical tones. Dove-grey satin robes, the simple ceremonial garb of the high priests of Ibis, covered the men from their shaven heads to their bare feet. Only their hands were exposed, palms pressed against the floor, fingertips pointing forward.

Behind them stood Solnarus, the Priest-King of Nithia. His flowing robe resembled those worn by the other priests, but he had cast back the cowl. His skin and garments were either white or the palest grey. Sunlight blazed through the temple's crystalline roof and bathed the Priest-King's serene face in a whiteness that some would have found unbearably bright.

Solnarus stared into the sun as if its warm brilliance nourished him. His skin was strangely light for a desert-dweller. His face and scalp were as smooth as a young man's, though nearly a century had passed since his birth—the Priest-Kings of Nithia descended from Atlantean kings, whose lifespans were thrice those of normal men's.

In Solnarus's eyes, a keen observer could see the wisdom of a century and more. The Priest-King's left iris blazed with a hue of blue so deep that it rivaled the azure of the sky. His right iris gleamed like polished amber. In a setting devoid of color, the Priest-King's contrasting eyes were at once startling and captivating.

Like the other priests, Solnarus chanted slowly and rhythmically. He raised his hands until his sleeves fell back to expose slender arms as pale as alabaster. He held a hollow globe of thin crystal in his fingers, a globe filled with fine white sand. Abruptly, he ceased his chanting.

"It is done," Solnarus sighed.

The six priests rose in a chorus of popping joints, straightening their bent backs and stiff knees. They did not seem weary, though they had knelt and chanted since dawn. They pulled back their cowls to reveal solemn faces and clasped their hands as they turned to face the Priest-King.

"The power of a god is within our reach," whispered a short, pudgy priest whose name was Milvius. He gazed despondently toward the center of the inner sanctum, at the only object in the entire temple. "Is it the will of Ibis that our people be shredded in the jaws of the Jackal?"

Five priests stepped away from Milvius, staring at him in open-mouthed astonishment. "Madness," one of them whispered.

Solnarus raised an eyebrow. "Perhaps it is not Ibis who condemns us, Milvius," he murmured. His bare feet shuffled across the floor as he walked toward the object of Milvius's attention. The Priest-King cradled his globe of sand as he stared morosely into the face of the Grim Grey God.

The statue had rested upon the floor of the temple for two millennia, the sole relic that linked the Nithians to their Atlantean ancestors. According to legend, the god had been artfully carved from a dull, silvery pearl twice the size of a man's head. Upon the marble floor it squatted toadlike, returning Solnarus's stare with its cold, graven eyes.

The Priest-King sighed and shook his head. "Ah, Milvius. I condemn you not for your tumultuous thoughts. Perhaps that which we have guarded for centuries—that which played a part in the very fall of Atlantis—"

An ominous boom drowned out the rest of his words. From the outer door it echoed, a peal of thunder that filled the high-ceilinged hallways and shattered the quietude of the inner sanctum.

Solnarus frowned, a row of furrows wrinkling his smooth forehead. "Verily, it may be the Grim Grey God that has sealed our fate, Milvius. But we have sworn by Ibis to protect it."

Five priests nodded solemnly, then gazed disapprovingly at Milvius. "Its power is evil," said one of them.

"The power of Chaos," whispered another.

"It is accursed."

"Forbidden," muttered two men, shaking their heads.

As Milvius nodded humbly, a splintering crash made him jump. He rubbed his jaw with shaking, spidery fingers. With a final, wistful look at the pearl statue, he turned toward the hallway to face the defilers who would soon swarm the temple. "The door crumbles, Solnarus!" he whispered, trembling.

"Peace, Milvius," the Priest-King said, his tone a balm that soothed the raw nerves of those who listened. He lowered his eyes to the sphere in his hands. "If we succeed, know you that Blackblade must suffer a fate far worse than ours. His own sword shall undo him; no more shall he crush cities like ours beneath his boot-heel. Our sacrifice sets a wind to blowing, and that wind is destined to disperse the clouds of Acheron before they obscure our world in foul darkness."

"*If* we succeed," Milvius quavered. "And if we cannot prevent him from seizing *that*," he gestured toward the statue, "who will stop him then?"

Solnarus's brow wrinkled again. "No one, Milvius. We are the last line of defense." He paused gloomily. "And know this: No priest, no sorcerer—perhaps not even a god—can undo what is wrought by the forces within the Grim Grey God. The ancient gods of evil imbued it with their power. Had the Atlanteans not wrested it from their ancient foes before it could be put to use, the world would already be a festering hell."

"They should have destroyed it," said Milvius. He flinched when the ram struck another earsplitting blow upon the door.

"No sane man would attempt to do so, even if he could. You have read the verses in the Eleventh Codex of Eibon. 'No one, neither man nor woman, may harm it, nor any thing of the world do it injury. And should the world be rid of it, the ancient gods within shall be reborn, and their ancient evil shall again darken the lands.' " Solnarus shook his head. "These passages and the others have haunted me since the day it befell me to become the guardian of the Grim Grey God. Long have I pondered their meaning—"

The crash of broken stone drowned out the Priest-King's words, and the demonic laughter of Blackblade sounded in the halls.

Milvius's eyes widened in terror. "The Jackal comes!" Sweat rolled from his nose and dripped onto his robes.

Blackblade rode into the spacious temple, roaring like a maddened giant. By his own order, none of his men followed too closely. He burst into the inner sanctum and brought his mount to an abrupt halt. The clopping of hooves echoed like the palpitations of a stone heart.

Solnarus stepped forward, clutching the glass sphere in steady hands. His face was smooth and dry, as serene as ever. He smiled wanly at Blackblade.

"Solnarus," the warlord of Acheron sneered triumphantly. "Kneel before your master, sniveling lamb of Ibis! Long has my blade craved your blood."

"You have reached too far this time, and doomed yourself to failure. You should have brought your brother! Verily, without Xaltotun's dark arts, you could not have crossed the desert or breached Nithia's gate. Nay, Jackal! Ne'er again will your blade take the lives of innocents."

Chuckling, Blackblade dismounted with an agility that should have been impossible for a man of his enormous size. He strode toward Solnarus, who stood unwavering. The other priests, like

Milvius, stayed at Solnarus's side, nervously eyeing Blackblade's blood-smeared, four-foot scimitar.

The Acheronian warlord swept his arms back, then swung his blade in a murderous two-handed stroke. The heads of two Nithian priests thumped to the marble floor as their severed necks jetted blood. Three others fell slain before the survivors could even move. The Jackal struck again, silencing Milvius's terrified wail. Sharpened steel sheared through the little priest's ribs, severed his spine, and shattered his shoulder blades, halving him at the torso.

Blackblade tore loose the upper half of the corpse, sliced out the heart and speared it on the tip of his scimitar. Grinning wickedly at Solnarus, he lifted the glistening organ to his teeth and tore out a dripping chunk. He licked his lips and spat a copious gobbet of blood into the Priest-King's face.

"Dotard," he mouthed, still chewing. "Now that the Grim Grey God is mine, nothing is beyond *my* reach. My armies will sweep across the land in a glorious tide of blood. The fist of mighty Acheron will soon grip the entire world and silence the whimpering of pathetic weaklings like you." He swallowed and noisily smacked his lips.

Solnarus made no reply. Blood from the slain priests had begun soaking into the hem of his spattered robe, but he stood fast, his gaze never leaving Blackblade's face. Only the Priest-King's eyes showed emotion, his blue eye gleaming like ice, his orange eye glowing like a hot ember.

Blackblade lunged without warning. His sword flew through the air like a striking serpent.

Solnarus raised his sphere into the path of the blade. Its fragile glass shattered in a spray of sand. Unchecked, Blackblade's sword bit into the Priest-King's neck and lopped off his head.

The body fell forward, but at the neck-hole from whence the blood should have spurted, there poured only sand. The head landed upright, its eyes rolling upward to stare defiantly at the astonished Jackal. "So, Jackal, it ends . . ." Solnarus's hollow voice echoed tauntingly from his lips. "You have smashed the Sphere of Souls . . . each grain of sand is a soul, an innocent life taken by your bewitched blade. Hell awaits you, Jackal of Acheron—"

Bellowing with bestial fury, Blackblade stomped the Priest-King's skull beneath his iron-shod boot and ground it into a pile of powdery bones and sand. He cursed and ranted as he trampled the

Priest-King's corpse until it was a shapeless mound that bore no resemblance to a man. Two rapid strides brought him within arm's reach of the pearl statue, which he reached for greedily.

Abruptly, a fierce wind howled through the temple. The light from the crystalline roof darkened as the sun was obscured. From above, a faint pattering sounded like rain, and yells from Blackblade's men filtered into the temple. Even as the Acheronian warlord gloated over his prize, the soldiers' cries faded to muffled whispers and were extinguished.

The Jackal hoisted the polished-pearl statue high into the air. "The Grim Grey God is mine!"

A splintering crash from above smothered Blackblade's shout of exhilaration. The roof shattered from the weight of the sand heaped atop it, showering the wide-eyed warlock with knifelike shards and burying him in a sandy grave. His death-yell was buried in a whirling, shrieking storm of sand that utterly engulfed the temple, the marble walls, the buildings without.

For twenty-three days the wind raged relentlessly, submerging the Holy City of Nithia in a veritable sea of sand. No lofty tower or brass spire was visible.

There would the Brass City lie hidden for some three thousand years, lost beneath the desolate dunes of what would one day become the eastern desert of Shem . . . hidden, but not forgotten. For one day howling winds would lay bare the secrets in the sand, and men would once more seek the Grim Grey God.

One
The Stowaway

Messantia's most infamous tavern, the Stowaway, lay unmarked at the city's outskirts amid a cluster of slovenly buildings. It marked the end of Merchant Street, which originated at the busiest harbor in Argos's capital city. At the harbor, the street was wide, paved with stone, and well-maintained by King Milo's taxes. But as it twisted, branched, and wound its way through the largest port city in any of the Hyborian Kingdoms, it dwindled to a narrow strip of dirt that was paved with naught but rubbish and traversed only by a dense population of rats. Here the locals named it Pirate's Lane, for those who trod upon it were less accustomed to hard-packed dirt than to wood-planked deck. They were seafaring rogues: stocky, tawny-haired Argosseans; lean, sallow-skinned Zingarans; and swarthy, black-bearded Shemites.

They clustered in the Stowaway's dim, wood-furnished confines like barnacles on a hull. Six of Messantia's boldest smugglers feasted on haunches of flame-roasted mutton, washing down their greasy repast with draughts of thick ale. A swarthy Kothian cutthroat

1

watched them with a predatory gaze, stroking his thick black mustache. A sweaty Shemite captain locked wrist and hand in an arm-wrestling match with a rival Zingaran, while a scarred, tattooed Nemedian collected wagers from the contestants' crewmen.

Of course, drinking and gambling were but two of many vices in which the Stowaway's motley patrons engaged.

Clad in the scantiest wisps of garments, wenches from a dozen lands moved among the throng, their bared hips swaying provocatively as they served ale, wine, and platters of steaming meat to patrons. Their voluptuous bodies drew many stares, though for the most part, their faces had a hard-eyed, jaded look. The tavern attracted the sort of men who preferred coarse, lusty harlots. Of course, no self-respecting doxy would go near a place with the Stowaway's reputation.

One would have to visit a dungeon to find a more ruffianly lot gathered in one room. Even so, the crowd seemed at ease—many of the rogues were bitter rivals at sea, but the Stowaway was neutral ground. Here they rollicked: drinking, wagering, and wenching away their plunder.

The crowd tonight was thicker than usual, for the crew of the notorious *Hawk* had put ashore after months at sea. Her captain was a pirate whose very name was cursed and feared by every seafaring merchant in the region. At the Stowaway's largest table sat this notorious rogue, Conan: a black-maned, blue-eyed giant from the frozen hills of Cimmeria. His crew—a motley band of villainous scum—surrounded him, laughing lustily as the *Hawk*'s first mate finished a bawdy lyric.

"By Crom, Rulvio, the most jaded strumpet would blush at your jests!" Conan guffawed, thumping the bearlike Argossean on the back.

Frothy Argossean ale slopped from Rulvio's leathern jack onto his hairy chest and drenched his baggy silken breeks. The first mate took no notice of the spill, quaffing the rest of his ale in a single gulp and belching thunderously.

Conan yelled for more ale. He leaned backward and playfully swatted the shapely backside of Rubinia, the Stowaway's comeliest serving-wench. She giggled and strolled away, her swaying hips and scanty shift turning the head of every man nearby. Conan's eyes drank in the sight wolfishly, and he gulped down another measure of strong ale.

"So, Captain," Rulvio rumbled, "say ye that we've enough loot for a fortnight of wenching in Messantia?"

"Aye," Conan affirmed. "The *Hawk* needs an overhaul anyway, and this lot of drunkards—" he nodded toward his sodden crewmen "—is ill-suited for any task save sailing or looting. And after tonight's windfall, the lads earned a good debauch."

"I've a mind to float in a sea of ale myself," chuckled Rulvio.

"Let's first discuss an urgent matter—privately," added Conan. He nodded toward the smoky shadows of the opposite end of the Stowaway.

Many of the *Hawk*'s crew had begun their debauch in earnest. One band diced, a few others had wenches in their laps, while many drifted to join other patrons, hear news, and swap lies about their adventures. Conan and Rulvio looked on, amused, and wandered to one of many dimly lit nooks in the Stowaway's squalid interior.

" 'Bel favors the thief what squanders his booty,' eh?" quoth Rulvio. His broad grin revealed teeth as crooked as his nose, which had been broken more times than he could remember.

Conan raised a bushy eyebrow. "Were it so, Bel would hold no sea-dog in higher esteem than you, Rulvio." The Cimmerian's blue eyes burned sharply, as if his wits had not yet been clouded by the Argossean ale. He lowered his voice and leaned closer to the golden hoop that dangled from Rulvio's sunburned ear. "We *have* been through some scrapes together, my friend. You shoved me to the deck and took an arrow in the leg for me, years ago when that Zingaran galley nearly ran us down. For that, I am in your debt."

Rulvio shrugged. "Had ye not slain a score of those Zingaran swine when they boarded us, our whole blasted crew would be rotting in Dagon's belly. Hah! There be no debt between us, Conan. I served under Borus before ye, and Gonzago before him, and neither could match ye as captain."

Conan accepted the compliment in silence. He demanded much from his men, but he rewarded them with fair shares of every haul. Still, a blood debt could not be settled so readily. And for what he had in mind, he would need the help of a stout fighter like Rulvio.

The Argossean's brow furrowed. "This ale has addled my wits, Conan, else I'd have seen it sooner. Why put ashore here, in a city with laws, and not in the Barachan Isles, where they welcome dogs like us?"

3

"Swear by Bel that you will not repeat what I am about to tell you."

Rulvio did so, his bloodshot eyes meeting Conan's somber gaze.

The Cimmerian withdrew a folded piece of parchment from his vest of supple, finely tooled leather. He laid it upon the table, thumping it with his scarred fist. "I found this in a cloak, aboard that little Zingaran ship we overtook today."

"Well, at least ye found something that the lads won't squander tonight," Rulvio said heavily. "Bel knows we'll guzzle the profit from that excursion before the sun rises. I'll not grumble about the cargo, but I would that we had caught the swine who made off in the skiff with the strongbox."

Conan waved aside the first mate's complaints. "We could not give chase—the cursed wind deserted us, and that fool Voralo gave chase in our boat and got himself and three lads killed in the process!" The memory stoked a fire of anger in Conan's eyes; the *Hawk* had eventually caught up with Voralo's drifting boat and its dead occupants, but their slayer had escaped, presumably to the haven afforded by nearby Messantia. Each man's throat had been slit deeply, vertically, their wounds unlike any that even Conan had seen. He chewed his lip for a span, then stared across the table at Rulvio. "But we may yet gain from that raid. Have you heard legends of a City of Brass?"

Rulvio snorted. "Aye. Though I be not fool enough to believe them. There's a knave in every blasted town from here to Turan who hawks maps to the Brass City. I doubt not that ye found such a piece of fakery—they be as common as lice in a beggar's beard!"

"So they are," Conan agreed, scowling. As a naïve youth, he had wasted many a coin on false treasure maps. "But this one is different; never have I seen its like. In my wanderings, I have learned a smattering of ancient rune-lore. The map bears inscriptions . . ." He paused as Rubinia arrived, a huge clay pitcher nestled in the crook of her elbow.

Rulvio's eyes had shifted away from Conan's. They lingered on Rubinia's full bosom, which strained at the thin fabric of her low-cut tunic as she bent over their table to refill their ale-jacks. When she finished, the Argossean's gaze followed her. "Forget this mad quest for the blasted Brass City, Captain. Why not spend the evenings carousing with us and pass the nights abed with that doxy until the

Hawk is ready to sail again? We be wolves of the sea, and on the sea we hunt—not in the dusty bowels of some landlocked ruin."

"You speak wisely, as ever, Rulvio. Assuredly the wench will take my mind off this map for a time. But I deem it worthwhile to spend a week or two on a foray into the desert of Shem, where these writings place the city. Accompany me if you wish. I shall go at it alone if you prefer to stay here—perhaps it were better if you did, or the lads may get into too much trouble."

"*Our* lads?" Rulvio winked. "Why, such refined fellows as they will of course obey every local law and observe every blasted custom." He pointed toward a group of a half-score of loud, inebriated knaves who had stopped throwing dice and started throwing punches. "Fenzini, you slack-wit!" Rulvio cursed. "Use the weighted dice in games with honest folk—not with your blasted mates!" He turned to Conan, grunting disapprovingly. "I must needs break this up before someone dents a skull." He cracked his knuckles as he rose from the wooden crate that served as his seat and staggered into the brawl.

Conan shook his head, though he was not too surprised by Rulvio's lack of enthusiasm for a venture into Shem. Still, the Cimmerian was determined to see if the map might open a vault of treasure that for centuries had eluded fortune-hunters. Many times he had single-handedly seized hoards of wealth, the very existence of which had been scoffed at by others. And he knew well that a few nights of revelry would end in restlessness. After months at sea, he welcomed a journey that would take him through Shem's lush wine country. If he struck it rich there, he could turn the *Hawk* over to Rulvio and live like a king, forgoing the freebooter's life-style of feasting one week and fasting for the next three or four.

He tucked the parchment into his vest and upended his ale-jack, gulping until he emptied it. Grinning, he rose and sauntered over to the mass of punching, kicking pirates that had begun to encompass the entire tavern. He ducked a flying clay pitcher, dodged a poorly thrown punch, and began to pull his besotted men one by one from the tangle of flailing limbs.

Two
Knives in the Dark

Through a thin veil of clouds, moonlight shimmered on rippling waters that lapped gently at the docks of Messantia. The Argossean capital, acknowledged as the queen of Hyboria's seaports by all but rival Zingarans, slept quietly under the blanket of night. In the darkness between moonset and sunrise, even the hardiest carousers snored in their bunks, or sprawled upon the paving-stones of alleys. More than a few lay facedown on the filthy floors of inns or taverns.

In spite of its shabby buildings, Messantia enjoyed the reputation of being among the safest of cities. At regular intervals, dutiful sentries patrolled even the darkest of streets. A lone woman could tread the streets of Messantia with aplomb, even at night. Of course, such safety came with a price, for King Milo's laws exacted severe penalties from those who violated the city's curfew. Messantia's complex justice system favored no one who walked the streets past curfew, save those in possession of the right documents.

Undoubtedly, some enterprising sentries accepted coinage in lieu of documents. Koralo, whose watch had just begun, was such a man.

His finely woven silver-and-blue tabard marked him as commander of the city's southeastern quarter. In fourteen years of loyal service, he had collected more wealth than many a Messantian merchant earned in a lifetime. He had also acquired a taste for the expensive wines of Kyros, a hefty gambling debt, and an appetite for certain exotic pleasures of the flesh that cost far more than the rarest wine. No matter how much gold he gathered, it slipped swiftly between his fat fingers.

Koralo's head and belly still ached from last night's excesses. His mood was as foul as the taste in his mouth as he led his three men in a routine patrol of the area known as Smuggler's Wharf. It was the most southern and eastern of the city's ports, the district farthest from the center of Messantia. Ships, bearing diverse and often illegally obtained goods, docked at the southeastern port, where they hoped to escape the attentions of Milo's industrious tax collectors. On a typical day, the pier was a hotbed of activity.

But at this time of day, as Koralo knew, even the smugglers slept. So he stared in fascination as a small boat approached, its sole occupant rowing rapidly but stealthily toward the end of the dark pier. The commander waited in the shadows at the far end of the pier, wondering why this man would so blatantly violate Messantia's laws. No vessels were permitted to put ashore at night, save in the presence of a Messantian cargo inspector.

Then Koralo saw the iron-bound trunk.

Koralo forgot his aches as he watched the boat approach. Pirate captains were wont to boldly smuggle their most precious booty into Messantia in just this manner, or so it was said. This might be the opportunity that Koralo had waited for—a chance to pay off his gambling debts and retire in luxury. His men, whom he had chosen carefully for a combination of brute strength and abysmal stupidity, would never realize that the "confiscated" trunk would be diverted from King Milo's storehouse.

Visions of flowing wine and submissive, nubile beauties filled Koralo's thoughts as the boat's bow gently bumped into the aged wooden pier. The stranger disembarked after an arduous struggle with the trunk. He was tall, clad in a loose-fitting mantle of dull indigo that blended into the shadowy night. A cowl concealed his face, and his footsteps were but whispers. He had tied a cloth pouch to the simple rope belt knotted about his waist, but no other gear—notably weapons—was in evidence. Koralo smiled. This would be easy. Like his sentries, the commander wore a bronze-studded leather jerkin and cap, more than adequate to turn the point of a knife or the edge of a sword.

The stranger carefully surveyed the length of the pier, then opened the trunk with a key that hung from a cord about his neck. He peered inside and froze, as if surprised by its contents. Cursing softly, he locked the trunk, shoved it into the water, and headed toward the cobblestone street. The stranger's swift strides carried him straight toward the shadowy alley where the sentries waited.

Koralo's eyes narrowed to predatory slits. He slid his saber from its well-oiled scabbard and whispered to his men. Two sentries cocked their crossbows, the moonlight affording them a measure of visibility. One man drew his broadsword and followed the commander into the street.

"Halt!" Koralo barked, raising his blade. "By order of King Milo—Set!" he cursed, dropping his saber. A thin, six-pointed piece of metal had sprouted from the wrist of his sword-arm. Had the strange missile veered slightly to either side, it would have struck him below his chin.

The stranger flicked his hand again. Blood erupted from the throat of the sentry beside Koralo; the man sank to his knees and died with a hideous gurgle.

The two remaining sentries rushed from the alley and trained their crossbows on the stranger. One arbalester died before he could trigger his weapon; a razor-sharp piece of steel pierced his eye and burrowed deeply into his brain. The other fired his bolt and cursed in amazement as the stranger's hand lashed out with inhuman speed and deflected the missile, which skittered across the stones. A moment later, that sentry was dead as well. Koralo retreated into the alley.

The indigo-robed man dashed forward and seized a dropped crossbow. In one smooth motion, he loaded the weapon and fired it at the fleeing Koralo, who staggered and fell without a single cry. The bolt had pierced his skull and killed him instantly. Its barbed, bloody tip protruded between Koralo's glazed eyes.

Methodically, the stranger went from man to man and checked each for a pulse. He fired a bolt into one sentry's heart at point-blank range. Without a moment's pause, he loosed another into Koralo's eye.

During the executions, the face beneath the dark cowl had registered neither pleasure nor distaste. The lips did not draw back in a grimace as the stranger extracted his small but deadly weapons from the bodies of the slain. He did not so much as flinch when he split the skull of one crossbowman with a saber and tore loose the steel star lodged within. The flesh of the bodies was still warm to the touch when the stranger dumped the corpses into the harbor. He worked with impressive speed and efficiency, wasting no time or effort to pause and wipe his brow or to catch his breath.

Indeed, Toj Akkhari had not risen to his exalted station of Master of Assassins in Zamboula by wasting time and effort. If dead men could speak, some two thousand would have attested to Toj's speed and ruthlessness. And tonight he moved with even more speed than usual. He was late for Jade's conclave. Toj's temper was typically as placid as a becalmed sea, but at present he was almost annoyed. King Milo's lackeys had cost him precious time, and Jade was waiting. Had Toj not been so impatient to meet Jade, he would have heard the approach of the inept watchdogs soon enough to have avoided them altogether. Toj preferred to shun the distractions of such routine killing, but one live sentry could have fetched a hundred more, causing Toj further delays. And not even Zamboula's Master of Assassins dared to keep Jade waiting for too long.

The meeting had been arranged by courier, when Toj had acquired something for which Jade would pay handsomely. That payment would be in the form of the Red Asp, a weapon Toj had sought for years. The dagger was said to have been fashioned from the horn of a serpent-demon and magicked with death-spells by the Seers of Mount Yimsha, those sorcerous masters of the dreaded Black Circle. The dagger's powers would render Toj the deadliest assassin that history would ever know.

Toj stalked through a labyrinth of dark alleys and dilapidated buildings. When he approached the center of Messantia's storehouse district, his well-honed senses warned him that hidden eyes observed his approach. He had expected this. He turned at an intersection, then followed a narrow lane of dirt flanked by walls of crumbling stone. The unmarked door of a small, grubby building opened as he approached it. Beyond the threshold, wooden steps led down into the dark bowels of the building. He swallowed the dry lump that had risen in his throat, took a deep breath, and began his descent.

The faint moonlight did not reach to the bottom of the steps. Toj was not surprised. Thieves and assassins of any status knew that

Jade held meetings only in the cover of darkness. No one alive had seen Jade's face, or so men said. Jade was cautious in the extreme—a characteristic understandable for one possessed of more wealth than many a Hyborian king, one who held sway over a strange empire that spanned a dozen kingdoms, from Aquilonia to Zingara.

Toj heard a telltale click from beneath his boot. The steps collapsed, turning the stairway into a steep ramp. Such was the assassin's agility that he kept his footing, but his soles slid along the oiled wood and he fought to keep his balance. Moments later, he reached the end of the ramp and tumbled onto the floor. Rolling instinctively to lessen the impact, he came nimbly to his feet. The flat hilt of a *shaken* throwing knife slid from his wrist-sheath into his left palm. It was one of five such knives concealed on his body. His right hand held several six-pointed *shaken*, still stained with the sentries' blood.

"Ashhadu salib muhadana." The voice sounded quiet and somehow distorted, though its tone was stern and authoritative.

"Jade?" Toj stammered, then quickly regained his composure. *"Ashhadu an la muhadan ilaha salib."* He switched to the cant that was known only among thieves and assassins of select guilds. Typically, he would have used fewer words and substituted furtive gestures of his head, eyes, fingers and hands. In the dark, however, Toj had to limit himself to the cant's verbal form.

"You'll not need your weapons here, Toj." Jade's voice bore a hint of amusement. An awkward silence followed this admonishment before more words were spoken . . . this time without humor. "You were to be here at nightfall, *majnun!*"

Toj stiffened at the insult. "Trouble on the voyage, Jade. A Barachan pirate ship—the *Hawk*—overtook my vessel and sank her a few leagues from Khorotas Harbor. I escaped in the tether-boat, but had to row into Smuggler's Wharf. The *Hawk* did not pursue me, fortunately, but four of Milo's fool sentries further delayed my arrival." He shifted his grip on the *shaken*-knife's hilt. In spite of Jade's assurance, the weapon had never left his hand.

"Word already reached me of your encounter with Koralo, whose coins will be missed at my tables of gaming and houses of pleasure. No matter. Have you brought it?"

"Yes," Toj lied. He noted with irritation that his palms had begun to sweat. "I shall tell you where it is hidden—*after* you give the Red Asp to me."

"I see," Jade said slowly. "Your lack of trust disheartens me, Toj. But there is no honor among thieves, or assassins . . . is there?"

Toj held his tongue. Did she know that he had lost the map? No, not even her spies could have divined this. Still, he cursed his foolishness. He had decided to pay a Zingaran merchant for sea-passage to Messantia, deeming it safer and swifter than a trip through bandit-ridden Shem. The trunk had been a decoy; he had hidden the map to the City of Brass in the lining of a dirty cloak that had lain beneath his bunk for the duration of the voyage. But in the darkness, surprised by the *Hawk*'s sudden onset, he had stuffed the wrong cloak into his watertight trunk and abandoned ship after dispatching the few crewmen who had gotten in his way.

Jade, however, could not possibly have discovered his error. If Toj had been watched since his arrival at the pier, Jade's spies might have seen him shove the trunk into the water. For that matter, they might have dived for it and found it empty, but Toj would have to take that chance.

The awkward silence passed; Jade continued. "You and your assassins have tainted our profession, Toj. You are little better than common sellswords who would slay even their kin for coin."

"You and your thieves steal gold or jewels, mere baubles. My assassins and I steal life . . . and for any man, is not life the most precious treasure he possesses?"

Jade laughed, a harsh and unnerving sound. "You are vile, Toj— but I need you. I know of none who possesses your skill at murder and lacks any shred of conscience. That is why I am giving you a chance to live."

As she spoke, Toj felt a sharp sting, like that of a wasp, in his thigh. He whirled with knife ready, but the darkness—so often his best ally—beset him for the nonce. "What is this outrage, Jade? You dare to—"

"Toj. Bold you are, to come here without map in hand and demand the ensorceled dagger that I stole from the vaults below the Temple of Set in Luxur. Yes, I have the Red Asp. Now I must know . . . did you study the guildmaster's map?"

" 'Examine it not,' you bade me," the assassin said, his calm voice belying his rising anxiety. Jade had hired him to murder the holder of the map: the Iranistani Guildmaster of Thieves in Anshan. The fool had stubbornly refused to relinquish the map to Jade.

Of course, when Toj had withdrawn the map from the slain

11

guildmaster's robes and escaped from Anshan, he *had* glanced at the chart drawn crudely on the parchment. However, Toj dealt in death, not in the translation of foreign scrawlings. "The map—"

"—is in the hands of Conan," Jade interrupted curtly, "the Cimmerian who now captains the Barachan *Hawk*. In fact, he plans to follow the map to the City of Brass on the morrow. Perhaps you were not so fortunate to escape his pirates and their cutlasses."

Toj sweated freely, his composure dissolving. "How so, Jade?"

Metal clattered on the stone floor near to Toj's feet. "Take the Red Asp, Toj. It is yours."

"But—" Toj stammered, then summoned a measure of composure. "Ah! I am to slay this Conan and retrieve the map. Of course. I swear it shall be done . . . ere the sun rises!"

"So soon, Toj? I think not. You see, I know something of Conan's incredible exploits, though never have our paths crossed. Only one possessed of that Cimmerian devil's unmatched strength and legendary luck could actually reach the City of Brass and retrieve what has lain hidden there for so many centuries. Lest you think to venture there yourself, know this: It is written that a dire curse haunts that city. Any who enter will fall victim to a slow, withering disease for which no cure exists. So you must wait outside the city for Conan. Then—*if* he bears the prize, dispose of him and bring it to me."

"An ingenious plan, Jade. I shall follow him, then, to the City of Brass. Just tell me where he lodges this night and I shall—"

"In the eastern district. The Stowaway, where rogues of his ilk are wont to squander their plunder. And do not think that you can cheat me, Toj. If Conan fails, I lose nothing. You, on the other hand, may lose everything. For if you leave here and do not return with the statue of pearl that lies buried in the City of Brass, you will die."

A cold draft of fear coursed through Toj's veins. With effort, he steadied his voice, so that his tongue would not betray the feelings in his gut. "What mean you by this, Jade? Poison?"

Laughter rang out again, harsh and cruel. "Me, a mere thief, *poison* the Master of Assassins? A rich jest, were it so. But also a futile one. Your Golden Lotus nectar would defeat any poison that even I could find. Nay, the sting you felt came from the tiny jaws of the *kalb* queen-beetle.

"She is one of your kind, an assassin of sorts, though not as swift as the notorious Toj. And she is tiny, no bigger than the tip of a seamstress's needle. Already she is burrowing through your flesh and crawling along your bones, seeking your heart. The food inside your body will fatten her as she wriggles through your innards. You see, the *kalb* Queen builds her nest in the heart of her host. Therein she will lay many eggs, and dozens of her young will hatch. These offspring will be tiny at first. But they will emerge . . . hungry. When you bring the statue to me, I shall tell you how to stop the *kalb* queen from building her nest. Only I have the knowledge that can spare you from this slow, agonizing doom."

Toj's composure fled, leaving raw panic in its place. "How do I know that you will keep your word, Jade? Why should I fetch the statue—I am a dead man no matter what I do!"

"Ah, Toj, you misunderstand. I have not given you my word, for as we both know, the promise of a thief has less substance than smoke in the wind. Think you that my offer is no better than certain death? By the next full moon, the *kalb* queen will taste the meat of your beating heart. You will endure suffering that lingers for weeks before the eggs hatch. When the *kalb* beetles . . . grow, you will writhe from torments so dire that you will beg for death. Only I can spare you this fate. No, Toj, I know you too well. You will do as I say—not for me, but for yourself."

Toj sputtered, his face reddening.

"It will be difficult," Jade continued. "Others may try to stop Conan . . . others with powers that may render even *your* arts useless if they reach the pearl statue first. We are not the only ones who know that the City of Brass has been found. My spies have brought news that troubles me. If these others should threaten Conan, eliminate them! And make certain that the Cimmerian succeeds, lest those others finish what the *kalb* beetle has begun."

Toj's voice was feverish. "What others, Jade? I must know everything. And tell me the secret of the *kalb* beetle now! I swear that I shall never again try to deceive you! What is it? Tell me now, or I shall refuse to go!"

The only answer to Toj's plea was silence.

Moments later, the first ray of dawn crept down the stairs and illuminated a small, circular chamber. Toj's voice echoed from windowless walls of grey brick. The room was empty but for the assassin and the exotic dagger that lay at his feet.

The stairway's collapsed steps had risen back into place. Toj's hand shook as he picked up the scarlet-bladed dagger. He held it gingerly, almost with reverence, and wrapped it in a makeshift sheath of cloth. For now, he would stow it beside the bladder of Golden Lotus nectar that he kept under his robes, beneath a leather strap that crossed his chest.

Toj composed himself. With a frown, he fingered the small, tingling wound in his leg. Swallowing the taste of bile that had risen unbidden into his throat, he ran up the stairs to seek out Conan the Cimmerian . . . the man he would mark for death.

Three
"Take Him Alive!"

Sweat streamed down Conan's neck as he hunched forward on the madly galloping horse. His long black hair swept out behind him like a pennant in a gale, and the wind was an invisible flail that whipped at his face. The Cimmerian wiped at his streaming eyes and glanced back over his shoulder, swearing sulfurously at what he saw.

He had thought that his steed would outpace his pursuers, but the brigands were steadily gaining. Conan could coax no more speed from his mare; he had taxed the poor beast to its limits. The chase had started at midday, the day after he left Messantia. He had ridden east and south, toward the meadowlands of northwestern Shem, avoiding the busy trade routes.

His course had taken him along the outskirts of Shem's populous city-states, following an abandoned, weed-choked trail. In many regions hereabouts, there was a price on his head. Were he caught, his past indiscretions and complete indifference to Shemitish laws might land him in a dungeon—or lead him to a more dire fate on an headsman's block.

But he had instantly regretted his decision to travel off-road when a disconcertingly large band of riders had descended swiftly from a tree-covered hillock, chasing him with the persistence of Picts on a blood trail. Why were they after a lone man?

Had there been a mere half-dozen or so ruffians pursuing him, he would have charged into their midst like a juggernaut. However, a coterie of this size would doubtless feather him with arrows before his sword would taste any blood. Shemites were accounted to be fine archers. Conan knew that Shemite raiders favored the short bow for its speed and ease of use, though it lacked the range and power of a crossbow or a fine Hyrkanian bow. But a man with an arrow in his gizzard cares not which weapon loosed it.

Conan cursed his decision to travel unencumbered by cap or mail. His simple garb consisted of a leather vest—somewhat soiled and bloodied from the recent brawl at the Stowaway—and loose-fitting breeks of silk that tapered near the tops of his sandals. His sword hung from his broad belt, bouncing with the horse's loping strides, and the hilt of his poniard dug through the thin vest and rubbed at his side.

The Cimmerian scrutinized the rolling meadows ahead, desperate for any terrain that might provide cover. When he reached the crest of a grassy hillock, he saw the pair of riders. They raced forward at the farthest reach of Conan's keen eyes. Hah! So these worthies behind him hunted prey other than himself, perhaps. Scanning the sward, he saw deep, widely spaced hoofprints that marked the trail of the pair who galloped yonder. Had he not been so distracted by the pursuit, he would have read these signs sooner. Mayhap his life at sea had dulled his sharp tracking skills.

If these brigands were after the duo up ahead, he could easily avoid them. Conan veered from the eastward road and charged due south. Before midday, by his reckoning, he should reach the great River Asgalun, which wound eastward through Kyros and Ghaza, two city-states famous for their wine. He grinned. A few goblets of Ghazan wine would slake his thirst better than the Stowaway's swill that now sloshed in his wineskin.

Conan's horse brayed and reared, and the smile fled from his lips as he pitched from the saddle and landed headfirst in a patch of thorny weeds. Through the tall grass, the immense snake that had startled his mount began to slither toward him. Its deep-crimson scales and black banding marked it as a deadly Shemitish blood-viper.

"Crom and Badb!" the Cimmerian bellowed and rolled aside as his panicked steed nearly trampled him. A handspan from Conan's face, the serpent's mouth opened wide, its forked tongue flickering between its scimitarlike fangs.

Conan rammed his poniard through the viper's triangular skull, pinning it to the ground in mid-strike. The serpent thrashed violently as the barbarian whipped his sword from his belt and lopped off the scarlet head. He yanked his blade from the skewered skull and crawled through the tall grass, lying low in the hopes that his pursuers would simply ignore him and press on. The pounding of hooves had drawn nearer. Perhaps they had not seen his horse throw him and would chase after the fleeing beast.

"There he is!" shouted a rider. "Bani, Vulso, Shua—split off and take him alive! The rest of you dogs follow me and tarry not, lest the princess elude us!"

Conan rose to a low crouch and peered through the weeds. His eyes narrowed to fierce slits as he watched the brigands separate. These Shemitish swine would learn the folly of trying to capture a Cimmerian. As they closed within a stone's throw, he leapt to his feet with a guttural snarl, sword in one hand and poniard in the other. Then he grunted in surprise, for he could now see that his foes were not mere bandits.

He faced a trio of *asshuri*, fighters who had earned their reputation as Shem's most dangerous mercenaries. Even the knights of Aquilonia grudgingly respected them.

They swept toward him at full trot, splitting to surround him in a triangle. The sun glinted on rivets of copper that studded their heavy jerkins of banded leather. The foremost warrior reined in and dismounted. He stared at the armed Cimmerian, who calmly stood his ground. The hook-nosed *asshuri*'s gaze shifted continually from his quarry's fiery blue eyes to his thickly muscled shoulders to his gleaming blades. Then the Shemite warrior dropped a hand from his bushy, blue-black beard and slid his broadsword from its scabbard. Conan noted with a grimace that its pommel was shaped like the head of a hawk, forged of gold. For an *asshuri*, an iron hawk marked the slaying of ten men in battle. Bronze represented twenty, silver fifty, and a gold hawk . . . a hundred or more slain.

The other two *asshuri* stayed in the saddle and kept their distance.

Afoot, their armor would weight them down should their prey decide to bolt.

The foremost *asshuri* stepped closer.

Brave fool, thought Conan. *He waits for me to throw my poniard at him, counting on my poor aim or his armor to save him—whereupon the others will disarm and seize me.* The Cimmerian grudgingly admired this foe, who had not even tried the coward's ploy of demanding that Conan surrender himself. Nay, this was a warrior emboldened by many triumphs in battle.

A tense silence thickened the air as the *asshuri* took another step.

Conan burst into action, twisting sideways and hurling his poniard end-over-end—but not at the man on foot. Its blade bit through the jerkin of one of the mounted warriors and sank to the hilt in the man's belly. He howled in pain and toppled from his horse, writhing on the grass as blood gushed from his wound.

Conan spun to face the unmounted *asshuri*. This warrior had already sprung into action, not slowed in the least by his bulky jerkin. His heavy blade clanged against Conan's scimitar as he parried the Cimmerian's murderous stroke. Wasting no breath on battle-cry or insult, he launched a vicious counterattack.

Conan gritted his teeth. The Shemite was every measure a gold-hawk swordsman. He had a maddening knack for countering every brutal blow that Conan struck. The *asshuri*'s precise cuts and thrusts showed mastery of a fighting style that prolonged combat and fatigued one's foeman; the attacks concentrated on Conan's scimitar, not on Conan himself. The Cimmerian could have fought in this manner until sunset without growing weary. Of course, Conan had more immediate concerns, namely the other mounted warrior, who was closing in. The beleaguered barbarian changed his tactics and began to back toward the supine Shemite, who lay unmoving.

The *asshuri* swordsman neither slowed nor pressed his attack. His eyes narrowed in suspicion, but he kept up his dizzying bladework. The longer he fought, the more complex his style became, until even Conan could not follow the endless series of remises, redoublements, and ripostes. Conan's scimitar flashed in response, a blur of flickering steel. The Cimmerian's movements were purely instinctive; only his unwavering speed and agility made him a match for the masterly *asshuri*.

"I have him, Vulso!" the mounted warrior shouted as he bore down on Conan.

"No, Bani—we take him alive!" the hook-nosed Shemite shouted.

Conan flexed his knees and bounded backward. He shifted his scimitar to his left hand and ripped his blood-smeared poniard from the fallen *asshuri*'s midriff. The man jerked and moaned weakly.

Bani's steed plunged headlong toward the Cimmerian. The *asshuri* rider leaned from his saddle and raised his sword-arm high for a vicious stroke.

Conan was forced to throw his poniard against his own backward momentum. Veins in his arm stood out like ropes beneath his skin as the hilt flew from his hand. With a moist smack, the slender blade plunged into Bani's eye. So powerful was Conan's arm that the tip of the poniard punched through brain and skull to jut out a handspan from the back of Bani's head. The warrior toppled from his saddle, dead before he landed on the sward.

Conan tossed his scimitar from left hand to right and moved warily toward his remaining foe.

"Nithing!" Vulso hissed. "We would have taken you alive." His eyes burned with fury.

"So says the dog to the lion," Conan growled. "You'll burn in Hell ere you take a Cimmerian—"

Vulso went from standstill to lunge, his extended blade hurtling toward Conan like a crossbow bolt.

Conan had anticipated this tactic. He paused for a heartbeat to time a sweep that would halve the *asshuri*. In that instant, pain seared his leg. The dying Shemite behind him had managed to thrust his sword through the Cimmerian's calf. Conan stumbled and parried wildly, his blade meeting naught but air. Only a spine-wrenching sideways twist saved him from impalement. His balance deserted him and he fell heavily to the ground at Vulso's feet.

Lashing out with his boot, Vulso caught Conan on the chin with a forceful kick that snapped the barbarian's head backward. The *asshuri*'s sword descended toward the stricken Cimmerian's neck.

It met steel with a clang as Conan managed to bring up his blade. He rolled and sprang to his feet with a fierce cry, ignoring the sword that was still lodged in his besmeared leg. Enraged, he set upon Vulso with the fury of wounded tiger. A mighty swing beat Vulso's sword from his grasp, and another bit into the jerkin, drawing blood from his side.

The *asshuri* dove to the ground and tore the blade from Conan's leg in a fresh spray of blood, throwing his shoulder against the Cimmerian's knee and knocking him down.

The two men struggled and rolled. They dropped their swords, useless in hand-to-hand combat. They seemed oblivious to the blood that gushed from their wounds as they pummeled each other, driven to frenzied rage. But Vulso's jerkin and cap protected his vitals from Conan's hammerlike blows, whereas the Cimmerian felt the full impact from the *asshuri*'s copper-studded gloves.

Conan seized Vulso's throat with one hand. The Shemite loomed above him, but the Cimmerian bent his good leg and brought it up, shoving the warrior aside. The agile Shemite kicked Conan's wounded calf and pounced on him again, driving a knee into his gut. Then it was Vulso's turn to clench the gasping Cimmerian's throat in a deadly grip.

Weakened from loss of blood, his lungs emptied of air, Conan felt his strength abandon him. He could not dislodge the *asshuri*'s hands. His arms dropped to the grass . . . and his fingers encountered the scaly severed head of the blood-viper. Fortunate that his hand was unscathed! A gurgle issued from his throat as he spent the last of his might smashing the serpent's skull into the wound that gaped in Vulso's side. The viper's poison-sac burst, spraying the *asshuri*'s insides with lethal venom.

Red-faced and red-eyed, Vulso dug his thumbs into Conan's windpipe and held on, though he trembled in agony. Moments later, wild convulsions shook the Shemite's body. Bloody foam frothed at his lips and dripped from his beard. His eyes rolled up and he slumped forward, lifeless.

But the venom had frozen Vulso's muscles. Stiff fingers still clenched Conan's neck in an unyielding grip of death.

The Cimmerian willed himself to move, assembling every fiber of vitality that yet lingered in his body. He succeeded only in releasing his grip on the viper's head. He was dimly aware of the approach of many horses. Was it the other *asshuri*, so soon? He decided that he cared not. A grey mist obscured his vision, and numbness settled into his leaden limbs. Even his torn calf had ceased to throb. Before all went dark, he managed to smile grimly.

His foe had passed first through Hell's gate.

Four
The Death Mage

A strange caravan proceeded quietly through the amber dusk that
heralded the coming of night in the northern Stygian desert. The
sky's rich hue was the only thing of beauty in the desolate dunes that
stretched from the Taian Mountains at Stygia's northeast border to
Harakht, the Hawk-God's accursed and ancient city. Sane men
shunned this region of the desert, for between Stygia and Shem
flowed the murkiest currents of the great River Styx.

Where life sprang from rivers in other lands, naught but death
floated in this stretch of the broad, black Styx. Beasts too blasphemous to name swam beneath her dark currents; madness and death
lingered in her watery bosom. Along her banks dwelt denizens both
vile and voracious—crocodiles large enough to swallow a man
whole, serpents of all sizes whose bites brought fever and disease,
and every other sort of reptile that slithered or crawled. Jackals and
carrion-birds lurked nearby, preying upon the weak, the sick, and the
dying.

Yet the caravan traveled at a leisurely pace along the dread river's

21

southern edge—the Stygian side—as if indifferent to the perils of the poisonous river. Twelve tall horses led the retinue in two files of six, adorned with chanfrons of gold and poitrals of heavy, gilt-edged cloth. They moved in unison, though they bore no riders and wore neither bit nor bridle. Their harnesses fixed them to a large, window-less carriage of a height sufficient for a man to stand upright within. Its black wooden sides, bedecked with elaborate symbols, bulged and curved in a shape not unlike that of a sarcophagus. The carriage rolled slowly on black wooden wheels that dug deeply into the sandy soil.

Behind this curious conveyance marched thirty-nine men-at-arms, equidistantly spaced in three files of thirteen. The glow of the sunset reddened their full suits of burnished plate armor. Great helms rested upon their elaborate gorgets, and the etchings in their pallettes, breastplates, and shields matched the symbols on the black carriage. Their swords were the sort typically wielded in two-handed fashion, but they carried these formidable weapons single-handedly, points raised in readiness. Above them, eleven archers stood atop the carriage, massive crossbows loaded and cocked. The mail and coifs of these arbalesters were fashioned from a burnished metal like that of the footmen below.

An ordinary cavalcade outfitted thusly would have perished within a day in the inhospitable desert clime, but this one had plodded along for seven days without stopping.

Anyone who witnessed the caravan's procession would have shut his eyes and blinked before he looked again. A wise man would then have shaken his head and departed hastily, deeming the sight to be a trick of the waning dusk or a bizarre mirage. A man of more courage than prudence, if he watched for too long, would see that which would blast his soul and plague him with nightmares until his dying day.

Beneath their gaudy barding, the horses lacked flesh. Like the archers, they were skeletons, devoid of skin, muscle, sinew or organs. Yet their bones moved in a hideous parody of life, blasphe-mously defying the laws of nature. The slow, methodical march of the escort belied its state as well. Beneath the helms were not faces of living men, but those of fleshless cadavers, with shadowy sockets for eyes.

The symbols on the carriage and the armor had not been seen this far west in seven hundred years. In a different era they had adorned the palaces, tapestries, and other trappings of the god-kings of Amentet. That evil empire's last king, Dûmâhk, had fallen in a great battle at Khyfa centuries hence. The angry Khyfans, loyal Mitra-worshipers all, had descended from their mountainous realm in a fervous avalanche, to cross Shem's southernmost border and decimate Dûmâhk's people. Amentet's defenders fought with fury; long and bitter was the holy war. But Dûmâhk and his people succumbed. Now only dust and lizards inhabited the scattered stones of Amentet's ruined cities, and the wail of desert wind was the only sound that echoed within her crumbling ruins.

But Dûmâhk's daughter had survived the devastation by fleeing eastward to Nebthu, taking with her a great many scrolls from Amentet's vast vault of lore. She read them to her sons, and they to their sons. Yet many of Dûmâhk's descendants cared little about the past and drifted to other cities, forgetting their heritage. The scrolls became a burden and were placed in the care of Set's priests at the great temple in Nebthu.

But not everyone had turned his back to his heritage. Though centuries had passed since Dûmâhk's fall, one descendant still lived who dreamed of Amantet as it was of old.

His name: Tevek Thul—the last keeper of Dûmâhk's faith. He lay now within his black carriage, stirring restlessly in a half-slumber.

In his dreams, Tevek beheld a thriving Amentet in its most glorious days, when blood had flowed from her cities' sacrificial altars in red rivers, and the god-kings had commanded absolute power. Tevek had read many accounts of Amentet—at first he had only studied the illustrations in these crumbling tomes, but curiosity had driven him to learn how to understand the runes that accompanied the drawings.

The priests of Nebthu had taught Tevek basic rune-lore when he was but six years old; they were impressed by his precocious grasp of their hieroglyphs. Tevek had consumed written words like a starving man at a banquet. Within two years, his skills had surpassed those of his elders.

As he dozed uneasily, Tevek's mind wandered back to the days of his youth, before he had discovered the Tablets of Epithur—keys to a power that had spurred him to attempt the restoration of Amentet's empire. In those days, he knew not of the clay tablets, only of the scrolls that comprised the richest treasure of his ancestors.

He had haunted the catacombs where those ancient scrolls of

Amentet lay, and he had read them voraciously. For years he stayed underground, steeping himself in the history of his ancestors. Nebthu's musty tombs and dank crypts became his home, and he began to loathe the feel of the sun on his skin. The only light he could bear was that of his dim reading-lamp. He shunned contact with people, for it took away from his reading. The priests left him food and water, but even they avoided him. His relatives disowned him, but he cared not. In his mind, they were traitors who should be stripped of their claim to Dûmâhk's lineage.

It was the last few scrolls that finally disgorged him from the bowels of Nebthu. These had been the most difficult to peruse, as if deliberately obscured by their scrivener. Not even Dûmâhk's wife had read them—they had lain apart from the others, wax seals intact.

Their contents had sent Tevek's pulse racing. They indicated that Dûmâhk, uncertain of victory over the Khyfans, had hidden the clay tablets containing Amentet's sorcerous knowledge. The scrolls, though diverting, contained no secret store of wizardry. They were naught but accounts of events long past.

No, the more valuable lore was cached in Dûmâhk's vanquished capital, hidden in the deepest of sepulchers beneath the crumbling temple.

Tevek abandoned his haunts at Nebthu and undertook the trip to the ruins, following the maps and directions enscribed on the scrolls. He traveled at night and hid himself from the sun by day. The physical demands of his trek fatigued him not. Tevek was accustomed to long intervals between meals; he had fasted for days at Nebthu while losing himself in a particularly fascinating scroll. And though he was rangy of build, he had inherited the iron constitution of his forefathers.

A lesser man would not have survived the wracking endured by Tevek in retrieving the clay tablets. Tevek had entered the ruins of Amentet as a smooth-skinned, black-haired youth. He had emerged as withered and wrinkled as a centenarian, with but a few wisps of black hair remaining in his long white mane. He cared not that his youthful appearance was lost forever. Had he not unearthed the arcane tablets from those ruins, he would never have risen to the position of power he held today.

Stirring, Tevek evoked his nether vision. His eyes remained shut as he transferred his sight to the hollow sockets of his undead subjects, one by one. A clear vista presented itself; only yellow-leafed palms, sickly shrubs, and camel-thorn weeds inhabited the region. At the horizon, he could see the walls of Harakht.

Nether vision was one of many gifts bestowed only upon those who achieved mastery of Tevek's dark calling: necromancy. Stygian priests, as well as wizards of diverse lands, claimed cognizance of this darkest of sorcerous pursuits, but Tevek deemed these charlatans ignorant of true necromancy. The formidable Seers of Mount Yimsha and the mightiest mages of Stygia would never wield even a tithe of the power commanded by Tevek. For he had memorized the immense Tablets of Epithur—the assemblage of arcane spells that spanned the centuries from Python's fall to Acheron's rise. After committing these to his infallible memory, he had destroyed all but three of them so that no other could benefit from their potent contents.

In his ebony carriage, Tevek smiled thinly. Not even the self-proclaimed prince of Stygian sorcerers, whom he was about to call upon, would ever be privy to the lost lore recorded by scores of long-dead archmages. Nay, great Thoth-Amon would lay his serpentlike eyes upon only three tablets. This trio Tevek had not reduced to rubble, for they contained annals copied from the Codices of Eibon—works whose very origins were deeply buried in time's vast cemetery.

Works that the prince of sorcerers had sought for decades.

Tevek had met Thoth-Amon once, years hence in Nebthu, and that meeting had left a lasting impression. The raw essence of evil had pervaded the very air about Thoth-Amon, whose mere presence had cowed the haughty priests of Nebthu. Tevek himself had felt the cold fire of Thoth-Amon's gaze, for the Stygian mage had questioned everyone at Nebthu regarding an ancient tome for which he searched.

Thoth-Amon believed that one codex among Eibon's eleven contained the key to the downfall of the accursed god Mitra, nemesis of Set. Tevek had read Eibon's verses twice, gleaning little from them. Though quaintly poetic, the writings delved into naught but the making and unmaking of idols, with specific references to icons that time had long since turned to dust. Spurious prose indeed, to have accrued such renown. Thoth-Amon had clearly been misinformed, to have wasted time and effort in search of those worthless writings. The fall of Mitra would please Tevek, but Thoth-Amon sought also to turn away that god's worshipers, to force them to swear fealty to Set.

Tevek would rather inflict an agonizing death upon them, to avenge the murder of his ancestors.

To this end, gladly would Tevek give the tablets to Thoth-Amon.

So he had slain a vulture and animated it to serve as his messenger to the Stygian sorcerer. Bearing a scrap of parchment, the bird had departed five days hence to bear news of Tevek's coming. Tomorrow, Tevek himself would reach the Oasis of Khajar, where the powerful but fatuous Thoth-Amon stirred his bubbling crocks of sorcerous stew. The need to seek assistance—especially from this pompous mage—irked Tevek considerably. But dominion of the dead did not, of itself, make one liege of the living. And it was against the living whom Tevek plotted . . . against the Mitra-worshiping scum who infested Khyfa.

Too long had the spawn of King Dûmâhk's murderers gone unpunished for their destruction of once-mighty Amentet. Tevek would see justice meted out.

To the last man, woman, and child, the Khyfans would suffer and die.

Five
Dungeon of Despair

An all-too-familiar reek assailed Conan's nostrils as he awakened. Most of the diverse dungeons in which the Cimmerian had been shackled were musty, filth-ridden pits that stank of death. Sighing, the barbarian lifted his head from the hard stone floor and vowed to commit crimes only in those kingdoms civilized enough to build their prisons aboveground and clean them up at least once every few years.

A distant groan echoed in the darkness, followed by an agonized scream that drowned out the squeaking and scurrying of rats. Conan brushed an enormous cockroach from his hair and squashed it against the floor. Irritated, he tried vainly to reach his stiff, aching calf. Heavy chains clanked against the manacles that bound his wrists, ankles, and neck. The links made only slow, shuffling movement possible, but they were surprisingly unattached to wall or floor. He was free to stumble around in the begrimed confines of his cell.

However, his calf protested when he stood. Conan's knee simply refused to unbend, forcing him to hop one-legged like a circus buffoon. His fingers encountered thick iron bars in two walls of the cage and stone at the other two—a corner cell.

The screams abated, giving way to agonized sobs. A soft but telltale hiss preceded each cry. That sound, accompanied by the faint, repugnant stink of roasting flesh, told of the goings-on in the torturer's chamber.

"Had enough, dog?" a harsh voice barked.

The only reply was loud, labored breathing and a low moan.

"We'll have it, sooner or later, fool! Better sooner, while you've lost only half your sight. Now tell us where you hid Her Majesty's tiara, or by Set, I'll shove this iron through your other eye!"

"Please . . . no. She wore it not . . . no! Mitra, mercy!"

Conan shuddered at the loud hiss that issued from the blackness, a rush of anger coursing through his blood as the poor wretch screamed like a damned soul in Hell. Though no stranger to torture, the Cimmerian was repulsed by its cruel cowardice. The torturer's malevolent chuckles fanned the flames of his ire, and he clenched his fists in helpless frustration.

The screams ended abruptly. The poor devil had either passed out or died—the latter might have been more merciful.

Conan wasted no time wondering why the *asshuri* had not simply run him through. No doubt he himself was in for it, too, either torture, execution, or both. Yet he was alive—wounded, but far from dead. A crude, blood-encrusted bandage encircled his swollen leg. His captors valued him more alive than dead, and that gave him an advantage.

A heavy door slammed, and booted feet approached. A dim, bobbing torch revealed a long corridor of cells, with Conan's at the end. The torch's bearer had an ugly face and a torso more hairy than a yak. These features, and his long arms, suggested closer kinship to an ape than to a Shemite. Of course, some maintained that there was little difference between *any* Shemite and an ape.

This repulsive brute's fingers clenched the thick hair of a man who was either dead or unconscious. A glimpse at the ruined eyes and gore-smeared face revealed the torturer's gruesome handiwork. Dragging the limp-bodied man by his reddish hair, the apelike Shemite lumbered halfway down the corridor before he stopped and tossed his charge into an open cell. He slammed its heavy door and slid its iron bar into place. The sound echoed as he stamped back out, and darkness again obscured the dismal dungeon.

Conan nearly jumped at the sound of a whisper from the cell opposite his, across the corridor.

"Crom!" he muttered, unnerved that he had neither seen nor heard this fellow prisoner.

"A cold god of bleak Cimmeria. And you—a Cimmerian, in Shem?" The woman's husky voice had an amused tone, strange in the bleak surroundings. Though the speaker's tongue was that of Shem, the accent was foreign—Zamorian, most probably.

"Aye—Conan. And have you a birthplace and a name?"

"I am Kylanna—from Zamora," she added with a sigh.

Conan's brow furrowed. Kylanna—royalty of Zamora, as he knew from his travels in that kingdom. She was the catch of a life-time for these black-bearded jackals! But they were mad to throw *her* into this slime-hole. He snorted in outrage. "Rarer than a Cimmerian in Shem is a Zamorian princess, stuck in an *asshuri* dungeon!"

"My father—Tiridates—sent me to Shem with an escort of one hundred men," she explained. "Rumors of an alliance between Shem and Koth reached his ears; he fears that these kingdoms will band together and attack him. I was to marry the prince in Shushan and formalize the alliance between Zamora and Shem. But these Shemite brigands waylaid us at the feet of the Mountains of Fire."

"A mere hundred guards?" Conan blurted in disbelief. "Tiridates was ever a drunken dullard . . . and old age has left him with the wits of a village idiot!"

Kylanna did not respond.

"Crom, girl," the barbarian growled sheepishly. "I meant no insult. Anyway, his hundred men would have fared better against mere brigands. It was *asshuri* who captured you—elite troops. No doubt some kinglet in these parts seeks to prevent the alliance of Zamora with Shem. Niggling nobles infest this land like flies on a dungheap. The whole lot of them should just fight it out on a field of battle, like men, and settle the matter once and for all. Only a cowardly swine would abduct a girl and pitch her into this slimy warren."

"He could not spare many soldiers," she replied indignantly. "Already he had moved most of our family from the palace at Shadizar to the keep in Arenjun, fearing that assassins might strike at his daughters. Koth's nobles will do anything to prevent a royal marriage between the houses of Shem and Zamora. Many men he sent as

29

a garrison, to protect his family. And with the threat from Koth itself—"

"No matter," Conan interrupted. Politics wearied him faster than the most arduous physical exertion. In Cimmeria, the best politician was a keen-edged blade. "The man they tortured here—was he among your escort?"

"Captain Tousalos." Her voice sounded strained, as if she were choking back tears. "When the Shemites attacked, he thirded the escort and scattered us in different directions. The others . . ." She paused, her voice wavering. "The others—"

"Slain, no doubt," he conjectured brusquely. "Until now, I never heard of the *asshuri* taking prisoners. But we are not their first guests here, methinks. Have they tortured you yet?"

His blunt question seemed to catch her by surprise; her despondent whisper came after a long silence. "Yet? They will torture me—a princess?"

"Perhaps not, if they have demanded a ransom from Tiridates."

"Then be silent and burden me with no more worries!" Her voice rose an octave. "It is true what they say about your race. You are savages—brutish barbarians with hearts as cold as the hills in which you dwell! You demean my father and speak to me as if I am some village tramp. It is you they should torture. Murdering louts like you deserve to rot in dungeons!"

Conan blinked, taken aback by her venomous outburst. He had been forward with her, but it was not his nature to bow and scrape before every man and woman who bore a title. Respect was earned, not given. Still, he reckoned that his manner had been too callous. Months of piracy in the company of scrofulous sea-dogs had taken its toll on him. Royal birthright aside, Kylanna was but a frightened girl ensnared in a trap of violence and deceit. Furthermore, Conan's upbringing had instilled in him a rough code of honor that tolerated no mistreatment of innocents, particularly women. Without giving the matter more thought, Conan spoke solemnly. "I swear upon Crom, god of my people, to free you from this place. Hell awaits me if I fail."

"Noble words for one so base," Kylanna scoffed. "I'll warrant that you've uttered them a hundred times—without honoring them once."

Conan bit back a stinging rebuttal. It would do nothing but affirm her low opinion of him. Only deeds would settle this aright. He would carry her all the way to Arenjun if need be and pick up his loot on the way back. Rulvio and the lads would keep for a few weeks. By Crom, they would keep for months if the loot held out that long!

Conan lowered himself to the floor to rest his good leg and conserve strength. As he did so, an odious possibility presented itself. The map! What if these thrice-accursed *asshuri* had confiscated it? They had not taken his vest, at least. His chains limited his reach, but he could run his fingers along the right side of the garment . . . there! The seam had not been disturbed. In all likelihood, the map still rested between the outer and inner leathers. He breathed easier, glad that he had sealed the folded parchment into his vest's hidden pocket.

From down the hall came a rattle, then the thump of boots on stone. The unsightly torturer was back. He stomped to the corridor's end and set his torch into a fixture upon the wall, directly between Conan's cell and Kylanna's. The Cimmerian stared longingly at the pair of keys that hung from a ring on the jailer's broad belt.

The foul-smelling fiend ignored Conan and unlocked Kylanna's cell door. He stepped within as Conan's pulse began to race. Even in the shifting torchlight, he could see why a prince of Shushan would desire the daughter of Tiridates. Her blond tresses wreathed a flawless face, with pale, rosy lips. In her eyes danced jade fire that could enchant a man's heart. A thin, scanty tunic accentuated her generous curves and clung to her full breasts. Her long, shapely legs, bare from mid-thigh down, trembled slightly at the Shemite's approach. The *asshuri* had not fettered her as they had Conan.

The hairy devil tore away her tunic and ogled her nude form. Conan seethed in helpless fury as the swine's intent became clear. "Cur!" he shouted, his voice like the roar of an enraged lion. "Touch her, and I'll tear out your black heart with my hands and feed it to the rats!"

The hideous head swiveled on its squat, fleshy neck to face Conan. "Heh!" the jailer chuckled. "Idle threats, from a man who's as good as dead. The noose awaits you in Kyros this night, dog. Ho! With the reward we get for snaring you, I'll feast like a lord tomorrow while you dangle from a rope. Now be silent and learn how a real man pleasures a woman—afore we trade her for Tiridates' gold."

Kylanna shrieked and backed away. The jailer pinned her against the wall, fumbling at his belt.

Conan strained at his chains, fury flowing hotter than molten lava through his veins. Steel links battled iron thews; blood streamed from beneath the Cimmerian's manacles as he grunted and flexed his arms in an effort that three normal men could not have matched. But the contest was hopeless, the chains forged so stoutly that only a sledge and chisel could break them.

"Conan!" came the pleading cry from Kylanna's cell, followed by the clink of metal on stone.

The Cimmerian stared dumbfounded at the ring of keys, which had slid to a stop mere inches from his feet. He wasted no time pondering how Kylanna had snatched them, for the jailer had roughly flung her to the floor then spun away, grunting incoherently. Conan fumbled with his manacles, choosing the wrong key first, then freeing himself of the steel constraints in a deft frenzy of movement.

The Shemite charged into the corridor as Conan shoved his arm through the bars of his cell door and turned the key in the lock. He forced his stiff knee to bend, hobbling like a lame beggar and cursing the pain that flared from his calf. With both hands, he shoved the door open, slamming it into the jailer's face.

The leering Shemite snarled and shoved it back, shutting Conan into the cell.

Conan hurled his shoulder against the bars and forced the door open again. In his hand dangled chains, weighted by thick iron manacles. He slipped through the door as the jailer's fist plowed into his belly. The blow would have sent a lesser man reeling, but Conan's midriff was sheathed in muscles of steel. He shouted fiercely and cracked the torturer's skull with a powerful blow from his heavy chains. Blood and brains sprayed the corridor. Conan seized the torch from the wall and called to Kylanna before the twitching corpse struck the floor. She made a hasty effort to cover herself with her shredded garments, then grimaced and hopped over the dead Shemite.

Conan bent to check the body for a dagger or some other weapon, ignoring the gush of crimson from the ruined head. The jailer had carried no arms. "Carry this," he said as he handed the torch to Kylanna. "That ruckus will assuredly fetch more of these *asshuri* dogs. Follow me and tarry not."

"Yes, *milord*," she huffed, "I'll free Captain Tousalos and look for others while you stand guard." She snatched the keys from him.

Her sarcasm was wasted on Conan, who noted only that she seemed to have recovered fully from her encounter with the scurrilous Shemite. The girl was either tough or haughty—perhaps both. Favoring his wounded leg, Conan hastened toward the only exit, a stout wooden door reinforced with iron bands. The girl glanced into each cell but entered only the one holding the torturer's victim.

"Arise, Tousalos!" Kylanna's frantic whisper echoed from the shadows. "Captain? Ah, Bel—no!" With a sob, Kylanna emerged from the shadows. "Dead," she said, her eyes downcast.

Conan nodded. "As I feared," he said with as much sympathy as he could muster. "Doubtless we shall join him in Hell if we further delay our escape. We must be away, now!"

He took back the keys and fitted one into the door's lock. Beyond lay narrow stairs leading down into a dimly lit corridor. Kylanna clutched at Conan's proffered hand, eliciting a faint grin from him as they descended. When they reached the bottom, nothing awaited them but a single flickering torch on the corridor wall. They passed by a chamber replete with torture instruments, and a pestilent pit of a room that might have been the jailer's. Heaps of charred rat-bones lay next to a soiled straw mattress; Conan's nose twitched at the reek that befouled the air.

The key opened another iron-banded door where the hallway ended. Conan pushed it open and surveyed the area beyond with some wonderment. The door opened to a fenced stockade. The prison was aboveground—a windowless, stone box squatting in a small compound that probably served as an *asshuri* base. A few wooden buildings rose from the muddy ground of the enclosure. When his eyes had adjusted to the light of what was either dawn or dusk, Conan saw no trace of their *asshuri* captors.

Eager to exploit this good fortune but unwilling to proceed without a measure of caution, Conan turned to Kylanna and raised his finger to his lips. He then pointed at the nearest fence and crept toward it. Kylanna left the torch behind and followed him. Other than the hoofprints of countless horses in the mud and the occasional impressions of *asshuri* boots, the place bore few signs of habitation. He whirled when he heard a sound from one of the small wooden buildings, then relaxed. It had been the snort of a restless horse.

They strolled toward the sound and entered the wooden structure.

Kylanna followed close behind, her small hand still engulfed by the Cimmerian's massive fist. It was now obvious that the sound had issued from the compound's stable. A familiar, pungent smell rose from rows of straw, and a trough of water lined one of the structure's three walls. Four horses—three of them fully saddled—shifted nervously as Conan and Kylanna approached.

Conan scowled, his suspicions aroused by this unexpected boon. Something sudden had transpired, else the *asshuri* would never have left their encampment unguarded. He reasoned that the absence of the *asshuri* might account for the bold assault on Kylanna; he doubted that the other rogues would have sanctioned the jailer's despoilment of so precious a treasure. But wounded or sleeping men might lie in the other buildings, and the Cimmerian felt it unwise to linger. Armed with naught but his makeshift weapon of chains and manacles, he would have the worst of a melee if the damned *asshuri* returned. It were better to escape on these mounts before his well of good fortune ran dry.

"We ride east," he whispered. Though the terrain lacked any landmarks that he recognized, the sun had become increasingly visible on the horizon. His natural sense of direction needed no more to establish a course.

The beasts shifted and shied from them, but Conan's horsemanship won out. Kylanna eyed the steeds uneasily, though she vaulted into the saddle and held the reins like a hostler. Conan noted that each of the horses, finely groomed specimens, carried saddlebags, rope, and waterskins. The *asshuri* had a commendable penchant for readiness.

Unaccosted, the strange duo trotted out of the compound's simple gate, which Conan closed behind them. He spared the time to survey their meadowy surroundings, noting that the enclosure nestled in a valley begirded by steep, sparsely forested hills. No path had been beaten through the meadows; the crafty *asshuri* chose different routes of access to avoid that very thing. From afar, no casual eyes would behold any sign of the compound's existence. To which of Shem's city-states did these warriors swear fealty? Conan reckoned that he would know soon enough.

As their horses scaled the eastern hillside and surmounted the ridge, Conan looked down at a fertile, green countryside that stretched in every direction to the limits of his vision. He recognized this lush landscape of vineyards. More precisely, he knew by sight the distinctive mark of Kyros, which adorned the massive gates of the walled city that rose from the greenery a mere half-league from the hilltop.

Kyros! From her grapes were born the finest wines Hyboria offered—and the most expensive. The royal family of Kyros wielded immense wealth and power, all of which stemmed from the flora of these valleys. Just as kings hired men-at-arms to guard their palace walls or protect their royal treasuries, the ruler of Kyros employed many companies of *asshuri* to maintain his empire of vines. Perhaps Kyros, as well as Koth, sought to prevent a treaty between Zamora and the dominant city-states of eastern Shem.

Conan's brow furrowed in annoyance. In Messantia, his treasure-hunt had seemed such a pleasurable prospect, free of the irksome artifices that now clouded his thoughts. Well, he would have none of it. Loot was all he sought from this foray—that and some honest bloodletting, should any rogues stand in his way. Too many obstacles lay to the east. The Cimmerian scowled and turned his horse around.

"We must ride north, not east," he advised Kylanna.

She had been occupied with adjusting her tattered garb, succeeding at last in a more modest arrangement. "North—to *Koth?*"

Conan nodded. "Aye. You can send a messenger to your father and have him come for you. I shall ride with you as far as Hanshali, a village on the road through the Kothian hills. Merchants and tradesmen control it, so your safety can be procured by simply negotiating for an escort to Arenjun. Mayhap you can pay for passage with one of the caravans passing from Argos to Zamora."

Kylanna looked doubtful. "I did not mean to speak such ill of you, back in the cell," she said. "And you did not hear all of my story. When our band rode toward Shushan, my saddlebags carried more than victuals. The king secretly sent a great treasure with me, as my dowry." Her voice faltered, as if doubting the wisdom of revealing the secret to the barbarian.

The Cimmerian waited patiently, his expression unchanged.

Clearing her throat, she continued. "The Tiara of Zakhraf, who was Zath's greatest high priestess of old."

Conan smirked derisively. In Zamboula's taverns, he had often heard the tale of that tiara's fate. "Hah! Lost decades ago, when the Kezankian hillmen sacked the temple in Yezud. Were it found, would Tiridates send a mere hundred men to guard it?"

Kylanna shook her head. "He did not wish to draw attention to me. And it was not lost—it was stolen. My father . . . obtained it from a Nemedian thief, who put a clever forgery in its place. *Before* the temple was burned."

"Impossible! No such thief lives. Even I . . . well, no man could enter the place. Four thousand hillmen perished before even one laid eyes upon the temple's interior."

Kylanna shook her head. "No, not impossible—not for Taurus of Nemedia. Though he may no longer live; in this you may speak truly. He disappeared years hence, but he procured the tiara ere he vanished."

"Taurus! I met him long ago, in Shadizar . . . but he did not disappear. The bite of a devil-spider sent him to Hell." Conan shuddered at the memory of his brief but harrowing enterprise with Taurus. By happenstance, he and the Nemedian had chosen the same night to rob the mage Yara's tower, unaware of a venomous guardian lurking within. Conan had never since met a thief of Taurus's skill. If anyone could have pilfered Zakhraf's trinket from the temple in Yezud, it would have been that crafty Nemedian.

"You knew him?" Her eyes widened in bemusement. "Well, I suppose that in his profession, he would have associated with all sorts of thugs."

Conan raised an eyebrow but let the insult pass.

Kylanna sighed. "Taurus was a friend of my father's, one of few who were kind to me. Tiridates often employed him for tasks requiring special talent. When I was a child, Taurus would bring baubles from faraway lands for my amusement."

"Aye, a decent enough rogue was Taurus . . . and more honorable than any Zamorian king," Conan added. Though he mistrusted Kylanna, he was now convinced that her story bore some resemblance to the truth. After all, the ruthless *asshuri* had tortured Captain Tousalos to learn the tiara's whereabouts. "But what of the tiara?"

"We hid it on the way. I shall reveal its hiding place to you—but not until you escort me safely to Arenjun's gate. I will tell my father that these Shemites stole the tiara."

"I think not, your majesty," Conan rumbled, his nostrils flaring. "You must tell me now; we can retrieve it ere we reach Arenjun."

Kylanna crossed her arms indignantly and glared at Conan. "You did spare me from a hideous fate this day," she said, as if trying to convince herself. "I am beholden to you for that, unseemly as it it. But what is to stop you from abandoning me when I divulge this secret?"

"Ishtar!" Conan exhaled. "Fickle wench—fetch it yourself and walk half-naked from here to Arenjun, if you mistrust me."

"Very well," she grumbled, wringing her hands. "Tousalos flung it into a pond at the foot of Devil's Thumb—a peak rising from the westernmost edge of the Mountains of Fire."

"Due north," Conan muttered, thinking aloud. "Our most direct approach is across the northern hills of Kyros and through the fields of Ghaza. No easy ride, that, even without *asshuri* dogs nipping at our heels. By Crom, we have wasted precious time on idle prattle when we should have been moving. Ride swiftly with me to keep up, if you would save your royal backside from further indignities!"

The whinny of Conan's steed smothered her outraged rebuff. Kylanna's eyes blazed as she urged her horse to a gallop, matching the Cimmerian's pace.

Six
Stalkers and Sorcerers

Toj scrambled down from his hiding place atop the *asshuri* prison, his thoughts awhirl. To avoid leaving footprints in the mud, he leapt onto the low fence in front of the *asshuri* stable and raced nimbly across its narrow wooden beams. A single horse lingered near the fence.

The assassin launched himself from a fence post into the saddle. He faced no mean challenge: Pursuing the girl and the Cimmerian in broad daylight might reveal his presence to them. But he dared not lose Conan again. Already he had been lucky—had the *asshuri* slain Conan, Toj would soon have joined him in Hell. He must protect Conan, or the Cimmerian would fail to retrieve the pearl god and Jade would not destroy the *kalb* beetle.

At first, the Cimmerian's trail was simple to follow. Toj's tracking skills had rendered this task effortless from Messantia all the way to Argos's eastern border. But the events of the past two days still befuddled him. First, the chase led by the *asshuri*, ending in Conan's imprisonment. Toj had stayed far back to avoid detection and thus had been too distant to help Conan escape. When some twenty of them had borne the barbarian away, the assassin had not dared to intervene. He had waited until nightfall and crept past the sentries into the enclosure. A brief span of eavesdropping divulged the Cimmerian's location. As he slithered up the prison's outer wall and onto its rooftop, the strange woman had ridden into the compound.

She had met with the *asshuri* who bore the accoutrements of a general. He had bowed to her and nodded respectfully at her curt commands. The two had stayed out of earshot, much to Toj's disappointment. Then, before Toj's incredulous gaze, she had stripped down to her tunic, rubbed dirt on herself, mussed her hair, and marched into the building. The general had the beard shaven from an *asshuri* corpse's face—one of the men slain by Conan—and outfitted the body in the garb of a Zamorian soldier.

"When the barbarian awakens, have the torturer begin," she had said, this time near enough for Toj to hear.

"Yes, milady. We shall depart ere dawn breaks."

"Belike he will slay your torturer."

"It is of no moment, milady. The dog is not *asshuri*—he is naught but a Shemite murderer whom I freed from the headsman's block in Kyros. The brute knows nothing."

"So be it, then—his blood stains your hands, Arostrio."

Toj had lain upon the roof, vexed that this woman had befouled his plan to free the Cimmerian from captivity. Conan must reach the City of Brass soon, before the *kalb* beetle laid its lethal eggs. But his curiosity had prompted him to lie prone upon the roof and watch the strange woman's scheme unfold. Besides, these warriors would have dispatched the barbarian already, had they been so inclined.

The assassin waited as several horses were saddled and led into the stable with the woman's ebony stallion. Muffled screams from a room below him had reached Toj's ears, at which time the entire *asshuri* contingent had gathered at the enclosure's gate and ridden away.

Conan and the woman had emerged from the building shortly thereafter. The woman had altered her voice and her demeanor, though . . . like an actress changing roles in some incomprehensible drama.

Even now, Toj could not hazard a guess at what the final act might be. He could easily have disposed of the meddlesome woman with a flick of his wrist, but in doing so, he would have revealed himself to

Conan. No ... instead, he would see where their path led. The woman presented no obstacle yet, and Jade had warned Toj that "others" would seek the pearl statue. Toj would slay the woman only if she further impeded Conan. And Toj reasoned that this would be a deed best done under the cover of night, while the Cimmerian slept. The assassin carried with him the means to deter suspicions of murder.

Indeed, the thin leather sack strapped to his back was crammed with cunning devices, rare poisons and herbs, and some few live creatures, all of which dealt death in myriad ways. Perhaps he would use the white Vendhyan scorpion for the woman—but no, the serpent's skull had advantages. With his Zembabwan bamboo pipe, he could blow an envenomed needle into the woman's neck while she slept. For such a purpose, he carried a small jar of his most deadly poison: powder from the black Khitan mushroom stalk mixed with venom from the Stygian emperor cobra. A drop of that blend was as deadly as a dagger plunged into the victim's heart.

The woman would die in a few silent moments, after which he would puncture her face with the skull's fangs. The wound—and the corpse's bloated, contorted visage—would mirror the attack of a virulent asp. Conan would suspect no foul play.

Satisfied with his plan, Toj followed the tracks of the Cimmerian and the mysterious woman. The two had already ridden out of sight, but their trail proved easy to follow.

The assassin shifted in the saddle, unaccustomed to its feel. He continued his assessment of the meddlesome woman. Whatever fate her scheme held for Conan, it could not be helpful to Toj. Tonight, he would end her involvement.

Tonight, she would die.

Some hundred leagues south of Kyros, the sluggish River Styx flowed past the Stygian city of Harakht, where dusky-faced Stygians clad in amber-hued robes bowed and crooned strange dirges before immense idols of their Hawk-God. Harakht's sentries admitted no foreigners; even Stygians who requested egress were subjected to knife-sharp inquiries, lest they be acting as spies. Many were searched, and Harakht's gatekeepers turned away any who were not devout worshipers of the Hawk-God or of Set.

This policy condemned many to death, for no water save that of the befouled Styx—and that of a single oasis—could be found within a day's ride or Harakht. Yet the oasis was avoided, even by those whose dry, sand-choked throats had not tasted water in days. Travelers in that arid waste heeded grim warnings whispered only in the light of day. And at night, no one dared to speak of what befell trespassers at the dreaded Oasis of Khajar.

There were worse fates than dying of thirst . . . much, much worse. For Thoth-Amon, Stygia's prince of sorcerers, dealt harshly with those who violated his domain.

Fully aware of these dire consequences, Tevek Thul nonetheless willed his skeletal steeds to venture into the oasis. He felt no apprehension at the imminent encounter. Tevek suspected that Thoth-Amon had already felt his approach. The necromancer relaxed his magical grip on his undead caravan, letting the sands of control trickle between his fingers. The horses and warriors toppled to the sand in jumbled heaps of bone.

Tevek exhaled deeply. His head tingled uncomfortably from breaking the psychic bonds he had formed with his subjects, and he paused to let the brief moment of disorientation pass. The animation of the dead required little energy to maintain once the bonds were in place, but the enchantment's dissolution took its toll. The longer that one left the bonds in place, the greater the strain at their severance. A lesser practitioner would have been rendered unconscious for a day. However, Tevek had scarcely used a drop from the deep well of necromantic energy he possessed. He had deemed it unwise to proceed with his minions, lest Thoth-Amon misinterpret his motives. The message borne by the vulture zombie may not have arrived; no acknowledgment of receipt had been made.

Tevek had longed to meet Set's champion again . . . this time as one worthy of Thoth-Amon's respect. He gathered his offering—the three clay Tablets of Epithur—and tucked them under his deceptively scrawny arm. Opening the trapdoor in the bottom of his black carriage, he stepped down onto the sands at the perimeter of Thoth-Amon's lair.

Nightfall had already drained the air and the ground of the desert sun's warmth. The earth felt cool beneath Tevek's bare feet, and a gentle breeze whispered through the dark palms and rippled across a sinister black pool. Its unwholesome surface reflected no moonlight or starlight, and its writhing currents endowed it with an eerie semblance of life. In spite of the breeze, a stifling silence enshrouded the oasis. No lizards stirred in the sand or swam in the pool; no birds roosted in the palms overhead.

At the center of the oasis loomed a massive, forbidding edifice. Constructed of gigantic sandstone blocks, its reddish exterior was worn smooth, its edges rounded. Tevek could not guess at the number of centuries this structure had stood, weathering the wind-driven storms.

The necromancer breathed deeply, relishing the comforting scent of cloying wickedness that pervaded the pool and radiated from the immense building. No maggots of Mitra had ever writhed in the innards of this dead place; the very air teemed with an almost palpable presence of immaculate evil. Tevek understood why Thoth-Amon seldom took leave of this comforting domain. He himself was, for similar reasons, loath to abandon his own necropolis.

On his way to the entrance of the edifice, he became aware of a curious sensation of *emptiness*. He paused and closed his eyes, focusing his mind to sense if any remains of the dead lay buried nearby. With practiced efficiency, he pushed the fingers of his mind into the hard-packed sand. He widened and deepened his search, but encountered nothing. As he had suspected, no charnel lay beneath the structure or the sand around it. He frowned. Evil as it was, this oasis lacked the burial chambers that nourished a necromancer's mind . . . and his body. He had expected to find catacombs beneath this sandstone edifice, and their absence unsettled him. All he sensed was a vague residue of carrion lingering within the sand at the bottom of the deep pool, but he could not see within. Water defied his spectral sight.

Tevek opened his eyes and waited impatiently for his vision to return. He endured a moment of blindness for every moment that he had employed his spectral sight. When the oasis's shadowy outline came into focus, he walked alongside the pool and boldly stepped up to the hulking megalith. Its shadowy entrance gaped like an open maw that led straight into Hell's throat.

The necromancer glanced at the glyphs etched into the massive arched doorway. Even Tevek, well-versed in obscure and ancient writings, had never seen their like. But he could guess their purpose; Thoth-Amon would lay sorcerous traps to snare or slay those not initiated into Set's priesthood. The practice was common enough in Stygia.

Tevek extended a hand from his voluminous sleeve and began to trace the sigil of Set in the air. Priests at Nebthu had shown him this sign, though he seldom invoked it. Green lines glowed in midair, as if Tevek were writing on an invisible tablet with a luminous stylus.

Behind him, the black pool was aboil.

Its gargantuan mass oozed *upward*, out of its bed in the sand, sprouting two armlike appendages and growing a bulbous protuberance at its apex. Its torso glistened and pulsated like a misshapen heart. Not one droplet of water fell from it, as if its surface had become a shiny skin. Monstrous hands, each large enough to engulf a man, reached for the necromancer.

Tevek's fingernail traced the last line of the symbol.

As quickly as it had taken form, the pool receded. But for a sluggish ripple on its surface, no evidence of its transformation remained. Tevek glanced over his shoulders. For just a moment, he had sensed the presence of the dead . . . an overwhelmingly powerful surge like that he had experienced at the ancient ossuary in Luxur's temple district, where for centuries priests had dumped the cadavers of their sacrificial victims into the same pit. The weight of fresher corpses above eventually compacted the desiccated mass below, slowly crushing bones into dust. Tevek had admired its efficiency.

He stared again at the pool, now certain that its oily waters concealed a vast trove of remains. Thoth-Amon had doubtless sacrificed thousands to Set in return for prodigious magical powers.

Tevek strode forward into an empty antechamber and descended a flight of stone steps. His soft footfalls raised whispering echoes against the smooth, worn stone. He needed no lantern; a simple invocation imbued his eyes with a red glow that pierced the veil of darkness. Moving well below the level of the desert, he soon entered a hall.

Serpentine cressets, set into walls of seamless stone, radiated sinister green light. Tevek let the red hue abate from his eyes, finding this new illumination to be more than adequate. Ahead, two rows of monolithic columns lined the spacious hall. Cryptic glyphs, like those on the doorway's arch outside, stippled the rounded stone pillars from ceiling to floor.

A simple throne, sculpted from glittering basaltic rock, dominated the opposite end of the hall. As Tevek approached, he held his clay tablets out before him and studied the throne's occupant.

Thoth-Amon had not aged visibly since Tevek had last seen him. Here was the same giant of a man, his skin the rich brown of mahogany. His only garment was a robe of white linen that stretched across his broad shoulders and swept the tops of his sandaled feet. Tevek greedily eyed the Stygian's massive ring of beaten copper.

This object—Thoth-Amon's sole ornament—had been forged in the likeness of a serpent that coiled thrice about his finger and held its tail in fanged jaws. Though copper in color, it was known as the Black Ring, for Set himself had imbued it with dark powers to aid his chosen champions. Beneath the sarcophagus of Ptah-nefer, an ancient predecessor of Thoth-Amon interred at Nebthu, Tevek had found a bronze tablet whose etched runes revealed the Black Ring's secrets.

It was that lore, etched in bronze, that had inspired Tevek to seek Thoth-Amon, for there he had read that *any* sorcerer could bend the Black Ring to a particular purpose. Ptah-nefer described in great detail the workings of the ancient talisman and the methods of channeling its power. With that power at his disposal, Tevek hoped to recover and control the object that would turn his dreams of vengeance into reality: the Grim Grey God.

He had only recently learned where the god lay, but its destructive powers could not be summoned unless one knew any three of the six names that comprised the god's full and true name. The high priests of Ibis knew only three names; the other three were recorded in grimoires of the blackest sorcery that dated back to Acheron. Knowledge of all six names would grant the power to destroy the god—something the priests of Ibis had doubtless sought to accomplish. But whoever knew all six names could do more than that—he could command the god's considerable powers. What better way to seek retribution, to doom the vermin of Khyfa beyond all hope? This time, Mitra would not save them!

Tevek could, with the Black Ring, divine all six of the names. Among his arcane lore was a spell that forced the departed to speak. Even those dead for centuries could be commanded to answer queries, but such an undertaking required tremendous magickal energy—more than Tevek possessed if he were to cast the enchantment upon a long-dead priest of Ibis. Only by drawing upon the Black Ring's raw power could Tevek succeed.

The sight of the ring sent a ripple of cold satisfaction through the mage's bones. He envisioned it upon his own finger. Soon, Tevek would grind the Mitran temples of Khyfa to dust and punish the descendants of Amentet's desecrators.

"Greetings, mighty Thoth-Amon," Tevek rasped, surprised by the dryness in his throat.

The dusky giant did not respond. HIs muscular frame sat motionless in its ebony seat. Eyes as black as his throne stared glassily forward, like those of a corpse.

"Thoth-Amon?" Tevek repeated, this time raising his voice. He shifted his tablets to one hand and lifted his cowl, uncovering his gaunt, pockmarked face. The necromancer's eyes and skin, in contrast to Thoth-Amon's, were pallid, yellowed grey. The palest of blue hues diffused his lips. Tevek's shocking white hair reached down past his shoulders; his square-cut beard curled outward at its end, halfway down his neck. The emerald glow from the cressets only accentuated Tevek's ghoulish visage.

Beneath his simple robes, Thoth-Amon's breast neither rose nor fell.

Tevek sighed. Perhaps the Stygian had freed his *ka* to roam a nameless spirit-realm, abandoning his body utterly. If so, Tevek might wait here for a long time. "So be it," he muttered, lowering himself to the floor. As he did so, the topmost tablet slid from his grasp and shattered on the black flagstones. Vexed, Tevek cursed and glared at the clay fragments.

A hollow moan issued from Thoth-Amon's motionless lips, quiet at first, as if from far away, but increasing in volume. The previously inert hands clenched into fists. *"Ai kon-phog, yaa!"* His voice howled through the hall like a fierce blast of frost.

Silence swiftly returned as the reverberatious died away. Tevek set down the remaining tablets, rose from the floor, clasped his hands, and mentally prepared his defenses, just in case.

The Stygian mage seemed to have regained his composure. His black eyes, alert now, swept Tevek from head to toe, the gaze as cold and predatory as a serpent's. Finally, he spoke. "Tevek Thul." Beneath the strong, clear voice was a rustling undertone, like the sound of slithering snakes.

"Yes, Dread Lord. Forgive my intrusion, but a matter of utmost importance has compelled me to—"

"—to end your insignificant life," the Stygian intoned. "What know you of *importance*, doltish robber of graves? Fah!" He gestured dismissively with his copper-ringed hand.

Tevek felt seeds of tension sprout in his shoulders. "I meant no offense, Mighty One. Did not my winged herald precede me?"

"My guardian would have destroyed any messenger—as it should have destroyed you. Your clumsiness has ruined a magical operation of *true* importance. For many of your months have I worked undisturbed, my *ka* searching the akashic records . . ." Thoth-Amon paused, the irritation in his voice replaced with a tone as cold and sharp as a dagger of ice. "All for naught."

"Your" months? Tevek had skeptically listened to tales of Thoth-Amon's powers, but perhaps he had underestimated the Stygian. Nevertheless, he stepped forward and spoke boldly. "Dread Lord, before you are two of Epithur's clay tablets."

Thoth-Amon's serpentine eyes flickered briefly to the shattered remnants on the floor. The ringed hand gestured. "Three," he murmured as clay fragments rapidly coalesced into their original form. "So Epithur's engravings *do* exist. The elusive Codices of Eibon were accurate, then. Perhaps I shall spare your life after all. Begone and never return, lest I squash you like the carrion-maggot that you are."

Tevek raised an eyebrow and abandoned his pretense of deference. He had not traveled so far to be kicked like a begging dog. "Years ago, the search for these consumed you like a fire! I deliver them now in return for a favor."

"And I have granted you one. Depart!" Cold, green fire flickered in the Stygian's black eyes.

"At once, Dread Lord," Tevek hissed between clenched teeth. "*After* you give your ring to me. I shall return it in a fortnight."

Thoth-Amon's sibilant laughter filled the hall like a blast of winter sleet. He held his muscular hand aloft so that green light glimmered on his ring. "Is that all?" he thundered, leaning forward. "A favor. Then you shall have it!" As he spoke, the Stygian extended his arm, his hand clenched into a fist. Emerald fire flared from the outthrust ring and spewed toward Tevek.

The necromancer's robes burst into flames. However, the wearer within had vanished; the garments lay smoldering upon the flagstones.

"Eh?" Thoth-Amon's brow lifted in surprise. Then he saw Tevek's shadow, extending from the robes to one of the hall's columns.

"Your bolts cannot harm me." Tevek's voice was muffled.

"Bah! A Keshattan shadow-mage's parlor trick," Thoth-Amon said dismissively. "It cannot save you from this!" He raised both hands at shoulder-width apart, palms facing each other, his fingers a blur of motion. A hole of opaque darkness opened in the air before him, its edges swirling. The black vortex widened as it spun, whistling hellishly, and Tevek's shadow began to stretch toward its center. The Stygian's words were a mocking roar. "Join your ancestors as your feeble spirit is sucked into the well of souls!"

"Aepe, ton-theon, anlala lai gaia! AEPE!" Tevek's desperate words rang in the hall as the tip of his shadow was sucked into the maelstrom.

"No!" Thoth-Amon snarled and leapt from his throne, slapping his hands together. The vortex shrank and disappeared with his gesture, but two shadowy shapes issued from it before it vanished. They hovered like nebulous grey clouds, then assumed humanoid shape and flitted toward the Stygian.

"Too late!" Tevek panted. "The dead serve me, Stygian—be they bone or spirit, corporeal or spectral, I am their master!" The words came with effort. Bones were not difficult to control, but formless shades could slip easily from his grasp. They taxed him to his limits; he could not dominate them for long.

Shadowy fingers groped the dusky-skinned sorcerer. One wrapped grey hands around his throat while another clawed at his eyes. Thoth-Amon gasped and blinked as he twisted away from his ghostly assailants. Cursing, he choked out a few harsh, guttural syllables. A green nimbus flickered around the copper ring. It crept up the Stygian's arm and eventually encompassed his entire body. Beneath his glowing shield, Thoth-Amon's face was a contorted mask; veins pulsed in his neck and at his temples. His muscular body trembled as if from great exertion.

The emerald aura pushed away the shades, who battered it with fists of fog. It rippled, but did not give way.

Tevek's shadowy form became hazy, then visible. Mastery of the wraiths had drained his reserves of necromantic energy and forced him to abandon his spectral citadel. With closed eyes, he focused his mind on the shadowy minions, who continued their assault.

Thoth-Amon's black eyes gleamed fiercely. The pulse at his temple quickened, and he began to expand his shield outward, forcing the wraiths farther and farther away from him. He uttered a strange chant; its words crackled in the air like bolts of lightning. He divided his green aura and propelled each half toward a shade, enveloping both in luminous bubbles. Then he closed his hands into tight fists, wrenching cries of anguish from the wraiths.

The bubbles shrank into tiny spheres, and the howling within was silenced immediately. Thoth-Amon sank back into his throne and rubbed his hands together. He glared down at Tevek Thul.

The necromancer sank to his knees, exhausted. *Beaten*, he thought dazedly. He hung his head, too weak to face the blast of fire that would soon issue from the Black Ring. The numbness faded from his shaking limbs, and he steadied himself. Ashen tendrils rose from his still-smoking tunic, though he noticed absently that the green fire had not actually burned the fabric. He retrieved his robes from the floor, seeing that they also were intact.

"Impressive," boomed Thoth-Amon, whose composure had returned. "It seems that the boy whom I met at Nebthu has acquired some measure of competence."

Tevek lifted his head and looked into Thoth-Amon's appraising eyes. He coughed and willed himself to stand, awaiting the mage's next words.

"At your age," continued Thoth-Amon, "I could manage no more than one wraith at a time—and not even the Seers of Mount Yimsha can drag spirits *from* the Well of Souls to this earthly plane." He lapsed into silence and mused for a time. "For what purpose do you covet my Black Ring?"

Tevek cleared his throat. "To excise the Mitra-worshiping scum from Khyfa and reclaim the city, Dread Lord."

" 'Twere a worthy purpose, in sooth," murmured Thoth-Amon. "The cult of accursed Mitra must be trampled into slime, that Father Set may assume rightful dominion over all. But on *your* finger, the ring would lack power to defeat the legions of Khyfa. You know not its workings." He smiled condescendingly. "Now must I must renew the operation that you disturbed." His eyes flashed briefly, but clearly he had forgiven—though not forgotten—Tevek's interruption.

"Ah, Mighty One, I seek the ring for no purpose so base as mortal combat."

The Stygian nodded and favored Tevek with an approving gaze. "Why, then?"

"With the ring, I—and I alone, meaning no disrespect, Dread Lord—can exhume that which was long buried in time's cemetery. You see, I have divined the whereabouts of the Grim Grey God."

Thoth-Amon gripped the arms of his throne. "Impossible," he muttered. "Every mage of the First Circle has scryed the length and breadth of the land for any trace of the Brass City of Nithia. Ibis shields it from us. How did you find it?"

"*I* did not, Prince of Magicians," Tevek replied. He felt his strength return, and with it, his confidence. "A common Zamorian found it. He was a smuggler who traded between Khemi and Anshan, in Iranistan."

"I know of Anshan. Continue," commanded Thoth-Amon.

"On his final trek to Anshan, he encountered the brass spire of Ibis's temple. A violent desert storm had exposed it. Though he knew nothing of its significance, he drew a map to it, which he sold to the thieves' guild."

Thoth-Amon's brow furrowed.

"On his way back from Anshan to Khemi, to avoid a Stygian border patrol, the smuggler crossed into my domain—through Nebthu. He died within sight of its walls, though not by my hand. A curious affliction had stricken him. It had withered the very flesh from his body . . . and it had turned much of his innards into sand. This I learned when I disassembled him later." A chilling smile touched Tevek's pale lips.

Thoth-Amon raised an eyebrow. "The curse of Solnarus!"

"Indeed. Like you, I have perused the *Book of Skelos*, so I knew at once that this emaciated husk of a man had ventured into Nithia." Tevek loosened the strings of a magically warded pouch made from the cured flesh of a young virgin. He dumped its contents—coarse, ashy dust—onto the floor. Though still weakened by his conflict with Thoth-Amon, Tevek had sufficient energy to perform the rite. He gestured and focused his mind on the fine granules, which stirred lazily and then formed themselves into the shape of a human skull.

The dusky-skinned Stygian nodded and drummed his fingers together, as if he knew what wizardry Tevek intended and was impatient to see it done.

"Tell me your name," Tevek commanded. His voice seemed amplified, as if it came from a chorus of throats. The questioning of the dead could be a tiresome practice. The departed could not lie outright, at least not to a necromancer of Tevek's skill, but they would mislead if given the chance. By an exhaustive process, Tevek had forced the smuggler to retrace his steps.

"Har . . . rab." The skull's response came as a distant echo, like the voice of a man at the bottom of a deep pit.

"Before you died, did you see a brass spire that rose from the desert?"

"Yes."

Thoth-Amon interrupted. "So you divined the location of the city. I must hear the rest myself, for this Harrab may have tried to deceive you."

Tevek nodded and cleared his throat, then focused his gaze on the skull. "You drew a map to the brass spire?"

"Yes."

"What became of this map?"

"Sold."

"To whom did you sell it?"

"Ib . . . har . . . am."

"Where did you sell it?"

"An . . . shan."

"The map—it was accurate?"

"Yes."

"Ibharam of Anshan—what is his profession?"

"Guild . . . mas . . . ter . . . thieves."

"Rest, Harrab." Tevek gestured, and the skull fell into dust. He took a piece of folded parchment from the pouch, knelt and carefully swept the dust back in. "The Brass City lies southeast of Shushan, in Shem's eastern desert. Only with your Black Ring can I safely retrieve the Grim Grey God—and when I command its powers, Khyfa will fall!"

"You said that you alone could fetch the idol. What is to stop me?"

"There is danger to you far greater than the curse," Tevek said softly. "*You* have sworn fealty to Set. In the ancient scrolls of Siptah's, I once read a warning that any follower of Set who enters the city will awaken Ibis and risk the destruction of the pearl god. Siptah wrote that the worship of accursed Ibis empowered Nithia with strong wards against those loyal to Set's purpose. Dare you to test the wards—can the Black Ring protect you from a god? As for me, my deeds serve Set's purpose more often than not, but I have sworn no oaths to him. My own gods are many: Ereškigal, Heret-Kau, Nephthys, Serkethetyt, Ta'xet, and Thanatos."

A scowl darkened Thoth-Amon's features, but the Stygian made no contradictory remarks. His attempts to destroy the priests of Ibis had failed too often for him to doubt that god's powers.

"Let me undertake this quest, Dread Lord," the necromancer continued. "Would it not please Set to see his worship resumed in Khyfa? When I command the Grim Grey God, I swear that ten thousand souls of Khyfa's Mitra-worshiping sheep shall be sacrificed to Set. Their blood shall desecrate Ibis's sanctuary there and anoint the stones of a new Temple of Set."

Green fire flickered in Thoth-Amon's black eyes while he contemplated the necromancer's words. He nodded solemnly, and his scowl retreated. Leaning forward, he lowered his hand to the floor. Like a living serpent, his copper ring uncoiled itself from his finger and slithered toward Tevek. "The Black Ring is yours for a time, until I recall it to my hand."

Tevek's brow furrowed as he knelt to receive the tiny snake. It wound itself about his finger and clasped its tail in its jaws, then again became an inanimate ring. Immediately he felt its power infuse him; his vision blurred as the Black Ring hurled its dark energy at his body and mind in overpowering waves. It seemed to him that he stood in the center of an icy inferno whose frozen flames flicked at him like black tongues, stinging him wherever they touched him. The agony was unbearable. Marshaling his willpower, he pushed the agony from his mind and rose to his feet.

The biting bonfire abated.

He stood in Thoth-Amon's hall.

" 'The Black Ring will serve those it consumes not,' " Thoth-Amon muttered under his breath, perhaps recalling the time when the ring had first become his. "Know this, Tevek Thul," he admonished, his voice clear and strong. "When you channel the Black Ring's power, you summon a demon that can serve you—or destroy you. Conjure no demon too great for you to master."

Tevek held up his hand and stared in wonderment at the ring. Through his veins surged icy rivers of power, which he could divert at will to serve his purposes. In a flash of insight, he realized that they had always flowed within him; their currents had driven his necromancies. The effort to perform his sorceries had been in the finding of these elusive currents.

With the ring, he would no longer waste time on such laborious searches. Evocations that heretofore had taken exhaustive preparation would become effortless with the Black Ring. The coppery coils possessed no intrinsic power—only the ability to focus energy that was already there. The cold fire he had felt before had not emanated from the ring . . . it had been inside him.

"Do not accustom yourself to it, necromancer," Thoth-Amon cautioned. "Even without my ring, I am more than a match for you." The Stygian stretched out his arms and spread them apart. In the air between his palms, the ghostly image of a white candle appeared. A thin, black flame sputtered from its wick.

"The Taper of Death—nay, it cannot be!" shouted Tevek in outrage, recognizing the Stygian's ploy at once. The insidious death-spell took days of preparation, but Thoth-Amon had cast it without apparent effort, and without the aid of the ring. Even the Black Seers of Mount Yimsha, who had formulated the enchantment, could not have cast it so quickly. Tevek had once labored to interpret their convoluted spellbooks, but had eventually deemed them unworthy of the effort. Thoth-Amon had obviously fared better in his studies.

"Doubt it not, impudent one," Thoth-Amon replied, a trace of smugness deepening his voice. "Your soul is melting. Only *I* can stop it. Your messenger did arrive, you see. My arts then made me aware of your find. While your skeletal caravan dragged you toward me, I wove this spell. I suffered you to enter my domain to test you, and to learn of your true purpose. Think you that Thoth-Amon is naught but a myrmidon of Set? Hah! You have much to learn, presumptuous heathen." His scornful words trailed off to a hideous chuckle. "Now your lesson begins."

Tevek gritted his teeth. Even with his newfound power, the death-spell could not be undone. Thoth-Amon had outwitted him.

"Go to the Brass City, retrieve the Grim Grey God and bring it to me," Thoth-Amon commanded. "For you spoke truly of the danger that lurks there for one steeped in Set's power. But the idol's powers will not be used for your selfish, small-minded schemes of vengeance. To subjugate Khyfa, you would presume to use my ring? As well swing a mattock to squash a midge." Thoth-Amon stared thoughtfully at the phantom candle between his hands. "When you return, I shall have my Black Ring *and* the Grim Grey God. Then the worship of Mitra, Ibis, and every other false deity shall be eradicated forever from the world. Take comfort in the certainty that if you succeed, the Khyfans will suffer—as will all who have opposed Father Set's purpose. And it is only for the furtherment of His purpose that I suffer you to wear my ring."

Tevek considered focusing the ring's energy to direct a withering blast of force at the smug Stygian. A pointless waste, he decided. The candle—his life-force—would continue to burn slowly down, even if Thoth-Amon were destroyed.

When the wick's flame died, so would Tevek.

The necromancer squinted. Had the candle's height lessened already? How much longer did he have before the spell reached its inevitable conclusion? He was wasting precious time! Without another word, Tevek spun and stormed out of the hall.

Thoth-Amon's sibilant laughter echoed on the stones and followed Tevek up the steps.

Outside, the necromancer spared no more time studying the oasis. He walked unmolested past the oily black pool and reassembled his skeletal coterie. *The Khyfans will suffer*, he mused repeatedly as his steeds carried him toward the City of Brass. Khyfa would fall, though Thoth-Amon's death-spell would soon claim him. His own life was not too great a price to pay for vengeance upon the Khyfan murderers. And he might yet devise a means to escape from the Set priest's web of death.

Though cold night had not yet settled across the desert sands, a bitter chill effused the air about Tevek Thul.

Seven
Varhia

Conan had led Kylanna out of Kyros without pause, and their sweat-lathered horses were exhausted. They crossed into Ghaza at midday. Conan finally halted at a small brook to let their steeds lap greedily at the cool water. He dismounted to work some of the stiffness out of his wounded leg, and to refill two waterskins. The Cimmerian splashed his face and let the water run down his chest and back. He felt instantly refreshed.

Kylanna squirmed in her saddle. She yawned and stretched, shading her face from the bright sun and searching the northern horizon.

Conan watched with amusement as the girl sought a more comfortable position for her shapely backside, which would no doubt ache on the morn. They had covered considerable ground; the Cimmerian had set a brutal pace and ridden hard across the hilly countryside. After a half-day of bouncing atop a galloping beast, all but the most accomplished of riders would be saddle-sore. Conan felt none of this himself, though his leg still ached from his recent tussle with the *asshuri*. Kylanna, for her part, had not complained at all. He was grudgingly impressed by her stoicism. In his experience, royalty were generally unused to the hardships of the road, for they often traveled in the plush comforts of carriages or atop cushioned mounts, while servants attended them. Evidently, this princess was different.

Kylanna's soft and curvaceous body concealed her toughness. Conan surreptitiously slid his gaze from her calf to her bared thigh, admiring one long, shapely leg. Her damp tunic clung to her full breasts, which swayed gently as she shook her hair to rid it of dust and sweat.

"I see no mountains yet," Kylanna stated in a disappointed tone. She smoothed her hair back and let it fall across her bare, deeply tanned shoulders.

Conan splashed more cold water on his face to cool himself off. By Crom, the sight of her could set a man's blood afire. "Aye, not yet." His throat had become hoarse, either from the ride or from his thoughts of the girl. The noble-born princess had vociferously expressed her opinion of Conan, quashing any thoughts he might have of proposing a different sort of reward for escorting her home. And Conan, though a barbarian, harbored no intention of forcing himself upon her. Though Cimmerians were savages, they took no woman without her freely given consent. Conan reluctantly took his eyes from her alluring body, swallowed a mouthful of water, and swung himself back into his saddle. "We must pass the night near Ghaza and ride northeast tomorrow afore we reach the border of Koth. Then we shall fetch the tiara and get you back to Arenjun."

"Why do we not ride due north? I know something of these lands, from the maps carried by my unfortunate captain. Does not this northeastern jaunt prolong our ride by a day or more?"

"We must avoid Duke Balvadek's lands. That potbellied old goat would have me gutted on sight."

Kylanna rolled her eyes. "What manner of brigand are you? By Bel, what murder or thievery did you commit to earn his wrath?"

"Neither," Conan answered with a roguish grin. "He has twin daughters, whom I met by chance when escorting one of Duke Reydnu's diplomats to Balvadek's castle. Reydnu rules over a nearby city-state, and was seeking an alliance with Balvadek, you see. Anyway, the wenches took a liking to me and told me of a secret way into their quarters, whereupon that night I—"

"Enough," Kylanna sighed. "Sicken me not with details of your rutting with these slatterns. So, Balvadek learned of your romp and was rightfully incensed."

"Nay, their husbands arrived the following morning, returning early from a campaign, and awakened the three of us. Those two armored fools, led into folly by their rage, rushed at me with drawn swords. They left me no choice but to hew down both of them in self-defense."

"Husbands—hmph! Even in Arenjun's Maul there are few cretins as scurrilous as you, to bed with wives and murder their men on the morn."

"They mentioned no husbands to me. Those two short-bearded, fumbling fools were doubtless as forgettable in bed as they were in battle. Anyway, Balvadek has since longed to see me swing from a gibbet outside his front gate. So today we ride northeast. You see, never has Reydnu cooperated in any way with Balvadek, before or after that ill-fated diplomatic fiasco. Their fathers feuded, and their fathers' fathers. Nay, there can be no peace between Balvadek and Reydnu."

Kylanna shook her head in disgust. "So Ghaza is safe? You are not wanted for crimes there, as you are in Kyros and every other city-state in this backward land?"

"No," Conan replied cheerfully. "That is, Ghaza is not safe for us. Few places in Shem would offer us haven. But Duke Reydnu has no cause to stick my head on a pike, and I know a border village with a small inn where we can obtain a room—"

"I shall not pass the night with you, barbarian," Kylanna laughed. "Nor shall I share my bed with the legions of crawling vermin that infest border-village inns. You shall find for me a suitable lodging with clean linens, a bathhouse, and proper food. Oh, and a seamstress as well, to fashion new garments for me. You may stay in the stable with the other beasts and lie abed with the hogs and rodents, with whom you share kinship. The worth of my tiara will more than compensate you for such trifling expenses as we incur." She reached for a full waterskin and took a long drink.

Conan stared at her incredulously. "Badb and Lir, wench! Were my purse heavy enough to afford such rooms, I would not lighten it thusly. We must avoid Shem's cities, and we can afford no dalliance. Clean linens—new garments—fah! Such a foppish place would be watched carefully by the rumormongers in Ghaza, and everyone from beggar to noble would hear of your arrival. Nay, we shall stay in the village of Varhia at the Sooty Boar, where the beds cost less than the ale and the proprietor asks no questions."

Kylanna wrinkled her nose in distaste. "The Sooty Boar? By comparison, an *asshuri* prison is doubtless a palace. Yet I suppose that some hardships must be endured on the long road home." She sighed heavily. "Very well, barbarian. Onward, to this offal pile of which you speak."

With effort, Conan smoothed the frayed edges of his temper and slapped the rump of his horse. He sullenly led Kylanna northeastward at a steady canter. The wench seemed to forget already that danger still dogged their path. The Cimmerian would see her safely home, as he had sworn to do. But he was a warrior, not a lackey, and her haughty tone set his teeth on edge.

Conan was beginning to regret this whole venture. His *Hawk* and Rulvio would wait, but Conan still needed time to follow his map before he returned to Messantia. If he could secure both the tiara *and* the treasure of the Brass City, he could hand over his ship to her first mate and crew. His newfound wealth would amount to more than ten years of piracy would yield. He would live in places of his own choosing, drinking and wenching at will, fighting whatever battles he wished for either profit or pleasure. Ensconced in these happy thoughts, Conan plodded onward, sparing the occasional backward glance to see that Kylanna stayed close and that no others followed.

Across meandering brooks and verdant landscape they proceeded, until the hills to the west hid the edge of the sun. Conan felt a strange mixture of relief and boredom. The *asshuri*'s failure to pursue them had made the day uneventful, and Kylanna had apparently deemed his unworthy of conversation. He judged that they would reach Varhia before nightfall. Conan was far from weary, but their steeds needed rest and Kylanna had begun to slump in her saddle.

The prospect of a seared joint of mutton and a frothy jack of ale bolstered him. As he recalled, the Sooty Boar's fare was rough, but hearty. The inn's patrons were primarily tradesmen or their men-at-arms, passing the night on the long road to or from Ghaza's capital city. Conan stretched and briefly looked over his shoulder.

Breath hissed between his teeth.

Had he seen a rider on a horse, far to the south, at the farthest reach of his gaze? Conan could swear that from the corner of one eye he had glimpsed furtive movement. He studied the landscape, but now saw only the lazily flowing brooks and sprawling fields of waist-high greenery. The terrain afforded no features that would conceal a man on horseback, so Conan reluctantly concluded that sun-lengthened shadows had deceived him. If someone were following them, the Cimmerian would surely have felt the presence of eyes on his back, like a clammy trickle of invisible sweat; that faint but unsettling sensation had saved him more than once.

Kylanna's gaze shifted to meet his. Her expression was one of mild curiosity, though she queried him not.

Conan simply turned around and led his horse onward, as if nothing unseemly perturbed him. If they were being followed, it was not by the *asshuri*. Those Shemites fought superbly, but lacked stealth. Only the crafty Picts, woodland warriors of a land far to the north and the west, had ever been able to deceive Conan's keen senses. Pictish scouts could creep unseen behind a stalking panther.

"How distant is this dungheap of a village?" Kylanna griped as she spurred her horse forward. "I have grown fatigued from this day's ride and am so famished that even the repulsive fare of your wretched inn may seem palatable."

"Not far." Conan ignored her haughty tone, preoccupied by the notion that someone followed them. He pointed to a patch of trees atop a distant ridge. "Past yon hilltop lies the trade route. We shall reach Varhia afore the sun sets." A mischievous gleam lit his eyes. "Doubtless your horse is as weary also, having borne the burden of your royal backside all day long." He turned away to hide his grin.

Kylanna stiffened and threw back her shoulders. "Oaf! Buffoon! You dare to jest thusly, after I have rewarded you so generously? Son of a goat!" She hurled other colorful phrases at Conan—many of them quite unladylike—before her temper cooled.

Conan, whose hide had thickened after years of sharp words from women of many lands, let her continue until she had exhausted her repertoire. His mind slipped back to thoughts of the unseen pursuer, but he dared not look behind again. It were better not to arouse suspicion. When they arrived in Varhia, he would know soon enough if someone trailed them.

As they came to the grove and crested the low ridge, the setting sun transformed the clouds into wisps of orange and violet. At the bottom of the ridge, a meandering valley nestled in the looming shadows of dusk. The trade route that wound through it was actually the bed of a river, long ago dried out. They followed it north until they sky darkened from azure to indigo.

"Varhia," Conan announced, nodding toward the sprawl of structures that lay ahead. He had traveled through here some years ago, and by appearances, the place had changed little. It was large for a village; some might have called it a small town. But Conan knew from experience that no constables or soldiers from Ghaza dwelt within its limits. As in many remote settlements, brawn or steel were its only laws. The Cimmerian found this arrangement agreeable, but deemed a few words of caution appropriate.

"Save your queenly words here," he advised in as neutral a tone as he could manage, "lest you attract too much attention. And let me haggle for our room and board." He glanced at her attire and rubbed his chin. "In that shift, you look too comely to pass unnoticed at the Sooty Boar. It were better for you to pose as a swordswoman than a harlot."

"A *harlot*? No wealth in the world would suffice for me to—"

"Know you aught of sword or dagger?" Conan interrupted.

Kylanna glared at him, but nodded. "My sisters and I were taught the rudiments, to defend our honor from ruffians of your ilk."

"Good." Conan took an *asshuri* short sword that had been strapped to the horse he had stolen from the encampment. He cut down his belt to fit Kylanna's slender waist. "Strap this on—and openly wear a dagger in your own gear. Then smear more dirt on your limbs." Conan dug the point of his sword across a scab on his leg until a thin trickle of blood welled up. "Smear some of this on your shift and on your blades."

The Zamorian eyed him doubtfully, but did as he suggested. When she leaned out of her saddle, she deftly spun her dagger and opened Conan's wound wider, wrinkling her nose in distaste as she daubed some blood onto her hands. "For appearances," she said with a straight face as Conan's jaw tightened.

"Do not use your real name here," Conan said. "In Varhia, you are . . ."

"Lyssa."

Conan shrugged. "As you like. Better to say that you are Zamorian, in any case, as befits your accent."

"Why not Lyssa of Ophir?" she asked in perfect Ophirean. "Or Lyssa of Nemedia?" Kylanna added, this time in Nemedian so flawless that her dialect—that of the capital city of Belverus—would have fooled a native.

Impressed, Conan folded his arms across his chest and smiled in wonderment. "It seems that some of King Tiridates' gold has flowed into the purses of fine tutors," he rumbled. "Why not Lyssa of Ophir, then? Better if we speak to no one at all, but if we must, methinks we shall escape notice. Let us hope that the innkeeper at the Sooty Boar has forgotten me. What a debauch I had there, by Crom! Conan of Cimmeria shall I remain."

Their horses clopped along the stones of the old riverbed and bore them to the outskirts of Varhia. Cool, gentle wind caressed them as they traversed the lush valley, and the songs of myriad birds lent a cheerful aspect to the sunset. Yet neither breeze nor birdsong could assuage Conan's lingering concern about their unseen follower.

As they approached the outskirts of Varhia, three swarthy men rose from a rough-hewn wooden bench. Two leaned upon tall, double-bladed axes and regarded Conan and Kylanna with undisguised suspicion. The third, who stood head and shoulders above the others, slid his broadsword from its worn scabbard. He stepped into the wide strip of dirt, his sword low but held in readiness. A ray of waning sunlight lent a malicious gleam to his dark eyes.

"Ignore them," Conan whispered to Kylanna, who now rode beside him. The Cimmerian's fingers closed around the hilt of his *asshuri* sword, and his fierce blue eyes met those of the tall Shemite. He did not slow his horse.

"Drawn rein, strangers," the Shemite said, his tone firm but polite. "It were better that you turn back and come not to Varhia."

"Since when?" Conan demanded. His hand never left his hilt, nor did his eyes leave those of the man in the road.

The Shemite's eyebrows shot up in surprise. "Have you not heard the news? Duke Reydnu is at war with Balvadek." He spat as he uttered the latter name. "Two companies of Reydnu's troops now occupy the village. Many local folk have abandoned Varhia. The border is closed to strangers—especially to those who come from the south, from where Balvadek's army may soon approach. Reydnu may deem that you are spies and hang you."

"Balvadek—of Kyros? We have not seen so much as one *asshuri* of Kyros this day . . . of course, we came not from the right direction," Conan added hastily. "But if Reydnu would turn away honest travelers from his lands, times are indeed hard for him. We seek only to stay a night here and depart at sunrise. Now turn aside, that Conan of Cimmeria and Lyssa of Ophir may pass." Boldly, he swept his sword from its scabbard.

The Shemite stepped backward, rubbed his bushy beard and studied the two strangers. His hands trembled, and his two comrades fidgeted and avoided Conan's baleful eyes. A tense silence lasted for several moments until the Shemite spoke. "You have the look of a hardened mercenary," he muttered. "Reydnu may traffic with your sort, as times are desperate. If your purpose here is to sell your sword, I can let you through." He lowered his voice. "The war goes poorly, and you are as unlikely a spy as I could imagine. Proceed, then."

"Aye," Conan agreed. He had no intention of embroiling himself in one of the bloody feuds that constantly erupted among Shem's city-states. He turned to Kylanna, thankful that she had restrained herself from speaking.

She stared at the ground as if she were lost in thought. Only when Conan cleared his throat did she look up and bestir her horse to follow him. She rode at his side. They passed the three bothersome sentries. The Shemites ogled Kylanna openly until a ferocious glare from Conan turned their gaze away.

"The Boar lies not far from here," Conan said as they passed by a smattering of farmhouses. He noted that these seemed bereft of beast or man. An encampment occupied one field. Tents clustered around the stone ring of a well, and several ash-filled fire pits had been dug nearby. Curiously, no soldiers or horses were in evidence.

Varhia sprawled across the valley in the manner typical for villages of Shem's wine country. The well-tended fields and rough-stone or wood houses soon gave way to the larger structures of the village proper. What village folk they saw went about their errands and seemed indifferent to the newly arrived pair of strangers. Two men, stripped to the waist and drenched in sweat, chopped trees into cord. Groups of peasant women gathered berries and vegetables from the fields, while others filled large earthen jars with water. Young boys raced to and fro on the paths and the road, carrying food, clay jugs, and various other bundles.

"There." Conan pointed toward a ramshackle jumble of wooden walls that rose higher than any of the houses. It leaned to one side, its grimy exterior featuring but a few crooked windows. The door—a huge square of wood that looked more like a gate—stood open. Men lounged against it and spilled from the interior, drinking, eating, laughing, or simply resting. "Ishtar curse these Shemites," Conan mumbled. "Methinks that half of Reydnu's retinue have taken up residence in the Boar."

"A pity," Kylanna said. "I had so looked forward to partaking of its hospitality."

Her sarcasm was lost on Conan, who clicked his teeth together in annoyance. "There is but one other public house—the Grape and Thistle, which doubtless suits your refined tastes better. Yet I doubt not that the officers have commandeered it." He scratched his square jaw and looked over his shoulder. "Some of those farmhouses back there may have been abandoned."

"Do you jest?" Kylanna shook her head. "Seek one if you wish, or a sheep's pen—nay, a sty might suit your tastes. As for me, I shall try the Grape and Thistle. Even if no rooms are vacant, some officers are gentlemen, and one may give up his quarters for a single night to convenience me. Such a place sounds safer, anyway. If the proprietor favors us, perhaps he can find a pile of straw for you in his stable. Where is this inn?"

Conan shrugged. "It matters not. We hold the wrong color of coin to procure rooms there. Nay, let us seek a villager and pay him for room and board."

"Has the Grape and Thistle a common room where entertainers perform?"

"Aye, I reckon so—jugglers and bards and the like."

"What coin do you carry?"

"Why?" Conan asked suspiciously.

"You are strong, are you not? While barbarians have few qualities of use, brute strength is chief among them. Well, there is a game of strength that was popular among officers of my father's royal guard. From what I have seen, you could not lose this game."

Conan had an idea of what she might be about to suggest. He picked through his woefully light pouch. "Twelve coppers, some few bronze bits, and one silver noble." His brow creased as he pulled the pouch's string's taut.

The pouch had been tucked into a vest pocket, where the *asshuri* could easily have found it. Never had Conan been imprisoned without his captors relieving him of wealth, however meager it might have been. Strange indeed that the Shemites had missed his map *and* his coinage.

"An adequate stake," Kylanna said confidently. "In the game, you and your challenger sit facing with elbows on the table, hands clasped, wrists locked. We wager three coppers to one that you can force the back of your challenger's hand to the table's top. You will then lose thrice and win but once."

Conan raised an eyebrow in protest.

"Then we wager three nobles to one—you must win then, of course, and then we raise the stakes. Three gold crowns to one."

The Cimmerian laughed. "Well do I know this game. Most officers are cowards at heart—weaklings who hide in armor behind the ranks of their men. They will be loath to pit their flabby arms against the battle-hardened thews of a barbarian."

"Leave that to me, if the odds do not attract challengers," said Kylanna. "By Bel, is it not enough that I must depend on a vagabond to take me home—must I also tend to such mundane matters as fare and lodging?"

"Betimes we shall see if your plan works," Conan rumbled. "If it fails, we must sleep upon the open ground and doubtless be soaked by the rain that pours nightly upon this region of Shem. That prospect troubles me not—by Crom, I have endured far worse—but you need rest for the journey tomorrow. And it would be unwise to beg these folk for quarters too long after sunset, especially in a time of war."

"Betimes we shall see," Kylanna said.

Conan guided them into the village proper, where a haphazard cluster of dwellings and establishments surrounded a small stone keep. The riverbed road led directly toward the modest but stout-looking castle, which squatted upon a low hill. Rough stones paved the dirt to form a wide, well-kept street.

Many buildings in this village center formed part of the original settlement, and though they were older, their walls were cleaner, their windows unmarred, and their roofs neatly shingled. Here trod the merchants and the stewards of Varhia. Some frowned in disapproval at the sight of these two horsed warriors who had intruded so boldly into their domain. Conan's fierce countenance deterred many a stare, however, and they reached the Grape and Thistle without incident.

The inn's sign hung from chains on a pole thrust into the stonework above the door. It swayed and creaked in the wind, a lonely sound that contrasted strangely with the echoes of merry music from within. Smoke issued from a vent atop the sloping roof, wafting the delicious aroma of roasted game into Conan's nostrils.

Seemingly from nowhere, a tall, well-groomed boy stepped up to Conan and Kylanna. Blond hair spilled out from beneath a hat of green cloth. A tabard of matching hue, woven with the inn's design—a thistle-covered vine bedecked with grapes—was belted at his waist, above leather breeks. "Hired swords of the duke's army, is it?" Excitement lit his eyes.

"Aye," Conan nodded. "You might say so."

"We had heard that reinforcements were coming. Welcome to the Grape and Thistle, the finest inn in all of Ghaza." The lanky lad swept his hat from his head and bowed low. "Aren at your service. Allow me to see to these fine steeds if you wish to seek rest or repast within our walls."

"Very well," Kylanna replied, in a tone more regal than any warrior could have managed.

Conan winced. "We depart at sunrise," he said. "How near is your stable?"

"Why, not far at all," Aren said amiably. He pointed out a building at the end of a narrow walkway. "And worry not, warriors. Your mounts will await you at the first ray of morn, rested and well-fed." He stepped closer and reached for the reins. "What news of the war?" the youth asked quietly, his eyes bright with curiosity.

"We bear none," Conan replied gruffly. "We came from the west and saw no men-at-arms."

Aren's shoulders drooped, and the gleam in his eyes receded. "But surely you have seen action this day, from the state of your gear and the lather of your mounts. By Erlik—" he winced and looked up at Kylanna "—begging your pardon, lady, but you've the look of battle about you!"

"That we have," Kylanna agreed. "A skirmish with bandits," she said dismissively. "We shall be grateful if you can procure a few items for us, ere we consult with the duke's officers. For my companion, a proper shirt—he prefers white, with long, loose-fitting sleeves. For me, a light tunic of green. Lead us to the stables, that we may inspect them whilst you fetch these garments."

Conan glowered in silent protest, but he went along with Kylanna as Aren walked swiftly to the austere building at the end of the alley. They halted before a closed gate, built of sturdy timber, wide enough for three horses to pass through together. Aren withdrew a key that hung from a cord about his neck, unlocked the stable's small side door, and stepped inside. Conan and Kylanna heard him work the crossbar that secured the gate, which swung open moments later.

These precautions did not surprise Conan. Horses were particularly valuable in these parts—especially those fine breeds that would likely belong to the Grape and Thistle's patrons—and thieves often targeted stables. The Cimmerian led his mount into the enclosure, which he surveyed with interest. From its floor of hard-packed dirt to its ceiling of sturdy beams, the expansive stable was as clean as any he had encountered. Conan had parted with good bronze to spend the night in quarters far worse than these. No scum or bugs floated in the water troughs, and no rat-spoor littered the shallow bins of feed. All but one of some twenty-odd stalls housed an occupant; some held two, though these were ponies or smaller breeds.

"We have only one pen left," Aren said apologetically. "A bit cramped for two, but for one night only, it should do. Well, please satisfy yourselves as to the suitability, lady and sir, as I tend to your request. The clothier's is scarcely a stone's throw from here, and they have exactly what you like. If you wish to unpack your gear yourselves, I can return afore you finish. Now there is the matter of payment for—"

Kylanna lifted a pouch from her saddlebag, which bulged with *asshuri* provisions: dried nuts and fruit, and pieces of flat bread that were hard enough to crack a tooth. She hefted the pouch. "Just speak to the innkeeper, Master Aren, and we shall see that your exceptional service is rewarded. Doubtless fresh garments, a hot meal, and a goblet of wine cannot help but increase our generosity."

Aren's polite smile disappeared for a moment as he shifted from one foot to the other and opened his mouth as if to speak. Then, smile renewed, he nodded and tipped his hat. He turned and dashed off on his errand.

Conan waited until the youth was well beyond earshot before glaring at Kylanna. "The innkeeper will not be so gullible," he grumbled. "And I am no fop, to prance about in nobleman's frippery!"

"It will mask your thews," said Kylanna.

"And deplete my coinage," Conan retorted.

"We must be presentable. There is more to this game than brute strength."

"Whether I am bedecked in silk or in mail, the locals are likely to recognize Conan of Cimmeria."

"Are they?" Kylanna scoffed, hands on her hips. "Verily, you must be a deity of sorts to the unwashed canaille of this village, but does your renown extend to these respectable quarters as well? I think not."

Conan's indignant and uncouth response was interrupted by the arrival of two shirtless youths in baggy breeches and sandals, who wheeled in a cart heaped with fresh hay. They glanced at the Cimmerian and the Zamorian with only casual interest. Wordlessly, they took up pitchforks and bent their backs to spread fresh straw upon the stable floor. Their long, damp hair bespoke a full day of labor, plastered as it was to their sun-darkened backs.

"You see?" Kylanna smiled. "There are those among even your caste to whom your legendary face is unfamiliar."

Conan shook his head and dismounted. He led his horse to the empty stall, which was farthest from the stable's gate. Riding tackle and harness lay stacked upon the shelves of the back wall, next to a long bench replete with the tools and supplies of a farrier. Conan saw some familiar implements among them—the smith's hammer and tongs, the anvil, and the iron bars and nails used in the making of horseshoes.

He shuddered to think what the innkeeper would charge them for just the stable. At the same time, he had long been away from the luxuries of civilization, and he admitted to himself that a haunch of roasted venison or rack of game fowl would satisfy his hunger better than a leg of charred, greasy mutton. For that matter, a bottle of Ghazan wine quenched thirst in a way that the Sooty Boar's bitter ale could not. And a damp night's sleep upon a pile of straw, though adequate for him, lacked the appeal of a dry bed. For all his objections, Conan realized that he had given in to Kylanna's absurd proposal as much for the rare experience that it represented as for the chance to liven up a dull evening.

Aren returned promptly, bearing their garments and some few extras—for Conan, a broad, blue sash, and for Kylanna, silken riding breeks that matched her new tunic. Kylanna expressed her approval, while Conan regarded his sash warily, as if it were a blue serpent and not just a strip of fabric.

"I shall advise Yarl, the innkeeper, of your arrival," Aren said.

"Duke Reydnu has set aside quarters for those who command his reinforcements." He bowed, hat in hand, and bustled out.

Conan held up the shirt and grimaced at the ruffles sewn to each cuff. While the thing, along with its bright sash, took after a fashion popular among Barachan pirates, it had an effeminate aspect that repelled him. The cuffs would hinder swordplay, and the sleeves would twist and tangle hopelessly in any close-in fighting. It was clearly a carpet-knight's garment. Reluctantly, he pulled it on over his vest, though his torso was too broad to permit him to lace up the front above his chest.

Kylanna changed swiftly in the stall, out of the stable boys' and Conan's sight. She came out and stared at Conan, a wide smile lifting the corners of her wine-red lips. "An ill fit for one of your ignoble descent," she teased quietly. "Truly, it suits you not."

"Speak no more of it unless you prefer a roof of rain clouds to that of this inn," Conan muttered. "By Crom, I would as soon face an army of *asshuri* than endure the barbs of your sharp tongue. Test my temper no further, girl! Let us get on with the game. More likely are we to end up fleeing town on horseback—or afoot, worse yet—with half of Reydnu's men in hot pursuit."

Conan fashioned his belt into a baldric and shoved a dagger into his boot. Kylanna's sword hung at her hip, its point extending down past mid-calf. She thrust her dagger into the other side of her belt and walked somewhat awkwardly. It was Conan's turn to grin. "An ill fit for a palace-softened princess," he commented, echoing her earlier remark. "The role of courtesan would befit you better." He gazed unabashedly at the generous cleavage revealed by the tunic's scooped neckline.

"No courtesan would condescend to accompany a brute like you."

"And yet a princess does so willingly."

With a huff, she stormed out. As she marched past the cart of hay, the two laborers stole sidelong looks at her and envious glances at Conan, who followed Kylanna around the corner to the Grape and Thistle's entrance.

The sun had slipped completely behind the ridge; the dark mask of dusk now hid Varhia. Above the inn's stout-looking door, a lone lantern cast a pale glow onto the silent, shadowy street. Conan and Kylanna walked across the cobblestones and up the steps to the inn's entrance. The bronze handles did not give in the slightest.

"Bolted," suggested Conan. "Odd, for a public house."

" 'Tis not so strange a practice. Many Zamorian villagers shut their doors to keep out the lower castes," Kylanna said.

"Aye, but thieves infest Zamora like fleas on a mangy cur's hide," Conan argued. "This is Varhia, where few doors are shut to anyone. Perhaps the officers have demanded privacy—"

The creak of hinges interrupted him, and the massive portal swung inward. A gaunt man with a narrow, jutting nose and a loose-fitting tunic of grey wool stood there, one hand on the door and the other on the hilt of a broadsword that hung from his belt. "You are the mercenary—" he paused, his brow furrowing "—the captains?"

They nodded.

"A messenger of the duke advised us to expect you. I am Yarl, innkeeper of the Grape and Thistle. Welcome." He bowed, beckoning them into the small, narrow antechamber.

He shut the noisy door behind them. Beyond the cramped, shadowy entryway, they could see the square, spacious common room. Four beams rose from the varnished hardwood floor to a latticework of ceiling beams. The place lacked windows, but a vent placed near the ceiling on each wall served to keep the air fresh. The entrance was in the southwest corner, where a corridor along the west wall ended at a stout-looking door that apparently led to the inn's rooms. A long counter ran the length of the east wall, and twelve tables of equal size filled most of the floor space. The northeast and southeast corners offered somewhat more luxurious seating accommodations in the form of cushioned divans. Subdued lighting came solely from a series of lamps on the wall behind the counter and from candles atop the tables.

The furnishings were clean and of a quality superior to those in most inns frequented by Conan. Some tables and benches looked new, as if they had never been thrown or broken. Apparently the patrons did not engage in brawls of the sort that the Cimmerian so routinely encountered in his travels. The place even lacked the smells of stale sweat, spilt ale, and old soot. Conan disliked the Grape and Thistle at once. In his absurd shirt and these prim surroundings, he felt awkward and out of sorts. Here was a house that catered to foppish nobles and snobbish officers. He was of a mind to rush out and return to the Sooty Boar, but he noticed Kylanna's clear expression of relief and heard her sigh of satisfaction.

"Quite satisfactory, Master Yarl," she said, nodding to the innkeeper and pressing several bronze coins into his palm. "For your stable boy, Aren, who treated us most kindly," she added. "Of course, we shall be much more generous to you, Master Yarl, for your personal attention and the hospitality that your fine inn affords to guests of the duke."

He bowed—not quite quickly enough to hide his avaricious expression—and tucked the coin into his belt-pouch. Then he led them into the common room, reciting an apparently well-used speech that extolled the supposedly unequaled virtues of his establishment. Conan doubted that such claims as he made could be true of the royal palace in Aquilonia, but he followed Kylanna's lead, nodding and pretending to be impressed by all the frippery shown to them. He stifled a yawn and watched Kylanna insinuate herself with the innkeeper. Soon he saw that she indeed had Zamorian blood, which flowed in the veins of the world's best thieves. For in short order, she had robbed Yarl of his wits and convinced him to let them play their wagering game in his common room.

Eight
The Watcher in the Woods

Toj squinted, shading his eyes with his palm. Still no sign of Conan and the woman. He coaxed more speed from his horse as he guided it across the ridgetop, through the trees and tall weeds that grew in abundance there. The Cimmerian had set an aggressive pace, taking advantage of the natural road formed by the dry riverbed in the valley. Toj had chosen the ridgetop for its superior vantage point and its cover of foliage, though the latter had proven to be a hindrance. Unable to match the full trot of his quarry, he had watched them outpace him and eventually move out of his sight.

That had compelled him to drive his horse to a gallop and risk exposure, in the likely event that Conan watched for pursuers. For some time, Toj had played at this game of hide-and-seek, until he became more certain of the pair's destination.

Toj possessed a fair knowledge of Shem's cities, for their squabbling dukes often availed themselves of assassins' services. It had been a year or two since he had personally done away with a target in Shem, but the lay of the land was known to him. This riverbed road wound its way from Kyros to Ghaza. Traders and travelers made frequent use of it, from Khorshemish in Koth across the Asgalun in Shem, or farther south to the forbidding seaport of serpent-ridden Khemi in Stygia.

Toj wondered at the lack of traffic through the valley. He believed that a village of no mean size lay ahead: Varhia, one of the larger settlements in this province. The Cimmerian and the woman would probably not travel at night, and they must rest their horses soon. Varhia was almost certainly Conan's destination. Strange that in spite of the village's proximity, Toj had seen no merchants or other folk. Either the assassin disremembered the maps of this region, or something unusual was afoot.

As the sun hovered just above the horizon, Toj passed through a particularly tall thicket. When he emerged, he looked down at the sweeping view of the sloping hillside to the east. His eyes narrowed as he saw movement far to the east. Instinctively, he took cover in the nearest copse and watched the huge host that approached from the southeast. The entire contingent was mounted, at least those that he could see. Their manner and garb bespoke their affiliation: *asshuri*.

He waited for a span and studied them from the shadows of the trees. These Shemite warriors were not of Kyros; Toj did not recognize their colors and devices. But he could easily see that they sped to a battle. Only in the rear of the host were any supplies in evidence, consisting of some few dozen mounts laden with bulky sacks, barrels, and spare battle gear. No tents or tools were apparent, indicating that this was not to be a drawn-out conflict. They rode to strike and swiftly crush their enemy, whomever that might be.

He looked upon the flank of the host, some ten—nay, fifteen—rows, thirty *asshuri* to each. At the forefront sat a tall man in a gilded saddle, his ivory-hued cape sweeping behind him in the breeze, his steed clad in fine barding. Surely, thought Toj, these warriors came from a nearby province, in light of their minimal provisions.

Shemitish nobles of these wine-producing regions were forever at odds with each other, and minor skirmishes were a routine matter. But this contingent represented more than a raiding party. Unless Toj misjudged their purpose and their direction of travel, their most likely objective was the taking of Varhia. Even if this was not their purpose, Toj could not risk disinvolvement.

What if Conan and the woman were in the village when the

asshuri struck? At best, this new development would hinder the Cimmerian's progress; at worst, if Conan were captured or slain, Toj would never secure the price that Jade had set on his life. He must away to Varhia and see to it that the barbarian tarried not in the village.

The assassin eased his horse from the thicket and prepared to ride down into the valley, where he intended to follow the riverbed road at full gallop and reach Varhia in time to intervene. Just *how* he would evacuate Conan was unclear at the moment, but he would solve that dilemma on the way to Varhia. Toj's talent for creative scheming had formed the rungs of the ladder he had climbed to claim the title of guildmaster.

So preoccupied was Toj that he almost overlooked an *asshuri* who stood in the tall grass not ten paces away. Toj halted immediately, chiding himself for his carelessness. Fortunately, the *asshuri* had not seen him. He was humming tunelessly and relieving himself beside a short tree. The man's lack of armor marked him as a scout. Toj saw no horse, but assumed that the scout had tethered it nearby.

Three *shaken* were in his hand a moment later, in case the Shemite turned. Toj dared not move; a snort from his horse or the snap of a twig might betray him. He would have thrown his *shaken* if the distance had not rendered the killing uncertain. To hurl the blades properly, Toj needed to be on his feet, moving toward the target. While on horseback, he might only wound the scout, who could then alert the whole host to Toj's presence. Patiently, he stood his ground. If the *asshuri* turned, Toj would throw himself from the horse and go for the kill.

A moment later, the scout sighed and straightened. He fumbled with his breeches as he swung around. He raised his head and paled visibly, staring aghast at Toj as if he looked upon a demon.

The assassin leapt from his saddle, sped forward, and loosed his *shaken* before the *asshuri* recovered his wits. Two flying blades slashed the scout's throat. A third shattered the teeth, plunged into the roof of the open mouth, and buried itself in the dying man's brain. Blood fountained from the gashed throat, but the *asshuri* was dead before his body flopped to the ground.

Toj hastened to the prone form to recover his weapons. The slaying had been swift and too silent to arouse suspicion among those in the nearby host. Satisfied, the assassin drew a slender, hook-bladed knife from a sheath strapped to his calf. He sliced away a piece of the dead man's tunic, then ripped the *shaken* from the ruins of the scout's mouth and wiped it clean of blood and brains.

As he retrieved his other blades, a warning tingle in his spine prompted him to glance over his shoulder. "Bel!" he hissed.

Two scouts stood behind him. One swung a heavy stick at Toj's unprotected head and caught him squarely on the temple. The other lashed out with his foot, his booted heel striking the back of Toj's knee. The guildmaster spun halfway around and tossed his single *shaken*, but another kick spoiled his aim. The thick wooden branch smashed down again. Toj dropped to one knee, then fell sideways, blood dripping from his nose.

"Is he dead, Mahkoro?" the branch-wielding scout asked.

"Nay, Baasha. Only halfway to Hell," Mahkoro replied, his palm pressed against Toj's neck to check for a pulse. "But after what he did to Aveni, I'll send the dog the rest of the way there. Aveni owed me sixty farthings, by Pteor!" Mahkoro wrapped his hands around Toj's throat and pressed in with his thumbs.

Baasha shook his head. "Before we kill him, we should find out what he was about. What if he is a spy of Reydnu's? Our *asshuri* brothers may be riding into a trap." The scout dropped his club and picked up Toj's errant *shaken*. "Look at this wheel of steel that he hurled at me . . . he must have used these to slay Aveni. Where in Zandru's Nine Hells did he come by such a weapon? Nay, Mahkoro, we must take this rogue to Balvadek—let go, by Zandru! Slay him not. Balvadek may wish to wring the truth from this dog, and we can do the wringing. A slow and painful death befits this spy." Baasha clapped a hand on Mahkoro's shoulder.

"You are right," said the *asshuri*, releasing his grip. "He is laden with gear, it seems, and perhaps he had valuables. Let's split whatever coins we find before we take him to Balvadek."

Baasha grinned. "Of course," he agreed.

They searched through Toj's robes, garments, pouches, and pockets, which were stuffed with a bewildering variety of weapons and supplies. A belt around Toj's waist was lined with heavy gold coins from various lands. All of the coins were spaced apart, tucked neatly into leather compartments stitched into the belt.

"This kept the coins from clinking together," Baasha observed. "A trick used by thieves and spies who would have no sound betray them while they skulk about their business."

"By Pteor, look at this dagger," Mahkoro marveled. He stared at the hilt that jutted from a sheath of soft leather fixed to the belt of loot. It was seamlessly wrought of gold and copper into a serpentlike shape, with the triangular head forming the pommel. A huge, flawless ruby glittered in each eye socket.

The men glanced at each other with expressions of pure avarice. Such a treasure represented five years of hard-earned pay, if not more, and it could not be shared.

Mahkoro was first to seize the dazzling hilt. He slipped it out of the sheath and drove it into Baasha's groin. The burnished steel blade ripped upward and opened Baasha's belly before the *asshuri* could step backward. Baasha grunted in pain and made a grab for Mahkoro's hand. He missed, but Mahkoro stumbled and nicked his arm with the dagger's tip.

Baasha staggered and grabbed his rent stomach. Blood dribbled from his mouth and gushed from his ghastly wound. He fell forward and twitched for a moment, then finally lay still. If Mahkoro had not turned away, he might have noticed that Baasha's blood had suddenly stopped flowing from his wound, and that his limbs had taken on a pale hue that was almost blue.

A grim smile of contentment played across Mahkoro's face. "You're mine," he whispered to the dagger. As he bent to remove Toj's belt and continue his looting, a twinge of pain struck him. He moaned in mingled surprise and agony. The dagger fell from his hand and he dropped to his knees. His arm burned as if the hottest fires of Hell seared it. Then he realized that it was not *heat* he felt, but bitter, unbearable cold. No more could Makhoro feel his fingers. Mercifully, his forearm grew numb, but the agonizing cold spread into his biceps and his shoulder, where it lingered for an eternity of torment.

Panic seized him as he saw the source of the spreading chill—the small wound from the serpentlike dagger. Poison . . . or sorcery? With his good arm, he rubbed at the frozen limb. It was bent, and he struggled to straighten it.

The icy forearm broke off at the elbow and fell from his fingers, its meat, muscle, and bones obscenely exposed. Mahkoro felt his gorge rise, but he did not live long enough to spew. The *asshuri*'s heart froze in his breast, and at that instant he knew no more.

The ornate dagger lay nearby upon the grass, its peculiar blade unstained by the blood it had tasted. In the waning sunlight, it gleamed like a reddish-gold serpent before Mahkoro's unseeing eyes.

Toj fingered his blood-matted hair, careful not to disturb the crust that had formed on his split scalp. He opened his eyes slowly and inadvertently raised his eyebrows. That slight movement threatened to open anew the deep wound from the blow that had knocked him senseless. How long had he lain here? Where were the *asshuri*— better yet, where was *here*? Toj forced his disoriented senses to focus . . . upon grass beneath him, the night sky above him, the cool but moist air on his skin. In addition to the intense throbbing of his head, he felt a mild ache from the back of his knee.

The assassin breathed evenly and deeply as he closed his eyes. It was the first step in a powerful discipline that he had mastered only through seven long years of study in the jungle-shrouded monastery at Xifeng, in a vast swamp of southern Khitai. There, inside a stone temple that had been ancient when Atlantis sank, eleven monks still whispered prayers to a strange god born from the spirits of five dragon brothers. In life, the dragons had fought among themselves, but in death, they found wisdom and their spirits joined to become one being: Xifeng.

Toj had discovered the monastery during one of his lotus-gathering expeditions into the deadly swamps of Khitai. The wizened monks freely shared their knowledge with those patient enough to learn. In seven years, Toj had learned only the bare rudiments of the first of Xifeng's five disciplines. For an apt pupil, each discipline took twice as long to learn as the previous one. Sima-Yan, the youngest monk to master all five, was more than two hundred and fifty years old.

Sima-Yan's whispered words echoed in his memory. "*Inhale . . . exhale*. There is no pain. *Inhale* . . . the pain deceives the mind. *Exhale* . . . trust not the mind, but heed the spirit. The mind is part of the mortal body, bound to the material world. *Inhale* . . . the spirit is essence, separate from the mind and therefore separate from the body. *Exhale* . . . can the spirit see the pain, hear it, smell it, or taste it? No, it is invisible, soundless, odorless, savorless. Can the spirit touch the pain? No, it is formless. *Inhale* . . . there is no pain."

Toj opened his eyes. He stood and stretched, oblivious to wounds that would have brought the most stoic of warriors to his knees. He ignored the trickle of warm blood that seeped into his collar. With a few of the many healing herbs that he carried with him, he would heal the cuts. They would not even require the nectar of the Golden Lotus, which was still in its bladder, strapped to his chest.

Unfortunately, the first discipline did not accelerate healing; it merely dispensed with the distractions that crippled the minds—and therefore the bodies—of almost all men. Without abolishing emotions such as pain, fear, hate—and love—the other disciplines could not be attained.

Sima-Yan had once demonstrated his mastery of the third discipline by plunging his *katana* sword through his heart, withdrawing it, and healing the wound as he did so.

Toj almost regretted his decision to leave the monastery. If he had remained to learn the third discipline, he could have rendered Jade's *kalb* beetle completely ineffective. But he would also have been unable to kill, save in self-defense, for the act of murder violated the second discipline. And he would have grown old in the learning, for he lacked the monks' longevity. Death would have claimed him long before he learned the fifth discipline. Ironically, it was mastery of this discipline that defended the mind and body from the powerful demon of time. The eldest monk of Xifeng had lived tenfold lifespans as measured by common men.

The assassin stood, flexing the muscles in his arms and legs to dissipate their stiffness. No longer troubled by his wounds, Toj reached for the pouch that contained his herbs of healing. He soon realized that all of his pockets and pouches had been disturbed. His dark gaze settled upon the dead *asshuri* who sprawled nearby, and his nose twitched at the stink that rose from their motionless bodies. In the pale moonglow, he espied the Red Asp, which lay next to a dismembered arm upon the sward.

Toj seized the exquisite hilt and admired the blade's smooth, reddened metal as he slid it into its sheath. So, these fools had paid the price for meddling with his magicked dagger. He noted that their corpses had nearly thawed from the icy bite that had doomed them. The spell's fabric unraveled slowly after doing its work. Blood dripped from their wounds, and moist droplets glistened upon their waxen skin. "Fools," he whispered to them, then raised his gaze to the moon. Fools indeed, but these fools had cost him precious time. By now, the *asshuri* host might have overrun Varhia and slain Conan.

After a brief and fruitless search for his horse, the assassin clamped his teeth to suppress the unwanted exasperation that welled within him. Left with no other choice, he adjusted his robes, tightened the straps of his boots, and ran toward the riverbed road and on to Varhia at a swift, surefooted pace. Toj possessed the lean-muscled, long-legged build of a Zamorian desert-jackal, and he sped toward the village with tireless determination.

Nine
Games of Blood

Have done with the northern savage already, by Erlik!" shouted Rigmus, general of Reydnu's army. Red-faced with excitement, he rose unsteadily to his feet. Expensive wine from his golden goblet slopped onto his silken white shirt and stained the cushions in the corner of the Grape and Thistle's common room. Oblivious to this display—one that had become more frequent as the Ghazan wine muddled his mind—Rigmus swayed drunkenly and leered at the barbarian's voluptuous companion.

The general's bodyguard, a monument of muscled flesh named Valeg, loomed over the small table at which he sat. Conan sweated nose-to-nose across from him. Knuckles whitened and biceps bulged as each man sought to force the other's arm to the table.

After two thrown matches earlier that evening, Conan had defeated nineteen challengers. Kylanna stood beside him throughout. To the Cimmerian's surprise, the princess had acted like a different woman from the moment of their arrival in the common room. She had put her feminine wiles to work, flirting with several hesitant contestants and cajoling others to take the seat across from Conan. Her smile widened, as did their purse of winnings. And the officers, sullen at first, seemed to warm up to the shapely woman and the wolfish stranger.

As the innkeeper soon saw, the contests seemed to dry the throats of Reydnu's restless officers. Many times had the innkeeper visited his cellar wherein the costlier vintages lay, and his coffers now bulged with coinage.

When General Rigmus arrived with his prodigious escort, the excitement soon reached a feverish pitch. The potbellied general's appetite for wagering surpassed his fondness for wine-swilling, and he spent gold in abundance to indulge himself. So confident was he of Valeg's prowess that he had immediately suggested a stake of ten golden Aquilonian crowns—the heaviest of Hyborian coins.

That first match had gone to Conan. The second, now in progress, seemed uncertain—and the wager had doubled.

Cords of muscle rippled under the sweat-sheathed flesh of Conan's arm. His absurd shirt, its sleeves rolled up past his massive biceps, was soaked throughout from his exertions. He drew back his lips in a snarl and stared fiercely into Valeg's beady, dull eyes. Therein he saw no flicker of thought, merely the stare of a mindless animal. The giant had spoken no words all night, not so much as a grunt. Could such brutish strength be born of a human sire?

Conan, in spite of his victory in the first encounter, began to wonder if he had merely surprised Valeg into defeat. He might have been gripping the hand of a granite statue, and this time that hand had not moved so much as a whisker's breadth. Conan's own wrist ached, and a sliver from the table lanced his elbow as he fought to keep his arm from sliding.

"Blue-eyes no beat Valeg," came the first guttural words from the crooked mouth.

Conan frowned as he recognized a peculiar, yet familiar, Kosalan accent, mangled though it was. Where had he heard it before? the memory eluded him as he struggled. Veins stood out in purple relief on his temples, and sweat poured anew from his forehead when he recalled an encounter from years past and surmised the nature of Valeg's inhuman musculature. In a hidden temple of Zamboula, the Cimmerian had fought Baal-Pteor, a Kosalan who had called himself a strangler of Yota-pong. In that barbaric and evil land, where men worshiped the bloodthirsty demon-god Yajur, priests trained youths to slay men by strangulation. In the bare hands of their executioners, sacrificial victims by the thousands had had their heads brutally twisted—nay, *torn*—from their shoulders. A man so trained would make an ideal bodyguard for a general too fat and weak to defend himself.

Valeg was a formidable foe. Conan had slain Baal-Pteor, but Valeg's mass lent him greater strength than Baal-Pteor's. Though Conan knew himself to be more than a match for nearly any man, he had not slept for nearly two days. He had ridden hard all day after escaping from the *asshuri* prison, and too long this night had he played at these contests of strength.

Valeg's broad face split into a grin, and he slammed Conan's arm onto the table, nearly snapping the bones in the Cimmerian's wrist. One of the tabletop's planks splintered under the impact.

Conan's defeat kindled flames of ire his breast. By Crom, he had once beaten a Kosalan strangler, and he could do it again! The passage of years since then had not sapped his strength. His anger pumped vigor anew into his cramped muscles, and he glared across the table at Valeg and smiled. "My left arm was ever my weaker," he challenged. "Another game, this time right-handed, and you shall taste defeat!"

Kylanna flashed a sly smile at Conan, then sighed in disappointment as she nearly emptied her purse into the general's outstretched palms. Conan's defeat had cost them almost all of their winnings. She stepped back to the Cimmerian's side and lowered her face close to his ear. "Well played, Conan!" she whispered. "You have learned this game, I see. Again we shall double the wager—forty gold crowns, enough to travel in proper comfort for the remainder of my return to Arenjun."

Slowly, Conan nodded agreement. He would test his mettle against this Kosalan. They lacked funds to back such a wager, but he now cared only about trouncing Valeg.

Kylanna faced the general and made a show of moistening her lips. "What say you, General Rigmus? Shall we double the stake?"

"A rematch!" the general exclaimed, spittle flying from his lips as he tucked the coins into a bulky sack that hung from his belt. He rubbed his hands together and leered at the generous expanse of Kylanna's exposed cleavage. "Forty crowns seems a trifle for such a contest. Why not a hundred?"

Exclamations of surprise at this outlandish sum rippled across the common room. A hushed pause followed as the onlookers waited for the woman's response. Only Conan and Valeg seemed indifferent to her answer as they stared fiercely at each other. Valeg cracked his knuckles loudly and flexed his huge biceps, as if he shared Conan's eagerness to have another go.

"Agreed, Rigmus," said Kylanna.

The general's beady eyes flickered. He slipped his sack from his belt and slapped it onto the table. "Now show your stake," he demanded.

Kylanna chewed her lower lip momentarily. "You would doubt my word that I shall honor our agreement, General?" she demanded in mock outrage.

"Show me your gold," he insisted.

"Not all of it is carried upon our persons," she began. "Much of it we secreted away, but all is within a half-day's ride."

"Hah! So you admit to your blatant misuse of our trust." The general swaggered toward her.

Conan readied himself to spring to her aid, and his hand strayed toward his hilt. A tense silence hung in the air.

Before Kylanna could protest, Rigmus spoke again. "In that case, I can name my terms for this contest. If my champion wins, you will have the pleasure of sharing my bed tonight." He smacked his wine-stained lips and chuckled lustily. "Of course, if your bravo should be victorious, the gold is yours."

Conan snarled, but Kylanna put her slender hand on his burly shoulder and spoke before he could protest. "Done," she said as her defiant gaze met Rigmus's piggish, drink-muddled eyes.

The general staggered forward and crushed her lithe body against his bulky torso, kissing her full upon the lips. "A taste of the joys that await you," he slurred, stifling a belch. "You are mine this night! No man is stronger than Valeg!"

Kylanna tore herself from Rigmus's embrace and slapped his face. "No man touches me so without my consent!"

Conan's hands clenched into fists.

Rigmus backed away and rubbed at the palm-shaped bloom of red that flushed his puffy cheek. "Uppity strumpet! When Valeg wins and I bind you to my bed, you'll regret that!"

Yarl chose that moment to intervene. His hand trembled as he poured a generous measure of his rarest Ghazan vintage into the general's goblet. Rigmus glowered but seemed content to let the matter rest. The moment of breathless tension passed.

The officers exchanged a flurry of side bets, and even the nervous innkeeper took part in the action. Of the coins wagered, the smaller pile favored the Cimmerian.

The buzz of speculation died down as Conan and Valeg leaned forward and extended their right hands. Yarl clapped to start the contest.

Knots of muscle rippled along Conan's sun-bronzed arm, and his fierce visage lent him an aspect that was more beast than man.

Valeg's face was devoid of expression. He snarled as he flexed his fingers, the smallest of which was thicker than Conan's thumb. His hand closed around the Cimmerian's with bone-crushing strength, and his biceps and forearm bore down with overwhelming force.

Conan's finger-joints popped loudly and his wrist bent, but he had braced himself for the brutal assault. Breath hissed between his clenched teeth as he struggled against the powerful Kosalan. He would prevail by sheer endurance. Valeg had tremendous strength, but Conan surmised that the man would tire sooner than he, as had Baal-Pteor. A sudden expenditure of strength would merely break like a wave on Valeg's rocklike arm. If he could but outlast the Kosalan. . . .

"Valeg! Valeg!" Shouts of encouragement sounded for the general's man, and many eyes gleamed in anticipation. Conan's arm had begun to give way. Derisive hoots and insults were hurled at him.

Valeg grunted, and the table creaked under the strain of the wrestlers' arms. Then the giant bore down, shoving Conan's hand to within a finger's breadth of the tabletop.

A low, bestial growl rose from the Cimmerian's throat. Sweat beaded and dripped from his limbs as they trembled from the strain, but neither fear nor defeat were present in the barbarian's expression.

Conan's growl became a roar as savage as a lion's. His wrist rose and wrenched the Kosalan's hand up, then down, smashing it onto the scarred wood. The table broke asunder when Valeg's arm struck it. As the wood cracked and splintered, the sack of gold tumbled to the floor in a cascade of coins—though none present scrabbled for them. Groans of dismay filled the air, and Rigmus in his gilt-edged tunic cursed and hurled his goblet of wine across the room. He then struck Valeg's face with his beefy hand.

"Son of a slut!" he raged. Ribbons of red drool ran from the corner of his mouth. "Have your thews become as weak as your wits? I deem you unfit to guard my person—no more will you enjoy the honor and the prestige of serving me!" He threw another goblet of wine against the wall. The innkeeper flinched at the impact but scurried away to fetch a new one.

Valeg's face clouded in apparent confusion, and his shoulders sagged, but he offered no words of protest.

Rigmus's drunken gaze swept along Kylanna's voluptuous body. "The gold is yours," he slurred. "But for that price, I will have you this night, wench."

"You'll have naught but a blade in your guts if you touch her again," growled Conan as he rose from his chair.

"Eh? And who are you, mercenary scum, to threaten the general of Reydnu's army? Your insolent tongue has dug you a deep grave!" With speed that belied his inebriation, Rigmus grabbed Kylanna's shoulder and spun her toward him.

Kylanna twisted away from Rigmus. "Conan, no!" she cried. "Do not—"

Conan's answering oath drowned out her protest, and his flying fist smashed into Rigmus's ear with a dull crack. The buffet snapped the general's head sideways and knocked his body backward. Blood squirted from one of his nostrils. His eyes rolled upward until only the whites could be seen, and he slumped to the floor, convulsing. Bloody foam bubbled from his mouth for a brief span, then he lay still.

The common room fell silent, flickering lamps reflecting on the shocked faces of Reydnu's officers.

"He's dead," murmured a hawk-faced sergeant. "The murdering dog slew the general over a doxy—"

"Cur!" yelled a bald, broad-shouldered captain, loosening the strap of his hilt.

"Swine! Barbarian!" hooted two swarthy lieutenants, snatching at their weapons. They darted toward the Cimmerian.

Conan stepped in front of Kylanna, hefted a table over his head, and hurled it full at the two lieutenants, knocking them back into their fellows. Angry shouts mingled with the muted crack of breaking bones.

The two men did not get up.

"Ishtar!" the bald captain swore as he leapt forward and slashed, his blade cleaving naught but air. Conan had anticipated the attack and bounded aside, even as he whipped his sword from its scabbard. The Cimmerian's counterattack swept out in a low, powerful arc, severing both of the captain's legs at mid-thigh. The soldier tumbled to the floor with an anguished moan, his sword slipping from nerveless fingers.

The sudden onset of violence seemed to paralyze the other officers for a moment, but they recovered. Weapons were drawn, and a few heartbeats later, Conan and Kylanna were surrounded.

The Cimmerian glowered, blood dripping from his blade as he shifted it from hand to hand. He swept the room with eyes that burned a baleful blue, and no man could meet that fearsome gaze. But Conan knew that against these odds, even he was doomed—he could not save himself and the girl. This lot of Shemite officers might be cowards, but they were also veterans who would overwhelm him by sheer numbers. He mocked them with a guttural laugh, for he would not cower like a frightened cur before the gaping maw of death. "Who dies next?" he rumbled.

A score of angry officers stared at him—men hungering for blood, blades gleaming in the lambent glow from the table lamps. But none dared to strike, and fear glimmered in all expressions . . . save that of Valeg. The brutish Kosalan's face registered naught but bestial hatred. He lifted a decorative but usable mace from its place on the wall and charged like a maddened bull, his arms swinging the weapon's head-sized ball of spikes toward Conan's skull.

The Cimmerian caught the blow on the flat of his sword, which bent and promptly snapped. The broken length of steel flew at Conan and sliced a flap of flesh from his scalp. The mace scraped his shoulder, its spikes digging a red furrow.

"Crom's teeth!" Conan barked as he plunged the handspan of steel—all that remained of his sword—into Valeg's side.

Unfazed, the Kosalan lifted his mace for a killing blow.

Conan bounded forward and grappled with Valeg, dodging in under the murderous sweep of the spikes. His momentum knocked the big man backward but did not topple him. The Cimmerian's knee slammed upward into Valeg's crotch, eliciting an agonized bellow. The Kosalan lost his balance and grabbed at Conan, who fell with him, their fists flailing as they struck the floor.

"Finish him!" screamed a short captain and a burly sergeant in unison, and a half-dozen men jumped into the fight, stabbing and slashing with reckless abandon at the two struggling men.

The hawk-faced sergeant lunged. His point nicked Conan's side but slid past, where it slipped between Valeg's ribs. Yet the Kosalan fought on as the sergeant jerked free his blade and cursed his own clumsiness.

Conan drove his elbow into the wound. Ribs snapped, their splintered ends piercing Valeg's heart. The Kosalan's last breath wheezed from him as the Cimmerian rolled aside and pulled the massive corpse with him to shield himself from the hail of blows landed by the officers. He groped for a dropped sword, but his clutching fingers closed instead around Valeg's mace.

The officers had ignored Kylanna, who had slowly backed toward a wall. But all the while, she had held her sword point-up, her legs apart in the stance of an expert swordfighter. Now she burst into action, her narrow blade flickering like the tongue of a steel serpent. An officer's head leapt from his shoulders in a crimson gush, while another man's entrails spilled from his rent belly. Two others fell back, grabbing at bloodied arms. Their blades lay upon the floor.

Officers cast looks of mingled fear and amazement in her direction as they retreated warily, then rejoined the melee with slower, more deliberate moves. Step by step, they forced Kylanna away from the tavern wall. Her sword whirled and twisted in a dazzling dance of steel that defied every assailant. Yet she wounded them not, and the odds clearly favored her attackers. Sweat poured down her face and shone on her breasts, which heaved beneath her damp, clinging tunic.

Conan had vanished in a mass of flailing sword-arms and flashing blades. Curses, howls of pain, the clash of metal, and the meaty smack of blades into flesh filled the air with a tangled din of butchery. Shemite after Shemite fell with a pulped skull, a torn throat, or a crushed torso. Some fell back or crawled away, clutching at less dire wounds but unable or unwilling to fight. In the blindness of fury and confusion, some officers struck their fellows, their very numbers working against them.

From a waist-deep mound of mangled, bloody flesh emerged the gore-smeared Cimmerian. He now clutched a dripping dirk, taken in the frenzy from a foeman. Splashed from head to toe with blood, he looked less a man and more a wild beast, his throat issuing naught but incoherent growls, his red-misted gaze flashing in search of more blood to spill.

Conan's eyes narrowed at the sight of Kylanna, who fought desperately against four opponents. He leapt over a mound of corpses and onto a table, rammed his dirk through one man's throat and snapped another's spine with a vicious sideways kick.

Kylanna quickly ran one man through. The last Shemite died moments later as he turned toward Conan, catching Conan's thrown dagger in his breast and Kylanna's downward slash through his belly.

"Bel, Badb, and Dagon," panted the Cimmerian, planting his hands on his knees and leaning forward in exhaustion. "Few woman—or men, for that matter—can claim your mastery of swordplay, girl! Even Valeria, Bêlit, or Karela might deem you a worthy foe. Where in Zandru's Nine Hells did you acquire your skill? Tell me not that Tiridates' elite soldiers tutored you, for no paunchy palace guard ever wielded a blade as deftly as you." With open suspicion, he studied her face.

Kylanna leaned against the wall and sighed wearily. She laid her blade upon a table and massaged her sword-arm. "Conan," she began slowly, "I have used you falsely. The battle has unmasked me. But for you, I would be at the gates of Gehanna."

"Aye, twice have I saved you," Conan said gruffly.

"Nay, only tonight, Cimmerian. Know you that when we met at the *asshuri* camp, I was in no danger."

"Crom, girl, are you mad? That torturer—"

"—was my man," she interrupted, "told to act the role of ravisher. I knew not that you would slay him, though it matters not. He was a murderer ten times over who had too often been spared a swift ride to Hell. As for my 'Captain Tousalos' in the other cell, he was one of my *asshuri*, whom you slew the day before. Never was he tortured; those screams were faked by another."

"To what end? Nay, tell me not, until I know your true identity. If you're a princess of Zamora, I'm war-chief of all Pictland." Anger flashed in his eyes. "And the tiara . . ."

"Does not exist," she said with a shrug. "A tale to lure you."

Conan smashed his fist against the table. "Sivitri is the name given me at birth," she continued. "I am truly a daughter of Tiridates, though he knows it not. Before that decadent old drunkard developed a preference for young boys, he kept my mother as a favored consort in Shadizar. I grew up in the palace there, but my mother paid me little heed, spending her days in the opium dens and her nights in whatever bed best served her purposes. She was weak in both mind and body. I vowed to become strong, to be master of my spirit and my flesh. It was after I could always beat the captain of the palace guard in our mock duels when Jade—" she stopped and cleared her throat. "—when she who became my mentor took an interest in me and gave me a purpose, and a station far better than I could have had were I acknowledged daughter by Tiridates himself."

"Jade?" Conan scoffed. "She is but a myth. I have thieved everywhere from Nemedian estates in Belverus to the Vendhyan towers in Ayodhya, and all men know that she is but a myth."

"A myth, yes—by her design," Sivitri replied. "For what is fame to a thief? It brings unwanted attention and eventual ruin."

Conan scowled but stifled his protest, for he knew this to be true. The best thief was one whose reputation was hidden, as well as his hoard.

"Speak not of her," cautioned Sivitri. "Those who say her name too often are wont to disappear. Anyway, know you that her empire is more vast than any king's, many of whom dangle like puppets from her vast web of strings. For her net stretches from the Hyborian kingdoms of the west to Kambuja—the southeastern corner of the world."

"I know of Kambuja," Conan muttered.

"Save Khitai, Stygia, and the Black Kingdoms, she has guilds in every land, or at least in every city deserving of the name."

"Guilds—of thieves?" Conan rubbed his jaw.

"Thieves, merchants, sages . . . and in Belverus and Zamboula, assassins' guilds. Some three hundred guildmasters in all—nay, belike it is more than that—pay obeisance to her in one form or another."

"To one woman?" Conan's brow furrowed.

His doubting tone sparked a flash of anger in Sivitri's eyes. "Were it a *man*, I suppose you would doubt it not. What are men but muscle-bound oafs who keep their brains in their breechclouts? How easily I used you, barbarian. A few doe-eyed looks at your thews, a careful display of my wares for you to ogle, and your senses—so keen on the hunt or in battle—are befogged."

"Were you a man, I would split your skull." Angrily he grated his teeth. But she spoke rightly enough . . . he *was* a fool, to have played into the lying wench's game. But what was her game? He could hazard but a few guesses, and the truth lay beneath waters too deep for him to fathom.

Sivitri's laugh cut sharply into his ears. "And so barks the hound to the tigress, before she tears out his throat. Sheathe your sword and your tongue, Cimmerian, for I swear by Bel, Zath, and Derketo that I shall not try to slay you. And I know enough of you and your ways to be certain that you would strike me down only if I attacked you."

Conan fumed, but uttered no denial.

"We waste time here. Only fools fight in a burning house, and we have just set this inn afire." She gestured toward the bloody heaps at their feet. "Belike the whole army will chase us to Turan when they learn of this deed. Let us away. I promise to explain my purpose to you, but not here!"

Conan growled and dug through a pile of corpses to strip them of coinpurses. He scooped up the stained gold from his match with Valeg and stuffed the lot into a spacious sack. He pried an expertly forged Corinthian longsword from the stiff fingers of a headless sergeant, all the while keeping an eye on Sivitri.

"I see." She shook her head. "Will you rid yourself of me? Will you slay me so that I cannot follow? Fate is a mistress who chooses her own partners, Conan, and she has chained us together for the nonce."

"I'll not harm you, but we part ways tonight. I owe nothing to you." He slipped a broad belt from an officer's waist and eyed it critically. "I'll leave you bound—"

The door rasped, and their heads spun toward it in time to glimpse the innkeeper's hasty departure.

"Crom's bones!" Conan swore in exasperation. "The dog must have hidden in the cellar and crept out while you distracted me. I'll not leave you to vengeful soldiers, for though you brought this battle upon us, you took a hand in evening the odds."

"I tried to stop you from killing that loutish general," Sivitri protested.

Conan growled in response and strode toward the door. "When the innkeeper rouses reinforcements, I'll be well down the road. If you stay in this slaughterhouse, I'll bear no blame for your death. Follow me if your must . . . and if you can." He broke into a run and flung open the door.

"What—" he began, before astonishment froze the words in his throat. He stopped so suddenly that he almost overbalanced, so unexpected was the sight filling his widened eyes.

The Grape and Thistle sat upon the crest of a low hill, affording a view of the city's southern quarter. There, fires burned and smoke billowed up into the night sky. In the light of the blaze, he saw mounted warriors—*asshuri*—at the outskirts. These had engaged an apparently confused throng of Reydnu's warriors, who were falling like ripe grain under the swords of the invaders. The battle had the look of a massacre in the making.

Conan could see at once that Varhia would fall.

A gaggle of men, chased by fighters on horseback, dashed along the street toward the inn. They pointed at Conan and yelled. He heard their voices, but the distance distorted their words. Even as they neared, the din of battle encroached upon the street's unnatural silence. "Balvadek's riders approach!" Conan shouted over his shoulder. He loped toward the stable, hoping that he could ride away before the *asshuri* swept into the northern quarter.

Conan kicked down the heavy wooden door, nearly hurling himself through it. Aren, true to his word, had tended to their horses. As Conan hastily fitted the riding harness on his mount, Sivitri appeared in the wrecked doorway.

"Six *asshuri* head toward us," she panted. "They have slain the men on foot before them."

"Too many for one of us," Conan grumbled. "It seems we are not to part ways yet."

"Not yet," Sivitri agreed. She tossed a blanket onto her horse, grabbed a harness, and fit it sloppily into place.

They rode at a trot into the alley, swords at ready. The glow of distant fires lit the narrow avenue, into which rode the *asshuri* raiders.

"We may never part ways, Cimmerian." Sivitri's calm tone belied their dire predicament. "We may burn together forever, in whatever Hell awaits us." A nervous laugh passed from her lips. "You once said you would rather face an army of *asshuri* than endure my tongue. The gods have granted your wish!"

Conan's face fell in dismay as he counted the enemy. Not six *asshuri*, but thrice that number, galloping toward them. The alley afforded no exit, save through row upon row of mounted warriors. Fatigue weighed upon his shoulders like a sack of stones, and every muscle from head to toe ached. But he was Cimmerian, with fire in his veins and steel in his hand. He would share the ferryman's fee with at least one Shemite.

"Crom!" Conan bellowed hoarsely. Even the battle-cry seemed to tax him. "Crom and steel!" He slapped his steed's rump with the flat of his blade and charged wearily but defiantly into the jaws of death.

Sivitri drew in a deep breath, waved her sword up high, and matched her horse's stride with his.

The Cimmerian met the foremost Shemite head-on, his sword clashing against that of his foeman in a shower of sparks. His downward stroke beat back the *asshuri*'s blade and bit through the man's light jerkin of leather. Skewered, the warrior slid from his saddle. Conan yanked his blade free but could not raise it in time to parry a stroke leveled at his neck. He twisted his head away and took the flat of the blade against the side of his head.

The impact knocked him off his steed, and his skull rang as if all the devils in Hell were howling into his ears. He blinked and looked up as two *asshuri* dismounted and rushed toward him. One of them—his gilded helm marking him a captain—slapped the other, who had struck at Conan. The captain shouted and raised his hand, but Conan heard not the words. Images and sounds blurred into a dreamlike mosaic for him, and his sword fell from his hand.

He rolled onto his side and saw Kylanna—Sivitri . . . whoever she was—saw her disarmed and dragged from her saddle, kicking and thrashing. Then the captain's boot smashed into his chin. Conan's fingers groped feebly for his hilt, but the lids of his eyes became leaden weights. He sank into a black sea of pain and knew no more.

Ten
Secrets in the Sand

Tevek Thul glided swiftly across the desert dunes of eastern Shem. He left no track and made no sound, for his feet never touched the sand. Had his coal-black cloak not shrouded his hand, a dim green glow would have radiated from Thoth-Amon's Black Ring, coiled around his finger. A tithe of its power had sufficed to propel him in this manner since his departure from Stygia.

By day, he had ensconced himself in his cloak to keep the sun's bright beams from burning his eyes. By night, he had flown across the trackless wastes that stretched between the River Styx and his destination: the Brass City. Few living things lay along his path, for the air itself sucked life from the ground, leaving naught but thick, almost unbreathable heat.

Tevek did not regret the absence of life, but rather its consequence: the absence of *death*. League upon league he had traversed without sensing so much as the shallow grave of a desert wolf. He had even slowed somewhat to extend his spirit-sight deeper, but to no avail. This arid waste unsettled him. He longed for the comforting nearness of even a small tomb.

Though the Black Ring infused him with sorcerous power, it could not nourish him. Tevek had not fed since crossing the Styx, where he had abandoned his undead retinue and his black carriage. He dared not squander the ring's power to convey them all through the air.

He could continue for a time without sustenance, but he knew well the limits of his physical body, and his quest in the Brass City might tax both mind and flesh to those limits.

The necromancer halted and slowly lowered his feet to the sand. From his robes he extracted a flat pouch—fashioned from the cured flesh of a virgin, like the pouch that held Harrab's crushed skull—and emptied the last of its contents into his cupped hand. Only a few pinches of the bone-dust lay upon the pale creases of his palm. He dug a talonlike fingernail into the base of his thumb until a drop of blood welled from it. This he mixed with the bone-dust while he intoned sibilant words in a dialect born of eons-vanished Thuria. *"Makanan-mati, coba, siya-lihat, lahat-mati!"*

The reddish-grey paste pulsed upon his palm, imbued with unnatural life, and shaped itself into a wormlike creature. Tevek lowered it to the sand that it might crawl. The thing etched a faint, finger-length groove into the dune, then stopped and coiled itself into a tight spiral.

Tevek studied the shallow furrow. By his reckoning, he would reach the place indicated within two, perhaps three, turns of the glass. But he would stray from the most direct route to the Brass City, and he was loath to tarry. Back at Khajar, in Thoth-Amon's den, the thrice-accursed Taper of Death burned lower and lower. Tevek weighed the consequences for a span before deciding to follow the line. He snatched the blood-worm between thumb and forefinger and popped it into his mouth, chewing slowly to savor the taste of blood and bone. It whetted his appetite.

Moments later, his feet left the sand and he sped in the direction of the line. The Black Ring would hold that course without wavering, until he willed it otherwise.

Tevek neared the settlement at dawn. Traces of a lightly trafficked caravan trail foretold its proximity, and it lay exactly on the line etched by the blood-worm. A useful cantrip that, though he seldom had occasion to evoke it. The library beneath Amentet housed many similar baubles of sorcery.

He lowered his feet to the path. Here, he would play the role of a road-weary scholar who wished to pass through on his way to Shushan. In several accounts he had read, travelers' writings described the desert folk of Shem as a fierce and wary lot. As he approached the base of a gradually sloping hill of rock, he saw supporting evidence.

The path narrowed as it neared the hilltop and led up to a knife-slash of a passage. A natural wall of steep rock encircled the settlement there. Fourteen men paced along the top of this wall, their rust-colored kaffiyehs and robes blending with the dull red rocks. Half of their number held bows in hand as they patrolled above the escarpment.

Tevek regarded them with disdain. Fools, so confident that their pitiful weapons could protect them. He could have destroyed them with little effort, but he preferred to conserve his energy. Striding calmly toward the cleft in the rocks, he squinted upward into the morning sky. Thin clouds veiled the unwelcome sun, and he was grateful for their presence. A beclouded sky would enable him to continue with a minimum of discomfort, once he fed here.

His strides carried him up the hill while the archers looked on. A few nocked shafts and held them at the ready. When he drew nearer, they loosened their grip on their bowstrings. After all, here was naught but an old, white-haired wanderer.

A stout Shemite, beard streaked with grey, stepped from a niche in the rock that had been cleverly hidden from view of the path. His tanned hand rested lightly upon the golden hilt of a curved dagger thrust into his broad belt. "No farther, old man, if you please," he said in a coarse Shemitish dialect, his tone more stern than courteous.

"Eh?" Tevek replied in a like tongue, though he was more accustomed to its written form. He could have crushed the Shemite like a desert lizard, but he deemed it better to act his part for the moment. "May I pass through?"

"Those who have business in Kaetta—or those who have coin to pay for passage—may enter and share our water. Have you either, old one?"

"Use your elders not so rudely," scolded Tevek, miffed by the man's tone. "I have both."

"I see. The Lord Ranjau records the names and callings of all who would enter his domain," the Shemite said. "What are yours?"

"Tovokles, Scholar Prime of the Royal Library at Aghrapur," replied Tevek with a touch of haughtiness. "And King Yezdigerd records the names of those who impede his aides, lest their discourtesy goes unforgotten."

The Shemite bit his lip, a trace of uncertainty in his eyes. "My apologies, Master Tovokles. I thought you a Stygian. Lord Ranjau and our people devoutly worship Mitra, and we turn away all followers of the accursed, soul-devouring Stygian serpent. But surely you came not alone, all the way from Aghrapur?"

Tevek shook his head mournfully. "No, not alone. My retinue lies dead upon the sands leagues past." He suppressed a smile at this private jest. "Brigands attacked us and left me for dead."

"Aye, you look it—meaning no offense, Master Tovokles," the man hastily corrected himself, his cheeks reddening. "Forget my earlier words. Though Turanian gods are not ours, we turn away no man in need. It is not the way of our people. You are welcome to our water for as long as you wish. I am Uzgaru, Gatewatcher. Follow me, that I may show you a proper welcome." He turned, beckoning Tevek to join him.

The necromancer's dry, pale tongue flicked across his chapped, peeling lips. It was not their water that he would drink. Worshipers of Mitra. Quite amusing.

Uzgaru prattled noisily as they entered the narrow, rock-walled passage that twisted gradually upward. Kaetta sat atop a plateau, affording a panoramic view of the desert for leagues in all directions. "You were fortunate to find us," the Shemite said. "Kaetta is the only bastion of civilization in this region. The nearest village is some hundred leagues distant. The spring that flows from this rock supports us in modest comfort, though we lack the means to raise crops or livestock."

Tevek half-listened to Uzgaru as the passageway widened and debouched to a broad circle, like a bowl surrounded on all sides by steep cliffs. Holes in the north face served as lodgings, it seemed. From the center of the bowl rose a four-walled structure with a flat roof, simple in form and unadorned. This would be the temple to Mitra, whose priesthood disdained the trappings that accompanied many religions. Nothing else had been built in the bowl save a ring of stone blocks that bordered the gently rippling waters of Kaetta's spring. The village could not have housed more than a thousand folk.

Of more interest to Tevek was the tingle he felt as Uzgaru led him nearer to the temple. A priest of Set would have been in danger here, for the Serpent Lord and the so-called Lord of Light were the bitterest of enemies. Tevek feared no contact with the priests of Mitra, though like as not, his own presence would discomfit them.

Mitra's influence was tangible enough here for Tevek to feel. He sensed something else as well, in the rock beneath the temple. A burial chamber . . . yes, a sizable sepulcher. Where there was life, there was death. The subterranean cavity radiated a repugnant warmth—the aura of consecration. A trifling problem for Tevek, who could defile it readily enough.

". . . service of worship on the morn, and thrice is the water blessed each day. Ah, good. Oradne has risen for the first blessing." Uzgaru had been discussing the roles of the village's three priests. One of these, bald and paunchy, emerged from the temple. His plain brown robe, belted at the waist with a horsehair rope, marked his calling. He approached and waved in greeting.

Fatuous fool, thought Tevek. Yet he would be on his way sooner if this misguided sheep of a priest granted him free access to the temple . . . and the crypts below. The taint of consecration had not diminished Tevek's appetite.

"My good Oradne, greetings," said Uzgaru. "This is Prime Scholar Tovokles of Aghrapur."

"Mitra bless you, Gatewatcher, and our guest. Welcome," the priest added, facing Tevek with curiosity evident in his face.

The necromancer wrenched a response from his reluctant throat. "My thanks, Oradne, for your hospitality." He felt an unexpected itch upon his hand and realized that its source was the Black Ring. What if the priest caught the scent of Set from it? Surely the ring was steeped in that god's essence. Tevek regarded the priest calmly. After all, it was this dun-robed dullard who stood in the shadow of peril, not Tevek Thul.

Oradne scratched the back of his neck, then shrugged his shoulders as if to shake off a morning chill. "Meaning no insult, Tovokles, but your face is pale and drawn. One of our women can prepare a repast for you, and draw a jug for a bath."

Uzgaru nodded. "Brigands, Oradne. He happened upon the path to us—"

"Begging your pardon, Gatewatcher, but I doubt not that Mitra's will guided his feet to us, as the Lord of Light has ever watched over those in need. Well then, Tovokles, I look forward to hearing your tale, but now I must tend to the morning blessing of the water, ere our people rise for the day. There is a spare chamber, modest but comfortable, among the priests' quarters."

"In the temple?" asked Tevek.

"Unless it offends your beliefs," the priest said. His smile did not warm his eyes this time, and Tevek took the meaning. A challenge, or a test.

"Of course not," the necromancer replied evenly. If the Black Ring revealed itself within the shrine, he would deal with the priests and any others who interfered. Once inside, it would be a simple matter to find the passageway down. . . .

"I'll find Beladah," offered Uzgaru. "She'll bring food, water, and fresh bedding."

"Yes, a day of rest will do you good, friend," Oradne proclaimed. "Come I'll show you the way." He seemed reassured by Tevek's willingness to enter the temple.

Tevek nodded in what he hoped would be taken as a gesture of thanks. His throat was unable to form even a lie of gratitude for these fools. The sooner he was away, the better. Not for him these sickening pleasantries, this tolerance of scum whom he should crush insectlike beneath the heel of his sorcery. He was no longer amused by this priest's pathetic games, and his even more pathetic faith in the protection of his temple.

Within the stone walls of the temple, the Black Ring seemed to gnaw like a living thing upon Tevek's finger, though it drew no blood. The necromancer tried vainly to subjugate it by willing it to cease; when it would not obey, he simply ignored it. The sensation would cease soon enough, and he would be on his way. Matters of greater import troubled him than the sorcerous sting of that copper serpent.

"It was built nine generations hence," the priest said, gesturing toward the rows of stone pews and the simple altar. "A haven in the desert," he added proudly.

"Not many in Shem profess Mitra as their god," Tevek noted. Since this windbag seemed intent to drone on, he may as well learn something of these sheep.

"Indeed," agreed Oradne with a heavy sigh. "We are few, but we spread enlightenment to those who trade with us."

"How often do merchants pass this way?"

"We have but one export here—opals of high quality from our small mining operation. Every fortnight, traders arrive to bid on our wares. They bring provisions that we lack. The quantity of gems is not so great as to tempt the larger bands of desert scavengers to attack us, and Kaetta is difficult to besiege in any event. We trust in Mitra to watch over us, and Uzgaru and his men keep the traders honest. Lord Ranjau is not greedy for wealth; he merely wishes to provide for his own in comfort and safety."

"A noble fellow." Tevek looked down and stifled a yawn. His gaze was at once drawn to the curious arabesques etched into the floor of the shrine. They were worn nearly smooth, but he found them to be strangely out of place in such austere surroundings. He had seen them pictured elsewhere, but their origin escaped him. When Oradne took him through a door at the rear of the shrine, the pattern was more pronounced. Fewer feet had trodden here.

They passed three doors along a narrow hallway and stopped at a fourth. Farther ahead, Tevek noted, the passageway sloped downward. From it issued the faintest of sepulchral scents, a fragrance so slight that only a necromancer might be aware of it. Tevek had fasted for too long—nigh on a week. Satisfaction lay not far now, and he would bide his time. This Beladah must arrive and depart first, then he would be left alone.

"Here you may sleep." Oradne gestured toward a cot fashioned of horsehair rope. "Beladah will bring a blanket."

A stone bench squatted beside the cot, and before the bench stood a dry basin ringed with water stains. Two thick candles occupied niches upon the wall above the basin.

"Oradne," Tevek began as he dropped heavily onto the bench, "farther down the hallway . . ."

"The catacombs? Seldom do we venture there, mayhap a score of occasions each year, when we lay to rest the shells of those whose souls have become one with Mitra. Naught lies in those dark passages but dust and fading memories. We mourn not our dead, for their spirits endure forever in the brilliance of Mitra's realm."

"Interesting," Tevek said, repulsed by this facile bit of doctrine. Then a flash of inspiration came to him. "In fact, King Yezdigerd sent me westward to learn of Hyborian traditions concerning the dead. He wishes to gain a better understanding of his neighbors, and he reasons that the customs of burial may convey insights into cultures. Later, perhaps, when my strength returns, I should like to venture there—just to observe."

Oradne shrugged. "I do not pretend to understand the motives of scholars, friend Tovokles. But you are free to observe what you will. If you wish a guide, one of us can—"

"As I have need, I shall accept your offer," Tevek replied, shaking his head in protest.

"Very well, then. Ah, I hear Beladah. Rest, and perhaps Lord Ranjau may dine with you this eve if you have regained sufficient vigor."

Tevek nodded again, weary of so much idle talk. Oradne smiled faintly, scratched his neck, and departed, nodding at a thin, jet-haired girl about to enter the room.

Baladah was not what the necromancer had expected. Women interested him little, and he had never lain with one—leastwise, not one who lived. The very warmth of their flesh and their breath, the color in their faces, the shine in their eyes and hair, these stilled any stirrings of lust. But this girl intrigued him, eager though he was to descend into the crypts below.

Her face and hands were pearly white, like her slender ankles and feet. Her conservative shift of pale green silhouetted her form. A woman, surely, but with the body of a waif, small-breasted and lean-muscled. Blue-black hair hung straight along the sides of a face devoid of unappealing color. Through the pallid flesh of her ankles and hands, he could see the angles and delicate framework of her bones.

"Master Tovokles?" she said timidly, hesitating in the doorway. In her arms she held a folded horsehair blanket, upon which rested a clay tray bearing food and a jug.

"Beladah," he replied, her submissiveness heightening his appreciation. She inspired in him a dark stirring. Perhaps he would act upon it. In the past, under the darkness of tombs, in depths so black that no moonbeam, star, or flicker of lamplight intruded, Tevek had done deeds that were beyond conscionable men.

The woman took a few tentative steps toward him and set the tray upon the stone bench. She lifted the jug and poured water into the basin. "To bathe, if you wish to," she explained. "I will return with some water to drink—Oradne must bless it first." She held out the blanket, waiting for him to take it.

He reached for the bundle with both hands before realizing his error. Distracted by her high, flat cheekbones, he had exposed the Black Ring. A lambent green nimbus surrounded its coppery coils, and she stared at it in wide-eyed fear. "Sorcery!" she whispered.

Before she could scream, Tevek focused his will. It was not too late to undo this mishap, and he knew well the weaving of the enchantment that brought sleep. But the ring itself twisted his intent, as if he had angered it by bringing it into a shrine of Mitra's. Tendrils of translucent green fire flared toward the girl's breast and lodged within to close like ghostly fingers around her heart. She gasped and pitched forward as her eyes rolled upward. Tevek grasped her wrists and broke her fall, instantly aware that the ring had slain her. The whites of her eyes stared sightlessly into his pitiless face, and he let her body slump to the floor.

Sandaled feet shuffled against the floor of the hallway and stopped in the doorway. "More comfortable now, I hope—" Oradne stopped, his mouth agape. "Mitra save us!" He made the sign against evil and dashed away before Tevek could loose the ring's power against him.

"Pray that he hears you," Tevek laughed. This subterfuge had exhausted his patience. He would desecrate the burial vaults and eat his fill. Any who stood in his way would perish before they realized their folly.

Tevek strode brazenly into the hallway and followed the long corridor that spiraled downward into the catacombs. His ring illuminated the narrow passageway and revealed more of the peculiar arabesques upon the floor. Unlike those in the structure above, here the walls of striated stone featured odd symbols.

The sight of these stirred Tevek's memory. The arabesques—he had seen them in drawings that represented Ibis's temples. The symbols were ancient glyphs, known only to the prophets of Ibis. Had Kaetta been built upon the ruins of the place where eons-dead followers of Ibis had worshiped? Here was something to trade with Thoth-Amon, for the Stygian had long sought to rid the world of Caranthes, High Priest of Ibis. What weaknesses of Ibis's cult might Thoth-Amon uncover here?

Tevek continued his descent. He heard the shouts and the booted feet of those who followed him, already summoned by Oradne. Let them come. The necromancer reached the bottom of the spiral, where the smell of the dead was much more evident. He looked down a long, wide corridor whose walls were pocked with niches— shelves for the shroud-wrapped flesh that lay there. The taint of consecration stank, but he would soon tend to that.

Tevek extracted a small, flat box of wood from one of his robe's many pockets. He worked the lid and dipped his finger into the black powder within—soot from the burned flesh of a beheaded murderer. Crouching, he swiftly sketched a circle and the six symbols of Thanatos at equal distances on its perimeter. He studied it carefully, for even the slightest flaw or break would foul the ritual.

Ignoring the increasingly loud sounds of pursuit, Tevek slid a dull-grey flute from the sheath strapped to his back. The instrument, carved from the leg-bone of an infant strangled by its mother, had been dipped in the blood of a virgin maiden and first winded beneath a full moon on the eve of her death. Tevek lifted it to his lips and played, his slender fingers working along its six slotted holes. The eerie melody echoed like the muted cries of a thousand unseen demons. The walls began to weep blood, which ran in meandering rivulets that pooled on the floor. A score of mouths yawned open in the once-seamless stonework and vomited forth a noisome black slime that stank of excrement.

Sequins of white light suddenly shimmered in the air and swirled, as if seeking escape from the noxious fluids that spewed from the ceiling and the walls. The lights flew straight at Tevek.

A cylinder of roaring emerald fire suddenly encircled the necromancer, matching the shape of the circle in which he stood. The white specks of light sparked and crackled as they struck the green flame, vanishing in tiny puffs of smoke like mosquitoes caught in a campfire. None escaped.

Tevek lowered the flute, and the blazing cylinder vanished. The pools of blood and gobbets of slime evaporated like shallow puddles beneath the hot sun, leaving only the stink of offal and carrion.

A troop of men, led by Uzgaru, rounded the bend at the bottom of the spiraling passage and stared. Several doubled over and clutched their stomachs, heaving at the stench.

A tall, swarthy man draped in full chain mail stepped up to Uzgaru's side. Behind him stood Oradne, flanked by two others in the plain garb of the Mitraic priesthood. "I am Lord Ranjau, faithful man of Mitra. Begone, vile servant of Set," he boomed. Symbols against evil adorned his pale green tabard, and he held his sword with point extended.

"Begone!" Oradne hissed, as he flung a cup of water at Tevek.

The necromancer made no effort to dodge the water, taking it full upon his breast. It dripped from him, hissing and smoking only where it contacted the Black Ring. He was surprised that it had come through his circle of protection, which would easily have stopped true holy water. Perhaps Oradne, when he had blessed that cup's contents, had enchanted it only against one sworn to Set.

Uzgaru lifted his two-handed scimitar and rushed at the necromancer. "Ranjau! Ranjau!"

Tevek laughed, a hideous sound that reverberated through the long catacomb. His voice deepened. "*Yotha-hie*, eyes to black, *Xet'ta*, steel to rust, *Hie-yotha*, bones to crack, *Ta'xet*, blood to dust!" He pointed his forefinger at Uzgaru, who jerked forward, puppetlike, clutching at his throat. His eyes bulged outward, then vanished within his skull. His scimitar and armor crumbled away from him in a shower of corroded flakes, and his body popped and twisted as if a dozen heavy mallets struck him at once. He collapsed, spilling scarlet dust from his gaping mouth and hollow eye sockets.

The others fell silent. The only sound in the catacombs was a droll chuckle from Tevek's throat. The necromancer had never seen the desiccation set in so quickly—the Black Ring had empowered the spell with a potency beyond Tevek's expectations. As well swat a gnat with a sledge, he thought. The rest of the helpless scum would flee when their leader fell. He formed the words of the chant again, his gaze fixed on Ranjau.

"Your necromancy cannot harm me, worm of the Pit," said Ranjau as Tevek spoke. "For I bear a sword forged in the lava-furnaces of the Taian Mountains, cooled in the holiest of Mitra-blessed fonts, and woven with prayers to protect its bearer from evil!" Encouraged by his pronouncement, the warlord advanced. He gripped the hilt with both hands and held the point outthrust. The others trembled behind him, even Oradne.

". . . *Ta'xet*, blood to dust!" finished Tevek as he extended his forefinger toward Ranjau's mailed torso.

From the sword's rune-etched blade flashed white fire that filled the murky catacombs with its brilliance.

Tevek's eyelids closed instinctively, his eyes unable to bear the burning whiteness. He blinked and peered through his slitted lids at Ranjau, who continued his advance. The spell had failed.

With a triumphant shout, the warlord swung his blade toward Tevek's neck.

The necromancer held his ground, trusting in the circle to protect him from the onrushing edge.

In midair, as the sword crossed the plane of Tevek's circle, a translucent shield of emerald appeared. The blade rang against it as if striking stone. Ranjau grimaced and clutched the hilt as the impact traveled painfully up his arm. Yet he swiftly redoubled his attack, making several tentative swings, each of which rebounded from the green barrier. Finally he leaned the blade against his shoulder and fell back a step, panting.

"Foolish worm," Tevek muttered. "Naught bearing Mitra's taint can touch me."

"Cower doglike behind your sorcerer's shield, then, and yap all you will," Ranjau countered. "Your foul spells can do naught against the power of Mitra. My sword has pulled your fangs, serpent. Even now do more of my men approach. How long can you stand against us? You shall soon be as dead as those who lie herein."

Tevek's eyes flickered. "You dare threaten me—think you that one of my power cannot crush you like the crawling insect you are?" Saying no more to Ranjau, he closed his eyes and began a slow chant. His voice deepened slightly with every syllable intoned, until the words sounded unlike any that a human throat could issue. His dirge caused the very walls to vibrate, and the slack-jawed onlookers felt their bones shake.

A cold draft of wind flowed through the corridor, as if the vent of an icy hell had suddenly opened. Tevek's mouthings reached a thundering crescendo, loud enough to reverberate within the deepest recesses of the catacombs.

Which indeed had been Tevek's intent.

His eyes opened, and the dirge ended abruptly, though a bitter chill still permeated the air. "Now, misguided wretches, witness the power that I draw from the bottomless well of Thanatos, the undying one, Emperor of the Black Beyond." Tevek turned his back and shouted down the long chamber, to the stirring, shroud-wrapped forms that lay there. "Arise, my minions! Arise, and rend the flesh of the living!" His words were strained, as if their utterance had over-exerted him. Tevek's hands trembled slightly.

From deep within the catacombs, they moved at his bidding. Whether deceased for untold centuries or for mere years, all heeded the necromancer's call. The rustling of their dusty shrouds on rough stone was a great sigh that echoed in the darkness. The echo gave way to the scraping of hundreds of bony feet that shuffled across the stones. Bound by the unearthly power of ancient words and by Tevek's will, the mindless, soulless army shambled toward its summoner.

A second band of Kaettan fighters burst into the hall. A few held aloft flickering torches that illuminated the nightmarish scene before them. The decayed corpses of their ancestors swayed toward them with skeletal arms outstretched. Those nearest to Tevek reached Ranjau first. Their shrouds, crumbling from age, had fallen or torn away as they slid from their niches along the walls. Clad in naught but tattered rags or the dust of their own desiccation, they approached, bony fingers extended.

The undead host parted as they passed the necromancer, whose face was a mask of fierce concentration. Tevek struggled to control their movements and to bend them to his purpose. Such was the peculiar drawback of the Thanatosian necromancy: The chant swiftly awakened all of the dead in the vicinity of its evoker—be there a score or a thousand—but every corpse thusly summoned required the constant touch of the mage's mind upon it, else it would turn against him. And the catacombs here reached deeper and farther than Tevek had supposed. Some half-thousand had heard his call, and these soon would work their way upward from the dusty bowels below.

Tevek sensed that the dead of Kaetta had slept soundly and were resentful of his intrusion. He knew by this that many herein had died quietly, from natural causes. More easily controlled were those whose lives had been torn from them—the victims of violence or malady—or those claimed by death before they could make peace with their gods.

The Kaettans' resistance to him accounted for their unsteady, jerky movements. But Tevek lashed at them with whiplike thoughts, driving them forward with relentless rage. For he ached to see these miserable villagers cower at his feet and whimper for mercy. He would grant none.

"Stand fast!" came Ranjau's rallying cry, as the men behind him shrank from the macabre scene. " 'Tis said that when you kill the

103

sorcerer, his magic dies with him. Slay this spawn of Set!" He waved his sword and stepped toward Tevek.

The warlord's words spurred several men forward. These were met at once by the front ranks of Tevek's eerie meiny. Bone met blade in a din of cracking and crunching. Steel hacked at clawlike fingers, and blades severed clutching hands from bony wrists as the Kaettans fought an army of their ancestors. But the macabre mien of the skeletal host seemed to drain the fighting spirit from Ranjau's warriors. Before the fighters could reach Tevek, every man found himself surrounded by groping claws and clacking teeth. Even the severed limbs twitched and grabbed at feet and ankles, tearing into warm flesh and spilling blood.

The archers nocked iron-tipped arrows and took aim at Tevek, their bows twanging as they loosed a volley. Uncertain of the integrity of his protective circle, the necromancer hastily dropped to a crouch behind the skeletal wall before him. The wave passed through the air above him to clatter harmlessly against bone and stone. His concentration had broken but for a moment before he again asserted his control. In the meantime, more of the walking dead came from below to swell the ranks of their worm-eaten fellows.

Ranjau's warriors began to scream as cold hands dragged them down and half-rotted teeth sank into their flesh. A few cried out in terror and turned to flee, but many slipped on slick patches of blood. Others tripped over twitching limbs. Blood from their torn throats drowned their appeals to Mitra, and a crimson wash soon spread across the stone floor.

Relentlessly, the expressionless host pushed forward, engulfing the priests and the archers and rending them limb from limb. Ranjau was the last to fall, his sword cleaving a skull as a pair of undead warriors seized his sword-arm. His blade fell to the floor with a hollow clang and was soon drenched in the spray of blood that fountained from his torn throat.

Tevek stood, his gaze still vapid, his pale lips pressed tightly from the effort he expended to command his retinue. He stepped out of his circle and spat contemptuously into Ranjau's upturned face. Taian forges and prayers to Mitra were no proof against the risen dead.

Go forth, he silently commanded those who now jammed the corridor. He projected his thoughts to every creature in the burial chamber. *Slay those who dwell above. Then come you here, to your place of rest, and slumber again.*

Weariness soaked into his skin like pelting rain, but his directive would be obeyed by all he had summoned.

All but one.

For when the villagers of Kaetta had met the doom decreed by Tevek, he would slake his thirst and vent his hunger here, among the dead. Then would he would permit himself a small dalliance before he departed for the Brass City. His mind had touched that of Beladah, who lay unbreathing in the temple above. She, too, had heard the chant and been bound by his summons, but he was saving her for later. When the clammy chill of death had banished all color and warmth from her flesh, he would seek such pleasures with her as only a necromancer could know.

From the temple above, he heard the pitiful screams of the dying as his legions undertook their dire mission. The sounds filled his ears with pleasing music, and a cruel smile danced upon his pallid face as he moved among the throng of the dead, up the spiraling hallway, to the cold arms of she who awaited him.

Eleven
"Into the Pit!"

Before he became fully cognizant, Conan sensed that he was lying atop a swiftly moving horse. Thick cords of rope bit into his wrists, and when his eyelids reluctantly rose, he saw that he had been bound to the steed's harness, behind its rider. Groggy and sore, he tried to shift his position, but the ropes permitted him no slack. The *asshuri* had lashed him belly-down, and there he would stay. Whenever the horse leapt over a large stone or a hole in the road, the impact traveled through his spine in a dull wave of pain.

Conan's every muscle ached to the bone, and his skull pounded as though a Pict were using it for a war-drum. But these injuries would heal, and he gave them no further notice. Why had the *asshuri* not cut him down in the alley? Doubtless he would find out. Shemites were a cruel and vengeful folk, and the *asshuri* were accounted as harshest among their people. He wasted no more thought on the matter of his fate. He would devote his attention to eluding whatever grim plans his captors had laid for him.

By the heat and the bright sky, he judged that he had slept until midday, or perhaps a few glasses past it. The terrain afforded no clues of his exact whereabouts; the horses traversed a nameless strip of road flanked by seemingly endless fields of vines. Much of western Shem bore the same features.

A low moan from nearby prompted Conan to crane his neck over his shoulder. This effort rewarded him with a stab of pain intense enough to make him grit his teeth.

Kylanna—or Sivitri—lay trussed upon the horse that rode slightly behind his. She, too, had been tied belly-down behind the saddle. Her hair hung down and covered her face. He noticed that several bruises had flowered upon her shapely arms, amid the nicks and cuts taken in their pitched battle. She had gone down fighting. This capture was no plot of hers, then, or so it seemed to Conan. He would be careful, though, never to trust the deceitful wench again.

Conan thought it likely that the *asshuri* would reach their destination soon. He could discern little in the way of provision, and no packhorses burdened by tents or other gear. Less than half a company was present, as far as he could see. But forty or fifty men were more than enough to guard two captives, though some of the Shemites sported bandages on their arms, legs, or heads. He looked toward the front of the host and drew in a sharp breath when he caught sight of the rider in the lead. A man from Balvadek's citadel, marked as such by adornments on his tabard. The other *asshuri* wore no garments that bespoke of rank or allegiance, but this man's dress marked him as captain. And the ivory-hued cape, the devices on his riding harness, they looked all too familiar. Duke Balvadek's lineage, perhaps a younger sibling, cousin, or nephew.

Small wonder, then, that Conan had been taken alive. The duke still sought him. Crom! All he had done was to bed a few wenches . . . and, in keeping with his usual luck, at a place and time that had nearly lowered a noose around his neck.

"Water," came the demand from Sivitri, her voice hoarse.

Conan sympathized. He could have drained a full flagon in one gulp, but he knew better than to ask a boon of these hook-nosed, black-bearded devils.

A few laughs sounded from the riders near enough to hear Sivitri.

"You'll drink your fill soon enough," chuckled the *asshuri* who was perched on the saddle in front of the woman. "Afore the duke quenches his thirst for *you*. Belike he'll send you for a dunk in the

107

baths first—the duke beds no wench who smells more like horse than woman."

"Swine! Offal! You dare to treat me like some common trull—"

"Nay, wench, no common trull could slay two of us ere we took you. A rare trull, the sort sought by the duke."

Several *asshuri* laughed again at the man's gibes.

"The fiends take your flea-bitten dog of a duke and gnaw his shriveled privates in Hell!"

Conan grinned. Sivitri's voice, cracked as it was, had not lost its sting.

"By Erlik," the rider on Conan's mount chortled, "this filly needs breaking in before the duke takes her. Mayhap we should perform this service for old Balvadek, as we are sworn to secure his personal safety. What say you, Deverro?"

"You went first last time, Uthan, after our little raid in Kyros. Remember the Brythunian doxy?"

"By Erlik's backside, Deverro, I'll not forget that blonde! 'Tis meet, then. You first, when we stop tonight in Saridis."

Deverro began to describe what he would do, in words as lewd as they were loud. Several *asshuri* offered their suggestions, some of which would have brought a blush to the face of a harlot in Shadizar's most iniquitous den. Raucous laughter arose, loud enough to drown out the steady pounding of hooves.

Conan scowled but held his tongue, for he knew better than to waste his breath on idle threats. He owed Sivitri nothing after her treachery, but he would as soon not see her used so brutally by these Shemitish bastards.

At least the ruffians had revealed their destination. He had passed through Saridis but once, before the mishap that had so angered Balvadek. The town served wayfarers, merchants, and *asshuri* of all callings, for it sat upon the crossing of diverse roads, where the borders of four city-states met. Ghaza, Kyros, Anakia, and Akkharia had each laid claim to the town at one time or another, but never had Saridis's folk acknowledged fealty to any dukedom.

By Conan's reckoning, the town lay a half-day's ride from Varhia, and a further half-day from Balvadek's citadel. The *asshuri's* conquest must have tired them, for they had struck late in the night. The Cimmerian looked forward to being taken down from the back of this damnable beast, else the constant pounding of its hooves would batter his bones to jelly.

The tabarded captain fell back, until he rode between Uthan and Deverro. "Lieutenant Uthan." The man spoke Shemite with a barbarous accent—no son of Shem, he.

Conan could see only the captain's back, and he did not wish to raise his head and crane his neck again. He deemed it prudent to let them think him fallen unconscious again, that they might reveal more of their plans.

"Sir?" Uthan's tone was at once respectful, a startling change from his former attitude.

"Take a half-score of your best dog-brothers and scout ahead, but use not the road. Have the men ride in pairs, but no brothers or friends together. Yesterday we lost Mahkoro and Baasha—our best scouts—ere we reached Varhia. Two companies of our dogs we left as garrison there, and this weary, wounded two-score that follow us home are ill-suited for an encounter with any remnants of Reydnu's army." The captain twisted in his saddle to survey the region behind him. "Ride swiftly, and meet us at the outskirts of Saridis. Spies and skirmishers may be afoot. Keep an eye on your back and a hand on your hilt," he admonished in the customary *asshuri* manner.

Conan, through slitted eyes, had glimpsed the captain's face as he turned around. The narrow, hooklike nose, crooked lips, and close-set eyes were those of Druvarik, youngest of Balvadek's brothers. The Cimmerian gloomily pondered the means by which the duke would avenge himself. The crow's cage, the lash . . . the rack?

Nay, the *asshuri*, as Conan recalled, preferred to rope a man by wrists and ankles to four strong horses and spur the beasts as one to a gallop, popping the captives bones from their sockets before ripping away the limbs. The victim might howl for a span of time as he bled to death, and that span must seem an eternity to one torn asunder so violently.

These Shemites made this savage drawing-and-quartering into a public affair. Women and children attended, that all might see how enemies of the state fared. Conan had once seen men wager on which arm or leg would first be torn off. And men of this region thought Cimmerians barbaric! Conan's people were indeed savages, but they dispatched enemies with sinew and steel, not with decadent tortures that slowly sucked the life from their foes.

The sun dipped slowly toward the horizon as Conan endured the remainder of the jolting ride to Saridis. Sivitri had succumbed to heat and exhaustion, for he noticed that she hung limply from the back of her horse. For his part, he seemed unable to turn his mind to aught but brooding over all manners of dismal deaths that might await him within Balvadek's citadel. The *asshuri* offered him nary a morsel, not even a sip from a waterskin, and the continual jouncing made sleep impossible. They intended to keep him too weak and weary to attempt escape, he realized. But if these dogs became careless and afforded him a chance, he would seize it, feeble or no. Conan's injuries and fatigue had not rendered him incapable of resistance—not yet. He longed for a chance to show these *asshuri* scum that a half-dead Cimmerian outmatched any among their ranks.

Soon the road widened, its surface becoming more even. They passed a few caravans of wagons, loaded with oaken barrels and guarded by bravos wearing irregular armor and weapons—mercenaries in the employ of wine merchants. These caravans gave the *asshuri* a wide. berth, exchanging no words. Captain Druvarik merely nodded to them and moved on. Here, on either side of the road, were dense orchards of tall apple trees, grown for the making of specialized wines—Saridis's chief industry.

The sweltering day gave way to humid, murky dusk as Druvarik's company neared a heavy wooden gate set into a wall that seemed to be of recent construction. Conan recalled no such fortifications at Saridis. This barrier's height might have matched that of a tall man. With a start, Conan noted that Balvadek's emblem, an upthrust sword enwreathed in vines, had been etched across the full breadth and height of the gate.

Conan could see that Saridis no longer claimed independence. Balvadek had been busy these past few years.

Uthan alone awaited their coming. He sat astride his mount, his face ashen and his arm bound in a sling.

Druvarik trotted forward to meet him. "What news, Uthan? Where are the dog-brothers who accompanied you?" His voice, though faint, reached Conan's ears.

"In Hell, sir." Uthan's querulous reply spoke volumes. "And Reydnu has raised demons against us," he added.

"Demons? That old dotard could not raise his manhood in a harlot's bed, to say nothing of demons. Belike it was a spy that caught you unawares, Uthan. I should flay the flesh from your bones for such an excuse—"

"Sir, my tale would change not after threescore lashes! We made haste as you commanded, though we found no signs of retaliation from Reydnu. Then, near a copse not three leagues distant from here, the rearmost of us—Akkesh—fell from his saddle. We halted at once, but Shimri and Abishai collapsed. Their throats spouted blood, and as they died, Pulha screamed to me that Akkesh's flesh was ice-cold, frozen like a Hyperborean pond in midwinter. The words had scarcely left his lips when he screamed and pitched onto Akkesh's body. I spurred my mount away—to alert you and the men, sir. The demon fleshed my arm with its strange claw as I escaped. 'Tis a miracle that its poison froze me not."

A sarcastic murmur or two rose from the others, but Druvarik merely sat in silence, as if pondering Uthan's account. "In battle, you are no craven," he muttered. "Yet show you their bodies to me, that I may judge what became of them. The duke must know the truth—as must I."

"Rather would I ride alone against every knight in Aquilonia than return to that copse," Uthan said, shuddering. "Erlik may not suffer me to survive if I do. Command me not to this doom."

"Your words do not befit a lieutenant, Uthan. Lead me to the slain, else I strip you of your rank here and now!"

Uthan shook his head.

Druvarik, in a motion as swift as it was deft, slid his slender-bladed sword from its scabbard and ran it through Uthan's heart. "Your fear dooms you, fool! To disobey my command is to die," he said, letting Uthan's body topple from the saddle. He withdrew his weapon as the *asshuri* thumped to the dirt, gasping.

"May the demon . . . freeze your bones . . . and drag you . . . to Hell . . ." he croaked, spitting blood. "*Sir.*" Then Uthan spoke no more.

"So fares the fool," muttered Druvarik, shaking blood from his blade. He straightened in his saddle and turned his mount so that he faced his men. "The dead will wait. Tomorrow, in daylight, I shall lead you in search for our dog-brothers. Tonight we sup in my father's hall and drink the wine of victory over Reydnu!" He thrust his bloody swordpoint skyward as he spoke.

"Victory!" Deverro raised his blade and cheered, apparently none too upset by his fellow lieutenant's demise.

"Victory, victory!" the others cried, mimicking Druvarik's gesture.

The gates swung outward while they cheered. Through them came a tall man who sat atop a huge black stallion. Dust and mud besmeared his ivory-hued cape and the rest of his finery. The gold rivets in his jerkin and high boots of lacquered black leather gleamed in the waning sunlight, and the hilt of a massive hand-and-a-half sword bristled with glittering gems. Thick black hair, streaked throughout with grey, streamed from a gilded, gem-studded cap that was more crown than helm. The man held his reins in one gold-riveted glove and stroked his full grey beard with the other.

"Duke Balvadek!" Druvarik gawked a moment before recovering his composure.

"Welcome home, my young brother," the duke said, riding forward. The sweat and dirt on the flanks of his magnificent horse did not diminish the beast's impressive appearance. "Yes, I rode to my border to meet you and celebrate the first of many victories to come in our campaign against Ghaza. And tomorrow," he said, steering his horse slowly toward Conan, "tomorrow we shall enjoy a little sport with this barbar. For too long has the foul murderer of my daughters' husbands gone unpunished." He stopped in front of the Cimmerian, swiftly took his heavy boot from its stirrup, and aimed a brutal kick at Conan's jaw.

Conan twisted, catching the blow on his cheekbone. He struggled against the bonds that held him, but their clever knots merely tightened further, and the thick cord bit into his wrists until blood trickled from them. Crimson ran from the furrow in his cheek, but he heeded none of his wounds. His gaze burned, a bonfire of blue fury. "Craven dotard," he rasped. "Loosen these ropes and face me in combat."

Balvadek's blade slid with a metallic ring from its golden scabbard. Age had not weakened him, for he wielded the immense weapon with but one hand. He held the point at Conan's throat. " 'Twere not meet for me, who shall one day be crowned king of all Shem, to soil a noble blade with the base blood of swine." He sheathed the sword with a flourish.

Conan, parched as he was, gathered his last measure of saliva and turned his head. He spat in Balvadek's face.

"Whelp!" roared the duke. He wiped the spittle from his beard and swept the sword out, swinging it in a downward arc toward Conan's neck.

The blade spun away before its edge met flesh.

Balvadek dropped the reins and clawed at his neck. The death-rattle wheezed from his throat as he slumped forward, his arm brushing against Conan's face before he slid from the saddle to lie motionless.

Hairs bristled on the back of Conan's neck. The duke's skin had been as cold and dry as the snows of Cimmeria. Uthan's demon had come! He writhed against his bonds while shouts of alarm rose from the *asshuri*.

Druvarik dismounted and hastened toward his fallen brother. The ivory cape covered Balvadek like a shroud.

Deverro shifted uneasily in his saddle. "How now, Captain? Is the duke slain?"

Druvarik knelt beside the body. Before he could lift the cape, he cried out in pain and surprise. Blood jetted from under his chin, staining his brother's cape. Wordlessly, the captain dropped onto Balvadek, his fingers clutching at the cape for a span, until the scarlet spurting from his throat stopped, and he moved no more.

Conan glanced downward at Balvadek's crumpled corpse. Druvarik had pulled aside the cape to reveal a metal object protruding from the neck. Would a demon have need of such? Conan felt the chill of superstitious dread fade at this revelation. He would say that a man had slain the duke—an archer in the apple trees, or a knife-thrower whose arm possessed incredible measures of strength and accuracy. Had that same slayer done away with Druvarik? Nay, 'twas a strange death, bearing a sorcerous taint that set Conan's teeth on edge. He cursed his helplessness. Tied to this steed, he could do naught.

"Aiee!" screamed Deverro. "Now the captain perishes. 'Tis Uthan's demon, come for us all! Flee—ride for your life!"

Shouts of panic rippled among the Shemites. Some rode into the village after Deverro, while others galloped back up the road the way they had just traveled.

"I'll not be slowed by your weight," snarled the Shemite upon the saddle before Conan. "Better to leave your carcass here for the vultures."

The Cimmerian twisted desperately as the *asshuri's* dagger slashed toward his unprotected throat. The ropes lacked enough slack for him to avoid the blade's sweep.

Again, his would-be slayer's stroke never landed.

The dagger flew from the *asshuri's* fingers, its hilt thumping harmlessly against Conan's shoulder before falling to the ground. A flicker of motion, barely perceptible, flashed in the corner of

Conan's field of vision. The dagger-wielding *asshuri* cried out in surprise at the blood that streamed from his hand. A thin metal disc had sliced the flesh between his thumb and forefinger and lodged into the bone. Another sank below his jaw and slashed his throat. Glazed eyes stared upward for a span before the Shemite flopped toward Conan, his face landing squarely between the Cimmerian's shoulder blades.

Conan grunted as blood soaked through his tattered leather vest and trickled hotly down his back. That disc's edge had been sharp enough to cut bone. . . .

He moved his wrists blindly, seeking the dead man's hand. A razorlike edge bit into his thumb, and he worked his bound wrists into position. Though his forearms and hands bled from dozens of stinging cuts when he finished, he managed to cut through the cord that bound his wrists. Pulling himself free of the loops of rope, he heaved the *asshuri* from his back.

The well-disciplined horse had pranced nervously but held its position. Conan reached his bloodied fingers toward the buckles of the harness. Moments later, his legs were free, and he pulled his stiff limbs into the saddle and sat upright. He perused the trees, where he had seen the movement earlier. Why had this assailant saved him? Conan did not think it the work of Reydnu. No Shemite was so subtle.

The only *asshuri* who remained were those who lay lifeless in the road. The gates of Saridis had closed with a boom while he was wrestling with the ropes. Of Sivitri, he saw no sign. "Show yourself, by Crom!" he bellowed at the trees. In the twilight, all his probing gaze could discern were the waving leaves and shadowy branches.

Muttering a litany of curses that involved gods of diverse lands, Conan dismounted and limped over to Balvadek's body. He wanted a close look at what manner of thing protruded from the man's neck, for the uncanny circumstances of that slaying still troubled him. Furthermore, he deemed that the duke no longer had need of his massive, jewel-encrusted sword. The Cimmerian hunched over the body and grasped the hilt with bloodied fingers, taking a measure of the weapon's balance.

All the while, Conan surreptitiously scanned the trees. He was more certain than before that whoever—or whatever—had dispatched those *asshuri* meant him no harm. But this unseen benefactor's motives were as muddy as a Khitan bog. What vexed him most was that he felt not even a presence in those trees. His honed senses would have warned him of the most silent of stalking panthers that lurked therein, but not so much as a warning tickle troubled him.

Conan hooked his foot under the duke, rolled him onto his back, and examined his neck. A *hilt* jutted there, elaborately worked in some refuscent metal. Fascinated, he crouched to pull the knife free. An unnatural chill still clung to the stiff corpse.

"Nay—touch it not!" came the warning shout, in the tongue of Argos. A man clad in robes of deep indigo leapt from behind a broad trunk and raced toward the kneeling Cimmerian.

Crom! Conan was taken aback by this stranger's stealth and speed, which would have shamed a Meruvian mountain lion. An almost tangible reek of danger troubled Conan's nostrils, and he instantly assumed a wide-legged stance, sword brandished. He did not back away from the duke's corpse. Afore this stranger plucked his dagger from Balvadek's neck, he would face Conan and answer a few questions.

"Raise your sword if you must," the man said, the sound of his voice like the rustling of dry leaves. He stopped a few paces from Conan, not short of breath in spite of his impressive sprint from the trees. "Raise it then, against he who saved you from these swine. Barbarian you are, if you would repay me in such base coin."

"Were your motive to save me, I would owe you a blood-debt," Conan answered, his gaze never leaving the stranger's hood-shadowed face. "I'll ask your name and your tale, stranger. You have my oath, sworn by Crom, Lord of the Mound, that I'll strike you only in self-defense."

"Crom? You're a Cimmerian, then. 'Tis said that only folk of those frozen hills worship Crom. I could see that you were no son of Shem—nor of Argos, though you wear Argossean garb. Know you that my name is Toj, and the story of my coming here would take longer than I have to tell it, and longer than you have to hear it. These *asshuri* think me a vengeful demon, and we should away before they have time to reconsider. In truth, my task was one of vengeance, the slaying of *that*—" he spat upon Balvadek's corpse "—vile heap of worm-ridden offal." He spat again, then muttered what Conan recognized as the most offensive of Argossean curses. Even the coarsest lads among the crew of his *Hawk*, loose as they were with obscenities, saved that particular epithet for special occasions.

"Time *is* short," Conan agreed, though he did not back away from Balvadek's body. An ugly suspicion had begun to take shape in his thoughts. "Tell me, Toj, are you embroiled in some wizardly matter? Your dagger seems to possess powers beyond those of an ordinary blade—"

"Aye, 'tis no common dirk, con—" Toj bit off his reply as he cleared his throat "—Cimmerian." He paused, his gaze flickering back and forth between Conan's fierce face and the hilt that jutted from Balvadek's thick neck. "Indeed, a spell most dire imbues the weapon. Avoid touching any part of it, lest you fall dead beside this unworthy offal-heap. I first learned of the Red Asp's powers from a spellcaster in Pelishtia who told me of the implement—of the icy death that awaits whoever touches that blade."

Conan's face tightened, and his muscles tensed. Not yet had he spoken his own name, but the stranger had known it. And if this Toj were Argossean, then Conan was a Pict! A trace of Turanian laced the man's otherwise flawless Argossean accent. Had Conan not recently been among Argosseans, he would not have noticed this. But why would a Turanian seek to protect him from Balvadek? Like the stranger's face, his purpose lay hidden in shadows. "What gain seek you—an Argossean—from Balvadek's demise?" Conan challenged.

"Vengeance . . . and gold," Toj replied evenly, gliding closer. "This rubbish murdered my father in one of his raids. My brother—the mage who magicked my dirk—offered our services to Duke Reydnu. He, being a reasonable fellow, agreed to reward us after we deterged Shem of this sub-human stain." He spat again.

Conan deliberately dipped the point of his sword and glanced sideways, inviting Toj to come even closer. Faster than a swooping hawk, Toj dived low and closed the gap to Balvadek's body. In that instant, Conan grabbed for the robes and simultaneously swung the sword's pommel toward Toj's skull. But the Cimmerian underestimated the robed man's speed. Smooth fabric slipped between his fingers, and the hilt connected with naught but air. Toj plucked free his dagger, rolled away, and vaulted neatly upon his feet, not off balance in the least.

Crom again! A circus acrobat would have envied Toj's agility. Even so, Conan had a trick or two up his sleeve. He feinted a leap to the right, shifting his shoulders in the same direction. Masters of hand-to-hand combat often taught pupils to observe the shoulders, which so often betrayed an opponent's intentions. Toj took the bait this time, stepping to his left as he tucked the dagger carefully inside his robes.

The Cimmerian hopped forward and spun, extending his left foot. He caught Toj squarely in the midriff and bowled him over. Conan's bare toes throbbed from the blow, for the muscles in that midsection were as hard as steel plating.

As he fell, Toj caught Conan's foot, dug his thumb into a spot near the ankle, and pulled. The Cimmerian felt his whole leg go numb, and he was scarcely able to tug it free of Toj's grasp. A burning sensation traveled from his foot to his thigh, and he hopped awkwardly backward on his good leg. Toj flexed his knees and jumped straight toward Conan. His heels thudded into ribs, and a chop from his fist knocked the sword from Conan's hand.

The Cimmerian staggered and sank to one knee, cursing. Last night's grueling battle and today's bruising ride had taken their toll. This wily Turanian would not easily be overcome. Conan braced himself for the next assault.

Toj's hood had fallen away in the scuffle.

The scarred face beneath startled Conan and caused him to rise hastily and step backward. Pale and drawn it was, the eyes fierce, shiny-black slits. Half of the small, flat nose had been sliced away long ago; the scar from the wound traveled across the cheekbone to the jawline. His lips were thin and cruel-seeming, his forehead high. The assassin's visage was at once repulsive and fearsome.

He regarded Conan with an expression of disdain. "Thick-witted Cimmerian! Have you naught but a clod of dirt in your skull? I have no quarrel with you—if I did, you would have met your Crom already. Against me, a lumbering, muscle-bound buffoon is as helpless as a babe."

He flipped his cowl forward over his head, but not before Conan caught sight of a strange scar, or perhaps it was a deformity. Toj's left ear had been notched from lobe to center. Three hoops of brushed silver, or some similar metal, held together both pieces of the ear.

"The pain you feel will soon abate. Then take you this advice: Leave at once. Tarry not in the village, for Reydnu has warned me that many of Balvadek's *asshuri* are mustered therein. Go about your business, whatever it might be. I am bound for Pelishtia—with *this*." A long, curved knife—not the ensorceled blade—seemed to appear in his hand. He bent and beheaded the lifeless duke with two swift slashes. Then he swathed the grisly object in fabric cut from Balvadek's ivory cape, knotted the wrapping and slung the bundle over his shoulder.

Conan felt some of the pain subside from his benumbed leg, but he dared not trust the muscles to bear his weight. He knelt and glared at Toj, his blue irises burning like those of a trapped wolf.

The Turanian scurried from corpse to corpse and dug his spiked metal discs from the flesh of the fallen. Some of the discs had sunk so deep that he was obliged to cut them free, which he did with the precision of a butcher in a slaughterhouse. He wiped his dripping hands on the tunic of an *asshuri* as he watched Conan seethe. "I would say well met," he offered. "But a lie told to a stranger is an ill farewell. If we meet again, it may be as enemies, man of Cimmeria."

Toj spun and disappeared into the trees, as silently as a breeze that stirred not a single leaf. The Turanian's stealth made Conan's flesh creep.

Conan rose, grunting from the fire that burned within his leg. He retrieved the huge sword and loosened the belt from the duke's headless body. Balvadek's coinpurse was tied to it, and the Cimmerian would have need of its contents when he reached the nearest village—that is, the nearest that lay *outside* of the late Balvadek's domain. Conan needed no admonishment of Toj's to make haste away from Saridis. He shook his head, sorely vexed that the Turanian had so easily bested him. But the man claimed involvement with wizards, and only a fool knowingly meddled in the schemes of sorcerers. Conan would ponder the strange encounter later, when the gonglike throbbing in his head had subsided.

As he hobbled toward the trees, he wondered what had become of Sivitri. Her motives were as mysterious as Toj's. By Crom, this simple treasure-hunting trip had become a complicated affair. Conan cursed the urge that had driven him from the flesh-pots of Messantia to seek whatever loot might lie in the place indicated on his map.

Muddled though his mind might be, Conan could not help but correlate his quest to the storm of troubles he had weathered. He had told only Rulvio of his intent to follow the map . . . and he knew his mate well enough to be certain of his loyalty. Could there be a connection between Sivitri's elaborate plan and Toj's inexplicable—if timely—intervention? He was more determined than ever to uncover the secret bounty in the Brass City.

Behind him, he heard enormous hinges creak. The gates were opening! "Set take these Shemites," he muttered as he hopped toward the trees.

"Halt!" a shrill and familiar voice commanded.

Sivitri!

As if to emphasize the command, a bow twanged, and the arrow from it plunged into the soil at Conan's feet. Slowed as he was by his nerveless leg, he could not risk a sprint for the cover of branches and leaves. He spun to face the speaker, sword at ready.

The gates swung all the way open, and Sivitri strolled out.

Behind her stood a short, heavyset man. His ill-fitting, gilt-edged robes sloped forward over his large belly and stopped just below his knees, where hosiery covered his spindly shanks. Four arbalesters flanked him—a pair to each side, bows held at readiness.

"Be at ease," Sivitri said as she strutted toward him. Conan noted that she had changed into fresh garments: a tunic of black- and crimson-striped velvet, and leather breeks that clung tightly to her supple curves.

"Crom, woman! What in Zandru's Nine Hells—" He swallowed, his throat drying at the sight of the generous cleavage that rose from her plunging neckline.

"Curb your tongue and sheathe your sword." Her imperious tone had returned, haughtier than ever. "Or should I say the late duke's sword, may Erlik roast his soul. And worry not, you are welcome to the weapon—indeed, you have earned it."

The heavyset man cleared his throat. "We all rejoice that the oppressor is slain," he added, in a lilting, nervous tone. "And I, Narsur, Magistrate of Saridis, welcome you on behalf of my people."

"What of your *asshuri*?" Conan growled.

"Those who were loyal to the oppressor are fled or slain," Narsur replied. "The others will bear you no grudge . . . without cause. Lay down your arms, honored guest. Saridis is a free village again, safe for travelers—and tradesmen," he added, rubbing his hands together. "But many spoke of a demon . . . does such a beast lurk nearby, or did you slay it?"

Conan shrugged and belted his sword. "What I saw was no demon." He strode nonchalantly toward Sivitri, knowing that the crossbows could have riddled his guts with bolts anyway, if Narsur's intent was to slay him. He yearned to know how the wench had gotten into the good graces of this paunchy old goat.

"Address me not as Sivitri," the woman whispered when he neared her. "In Saridis, I am known as Zeganna. I shall explain all presently, in the late duke's private dining hall—beyond Narsur's prying eyes and keen ears."

Nodding, Conan walked beside her toward the magistrate. If he could hear the tale while he slaked his thirst and satisfied his hunger, so much the better. "So, *Zeganna*," he said with a sigh of exasperation, "how did you escape from the *asshuri*?"

"It seems that a rebellion began to brew here, not long after Balvadek's *asshuri* seized Saridis by main force. Narsur told me that the duke, worried by the rumors of rebels in the area, rode personally to Saridis, which is how he happened to be present. Narsur's agents would have killed him this night, had he not died outside the gates." She glanced back at the duke's sprawled carcass. "Did you behead him, then?"

"Nay," Conan answered gruffly. "Uthan's *demon*—actually a man of flesh and blood—did us all that favor."

"What man?"

"He named himself Toj, though I wonder—"

"Toj? Was he Turanian? Did his ear bear a strange scar?" Sivitri asked querulously.

"Aye—on both counts," Conan said. He took no comfort in knowing that Sivitri knew about Toj . . . as he had speculated. "You know him?"

"I know *of* him." She shivered, though the early evening air was warm enough. "This—" she gestured sweepingly "—has the look of his work. Uthan was more right than you know. Toj may be a man in the flesh, but his blood is as cold and cruel as a demon's."

"He rained death upon the *asshuri*," Conan said, scratching his chin. "Twice he saved me, though I know not why. I tried to detain him, but an eel is less slippery than he. While he lingered afterward to collect his strange weaponry, he spoke to me of revenge upon Balvadek."

"We are in more dire trouble than ever, Conan. But say no more—speak not of this to Narsur!"

"What has he to do with—"

"Later!" she whispered tersely as they neared the magistrate.

Narsur smiled vapidly at Conan. "Will your stay in Saridis be for one night, or perhaps for two, honored guest? Doubtless you have urgent business elsewhere, with which the oppressor interfered." His tone indicated quite clearly that the sooner Conan left, the better.

Sivitri spoke sharply to Narsur. "Arrange two of the finest *asshuri* horses for us—and provisions for a seven-day ride. Conan and I shall depart at first light tomorrow."

"As you wish, Lady Zeganna." Narsur promptly delegated this task to one of the bowmen at his side, who nodded and walked swiftly through the gates. "Need you aught else?"

"Yes—*privacy*," Sivitri snapped. "Is the table in the Amethyst Room yet laid with the fare I requested? And the wine from the reserve stock in the citadel's cellar?"

"My personal servants were seeing to this. Everything has been arranged," he replied, miffed. Whirling, he walked away with his archers in tow.

Conan wondered exactly what had been arranged, and if it might involve more than dinner. "Seven days?" he snorted. "By Crom, I'll not ride with you for one! I am no dog of yours, *Lady* Zeganna, that you may pull me about on a leash. Conan does as he chooses. Tonight I choose to sup with you, and tomorrow I take my horse, my provisions, and my leave of you and your schemes."

Sivitri's expression would have soured new milk. She lowered her voice and stared into his eyes. "Choose you, then, to ride onward to the Brass City? It slumbers like a sand-covered giant, three-days' ride from Saridis. Seven days, Cimmerian. Three days to reach the giant, one to pilfer his treasure, and three again to return here."

Conan slapped his hand onto his sword's pommel and gripped the hilt until his knuckles whitened. "Bel's beard, wench! Where I ride is no business of yours, and I know not of any Brass City."

"You are fortunate that your skill in battle far surpasses your skill in lying," Sivitri said with a faint smile. "You spoke to Rulvio of the Brass City, when you drank with him in Messantia." Her smile widened at the surprise written clearly upon Conan's face. "Yes, I heard nearly every word you spoke in that wharf-rat's hovel. For in Messantia, many know me by another name—Rubinia, a mere serving-wench."

Conan sputtered as he summoned Rubinia's image from his memory. He recalled mostly the generous swell of her bosoms and her delightful backside. With effort, he envisioned her smooth, oval face and high cheekbones . . . but moreover, the similarity was in the eyes. Her irises seemed to shift colors with her mood, from a blue as bright as the Southern Sea on a cloudless summer day to a pure green like that of emeralds sparkling in a torchlit treasure-vault. And Sivitri's blond tresses, if darkened by dyes and styled differently, could match Rubinia's ebon plaits. Aye, were they not the same person, belike they were twins?

Sivitri said nothing more, but her smug look did little to brighten Conan's mood. The Cimmerian followed her through the gates and into the village, his mind awhirl from the events of the past few days. He made no effort to converse, and she seemed content to let him ponder.

Toj tossed aside the gory, cloth-wrapped bundle that held Balvadek's head. He hoped that the Cimmerian would believe his tale. The impromptu meeting had been necessary but unfortunate—Toj had taken such pains to hide his presence thus far. It was the woman's fault, really, else the Cimmerian would already have reached Nithia.

Now was the time to eliminate her. But he must do so without raising the Cimmerian's suspicions and causing further delays. A slow poison would be best, one that bore the symptoms of a pestilence, albeit one that took a while to set in. And here was an opportunity to introduce it, without risk of confronting the Cimmerian again. Toj moved swiftly through the woods toward the outer wall of Saridis. Its rough surface, though sufficient to repel an encumbered soldier, was pocked with enough footholds for him to scale it with little difficulty.

From atop the wall, he watched Narsur hasten toward the citadel that rose from the center of Saridis. Toj knew this corrupt little noble, who had once paid the Zamboulan assassin's guild handsomely to eliminate a rival. Waiting until the street below was deserted, Toj slid down the inner wall and hurried into the village to intercept Narsur. Moments later, he stepped from the shadows and stood before his quarry.

Narsur jerked backward in surprise. "Eh? Toj—what, er, why are you here?"

"Merely to ask a simple favor, before I leave for Zamboula," the assassin replied. "A small service." He sifted through his robes, digging out a cloth packet and a clay phial. From the packet he took two small crystals, one dull red and the other clear. He shook a drop from the phial, which both crystals soaked up immediately. Then he folded the crystals back into the cloth and held the packet out.

Narsur eyed it dubiously. "What favor do you need?"

"The woman who is with the Cimmerian—she asked you to prepare food and wine? And if I guess rightly, she will need horses and provisions tomorrow."

The paunchy Shemite's expression clouded. "She wanted a table set, yes. But—know you who she is?"

"Indeed I do. Think you that I do this blindly?"

"By Erlik, are you asking me to—"

"To save yourself from a lingering and painful death." Toj's face seethed with menace. "A small service, one without repercussions for you—if you perform it promptly. Fail me, and die in agony before sunrise."

Narsur gulped. His shoulders slumped. "Tell me what to do."

Toj dropped the packet into the Shemite's outstretched hand and sealed the doom of the meddlesome woman.

Twelve
The Amethyst Room

Beyond its outer wall, Saridis resembled most of the larger villages found in Shem's wine-producing region. Its chief peculiarity was the wall itself, the raising of which must have taxed Balvadek's treasury. The stone barrier encircled a sprawling settlement, sparse of any sizable buildings save those surrounding the citadel in the center. The wide road led past a profusion of wooden shacks and tiny, lopsided stone houses. No inns or shops lined the road for some distance from the gate.

Finally, as Conan and Sivitri neared the tall citadel, Conan saw tent-stakes and trampled grass that marked a large area where all trade took place. Wagon-tracks led away, to the other side of the village. After sunrise, the merchants and peddlers would hawk their wares from carts, shaded beneath striped canopies. Shemites and foreigners would haggle in a dozen languages over bronze chits or copper bits, buying or trading all manner of goods: fruits and meats from farmers, lumber from woodcutters, and metal goods that ranged from pots of iron to weapons of steel. Conan doubted that in

Saridis this common trafficking amounted to a tenth of the commerce in Shemitish wine.

Sounds of merry music and rollicking laughter drifted to the Cimmerian from across the pavilion. Ahead, then, lay the taverns and wineshops where villagers—workmen and merchants alike—doubtless celebrated the lifting of Balvadek's boot-heel from their windpipes. The narrowing road took the pair through this district, where a festival of sorts jammed the way to the citadel. Doe-eyed, dark-haired vixens, clad in naught but scanty shifts and narrow strips of colorful cloth, strutted boldly among the revelers, hawking their fleshy wares. Men with barrels strapped to their backs sold their private blends of wine or ale for varying prices; others carried trays of sweetmeats giving off aromas that tantalized Conan's nostrils and awakened his palate.

They shoved their way through the throng, which was thickest near a group of musicians who played pipes and sang for an audience of laughing, dancing village folk. Conan seldom saw this side of Shemitish life. They were a people of extremes—they warred with as much abandon as they reveled. He shook his head and pushed by an *asshuri* he recognized from the ride, who smiled at Conan, guzzled from a clay jar, belched, and called for more.

When the two passed the last of the crowded taverns and neared the narrow, open gate at the base of the citadel, Conan saw several dozen *asshuri* in attendance. They sat atop their mounts and regarded Conan with somber expressions as he followed Sivitri into the tall, square tower. More leather-armored warriors stood in the courtyard within, watching with unveiled interest. A grey-bearded man worked the iron-bound inner door with his key and held it open as Conan and Sivitri stepped into the citadel's great hall.

Immense tapestries nearly covered the roughly hewn blocks of grey stone that comprised the walls. These ivory-hued hangings, embroidered with colorful, intricate designs, hung from the high ceiling and nearly reached the hard-packed dirt floor. Dour-faced fighting men and some few women sat on narrow benches at scarred wooden tables, conversing, eating and drinking. When the two strangers arrived, everyone paused awkwardly to stare with curious but not unfriendly faces. Presently, some of the occupants looked away or spoke in hushed voices.

Sivitri ignored them all, approached the far wall, and began to ascend a stair, its risers so narrow that Conan had to turn sideways and press his back against the wall as he followed her up. Citadel builders often limited access to upper levels in such a way, for these scant ledges prevented a large body of invaders from bringing their numbers to bear. Archers could repel intruders easily, and one skillful swordsman could wreak havoc at the top of the steps.

The keep's upper level featured other fortifications. The stairway led to the mouth of a long corridor, wherein narrow slits provided archers or other defenders ample opportunity to do away with trespassers. There were but four doors along the hallway, each closed. Sivitri proceeded calmly and stopped midway down the corridor, before an iron-banded portal carved with Balvadek's royal insignia. Set into the wood were sizable amethysts that formed points for the carving. Sivitri looked carefully over her shoulder, then turned and pressed her thumb against one of the gems. She maintained the pressure as she pushed open the door. A dull clank, like the drawing of a heavy bolt, issued from the vicinity of the jamb.

Conan duly noted this. He suspected that by merely pushing open the door and not applying pressure to the amethyst, some trap might be triggered. He appraised the gemstone. As a pirate captain, he had learned well the market value of precious stones. If sold in any city from Messantia to Aghrapur, a cut and polished amethyst of such size would be worth a hefty purse of gold.

"Narsur was good enough to show me how this works," Sivitri explained. "The Amethyst Room," she added unnecessarily as they entered. "Ah! True to his word, he has set a table bounteous enough for even your appetite."

"We shall see," Conan replied. He looked around the room, which was as sparsely furnished as the hall below. Naught lay within but a table, its length half again Conan's height. Six matching chairs with well-cushioned seats and arms and high, padded backs awaited them. No windows or vents had been cut into any of the walls. More tapestries—smaller versions of those in the hall below—covered most of the wall space. The thickness of their fabric, Conan noted, was such that it would absorb all but the loudest of sound. An ornate silver candelabra sat atop the table. All nine of its tapers burned, casting flickering shadows on the walls.

Conan recognized this chamber as one well-suited for private discussions. He let his gaze wander casually across the floor and along the ceilings, noting that every gap or seam had been carefully plugged with mortar.

Sivitri systematically lifted each tapestry and examined the wall behind. She breathed a sigh of relief when she let the last hanging drop back in place. " 'Tis said that one of these walls is false, affording a niche for eavesdropping—though only the dead may know the truth of this. We must carefully consider our every move from this moment forward, or Toj will find me. What a strange mix of ill luck and good fortune that you encountered him here, outside the gates, in time to thwart Balvadek's vengeance." She dropped herself onto a chair and stared morosely at the platter of boiled venison and potatoes, thick slices of cheese, baskets of apples and bunches of grapes heaped upon the table. "Eat your fill, then, while I relate the tale of how our fates became entangled. Will you not take a seat?"

Conan helped himself to a generous chunk of meat, which he wolfed down before answering Sivitri. "Why should I believe any more of your lies?" he asked. He reached for a pitcher, poured wine into a large clay jar, and set it down in front of her. "Here. You drink first."

Without a moment's hesitation, she drank deeply from the vessel, then pushed it back across the table. "You think I would poison you? If I wanted you dead, at my command the *asshuri* would have slain you days hence, ere I staged your 'rescue' of me and our escape from their encampment. And with one word to Narsur and his archers at the gates, I could have ordered your death."

Conan gulped down a draught of the sweet apple wine, but its taste somehow turned bitter in his mouth when he thought on her words. He was no man's—or woman's—puppet, by Crom! Yet he could not refute her claims. He bit into a potato and chewed noisily, waiting for her to continue and actually anxious to hear her explanation. Across from him sat a woman of mystery, to be sure.

"I need you alive, man of Cimmeria," Sivitri went on. "Bel knows why, but she whom I serve is convinced that only you can retrieve the greatest relic from the Age of Acheron—from the sandy ruins of the Brass City."

Conan mouthed a protest, but she quickly quashed it.

"Oh, deny not that you seek it, barbar. Be you a pirate at sea or a thief upon land, your thoughts turn ever to the next haul of loot. You see, I know something of pirates and thieves, for she whom I serve rules over the greatest empire of them—an empire that spans a dozen kingdoms from Aquilonia to Turan, Iranistan to Zingara, and to the Sea of Vilayet and the Western Ocean."

"Jade, empress of a half-continent of rogues and scum," Conan said through a mouthful of potato.

Sivitri's eyes flashed in sudden anger. "I cautioned you once and I do so again—do not name her outside these walls. By habit, I do not say it, though here we may speak freely enough. Still, you besmirch her name when you rasp it across your barbarous tongue. Were it not for her long reach, we might be chained in a dungeon. I recognized Narsur as one of her chief Shemitish agents, a man who operates Hyboria's richest wine-smuggling ring . . . from this very village.

"When I spoke the secret words to Narsur, he acknowledged me as one of her Council of Three. He told me that she had suffered Balvadek's boorish reign only long enough to drain the duke's treasury and complete the building of the wall and this citadel to protect the smuggling base. Narsur timed the 'rebellion' here to coincide with Balvadek's attack on Varhia. Now Narsur is magistrate of a walled fortress; no Shemitish kinglet will dare to attack Saridis again. And gold from the trading of stolen wine pours from Shem into her coffers."

"How came you to be in Shem so quickly after spying on me in the tavern?" Conan lifted a slice of venison, his eyes never leaving Sivitri's face.

"A sleepless night that was, to be sure—for me. While you brawled that night and slept off your ale that morning, I rode to intercede."

"Why?" Conan leaned white-knuckled fists against the heavy tabletop.

"For six years—in fact, since the very day she learned of its existence—my mistress has sought a long-lost treasure said to lie within the vanished walls of the Brass City. You see, when I first knew her, she was young, perhaps my age." Sivitri smiled wistfully. "She took me in and showed me kindness that none would believe of her now." Her smile faded as quickly as it had come. "She survived her father, who had been Guildmaster of Thieves in Arenjun . . . a position of great wealth and power. With diplomats of gold and armies of guile, she expanded her borders until they encompassed other guilds. Those guildmasters who did not acquiesce faced dwindling profits or daggers in the dark—she is not averse to working with assassins.

"Her influence grew, but her success seemed to feed upon itself.

Still she craved more wealth, more guilds . . . enough to hold sway over Hyboria's mightiest kings. What I tell you now, Cimmerian, none know but me. She confided in me that when she was a girl of but eighteen summers, a baron captured her and . . . took her, by force. He used her brutally, for vengeance against her father. Of course, the swine was eventually caught and put to death in a most suitable manner—"

Conan grimaced at Sivitri's gruesome description. He had heard tales of Arenjun's guildmaster, a cruel and ruthless man by all accounts. None had wept at that old villain's deathbed!

"Anyway, the man himself died, but her loathing of men burned hotter and hotter over the years. The memory of that ordeal, or rather of the man who had subjected her to it, stoked the coals of that blaze until it could never be extinguished. I think it is the same fire that drives her to dominate men of power—kings, dukes, and such like.

"As you might know, my mistress trusts none but women. I am one of her Council of Three. The other two are queens—of which lands you need not know, though their names would no doubt startle you. This woman employs men, whom she uses as tools. They are discarded when their work is done. She has chosen you as a tool— she intends to take from you the treasure that you now seek. But I tell you that one of her most effective tools is Toj Akkhari, Guild-master of Assassins in Zamboula. Never did a murderer live whose blood was colder than his, or whose daggers were quicker."

"By Erlik, you may speak truly enough on this matter," Conan nodded. That berobed acrobat had danced nimbly past him as if he were standing still—a claim few men could make.

Sivitri reached for the jar of wine. As she sipped from it, her hand shook. "My ruler may suspect my treachery, Conan. She may have sent Toj to slay me."

"What treachery? Crom, woman! Seek you to overthrow Jade?"

Sivitri's face paled and she sloshed wine over the rim of the jar when she laid the vessel upon the table. "Mother of Mitra, never! I love her, Conan, as only a sister can love another." With her words came an unexpected burst of tears. She wiped at her face and turned away in shame.

After an awkward pause, Conan nudged the wine jar toward her. "Steady yourself with a drink . . . Sivitri. Crom take me for a bigger fool than any village idiot, but I believe your tale thus far. Now finish it, if you can."

She inhaled deeply and rubbed at her eyes. "My quest is one of treachery, but also one of love. I would save my mistress from herself, Cimmerian, though it cost me my life. She must never have the treasure that might await discovery in the ruins of the Brass City. It would destroy her—strip away the threadbare cloth of the woman who took me in when I most needed help.

"What she seeks is an ancient talisman whose secrets neither man nor woman was meant to discover. It is said to be older than Acheron, as old as Atlantis, perhaps. Legends have given it many names: the Dark Pearl of Atlantis . . . the Ashen Bane of Kull . . . the Grim Grey God."

Conan snorted. "The dust of superstition lies thickest upon the more valuable of ancient treasures. Wipe the dust from gold and it is still gold."

"So say you. But I have read of the Grim Grey God in a tome that the guildmistress procured when she began her search for the god. Though it is said to be carved from an immense pearl, the god is no mere treasure. She seeks it for the powers it is rumored to possess. Long ago, a lesser god of Atlantis goaded two greater gods—who had ever been rivals—to make war upon each other. Soon, all but mighty Ibis fought bitterly. The cataclysm that followed nearly ripped the world asunder, and it destroyed many of the very people who worshiped those gods.

"Ibis stopped the gods before they could destroy the world. He punished the lesser god, who had started the conflict, imprisoning him within a pearl from one of the gargantuan oysters of Atlantis. Ibis charged his priests with the task of guarding that pearl, which had taken on the ugly form of the lesser god, who slept restlessly within. Ibis whispered that god's true name to his high priest. If uttered, that name will awaken the slumbering god and free him, though the god be bound by the one who knows his name.

"The tablets did not say why Ibis did not simply slay the lesser god, but—"

"I have heard that one god cannot destroy another without destroying himself. A priest once tried to explain this to me, though I paid little attention to his ravings."

"Perhaps so," mused Sivitri. "But whatever the reason, it matters not. The ruler of thieves has somehow learned the secret name of the Grim Grey God, and she intends to awaken him. With a god—even a lesser one—to do her bidding, none shall stand in her way. She means for you to recover the god from the Brass City, then she will take it from you. Often has she worked a scheme thusly . . . Bel!" Sivitri's face paled suddenly, and she rose from her chair.

"What?" Conan instinctively reached for his sword-hilt as he rose to face the door behind them, his muscles tensing.

"Toj is not after *me*, Cimmerian. Do you not see? He was sent to slay *you*. That murdering Turanian has stalked you since you left Messantia, I doubt it not, and after you find the ruins and retrieve the god, he—"

"He will find that a Cimmerian is no easy prey," Conan rumbled. His hand lifted from the hilt to the jar of wine. He sat upon a corner of the table, scowling fiercely as he drummed his huge fingers on the polished wood of the tabletop. In spite of his outward bravado, he knew the wiry assassin to be a deadly foe. There were few precautions a man could take against those strange knives, which the assassin hurled with such lethal speed and precision. And the way he had vanished into the trees . . . Conan would have an easier time sighting a snake in the grass than the wily Turanian.

Sivitri settled back into the chair and took another sip of wine. She rubbed her lips together and frowned, as if the taste were not to her liking. "She craves the god more than I thought. It must never reach her, Conan. Even though she knows its true name, the god is evil beyond reckoning. I have seen the tablets, scribed by the long-dead high priest of Ibis who first guarded the idol. His etchings foretell events most dire. After the god first awakens, the speaker of his name will succumb wholly to evil and suffer a fate more horrible than a thousand lifetimes of agony in the deepest Acheronian torture-pits. My sister scoffs at this prophecy, and I cannot convince her to set aside her obsession. I would spare her from this, Conan. We must find the god, that I may take it to Caranthes, priest of Ibis. Only within his temple can it be safely kept."

"If it be made of naught but pearl, why not destroy it?" Conan frowned, bemused.

Sivitri laughed cheerlessly. "Were it only so simple. The tablets also say that no one can destroy the god, unless he knows the six parts of its full and true name. The priests of Ibis knew but half of the name—that is why they could do naught but guard the relic for centuries."

Conan settled into a chair with a sigh of exasperation. "I care not what happens to Jade. Why in the Nine Hells of Zandru should I continue on this mad quest to the Brass City? If I risk my neck to seek the treasure—and defeat Toj before he sinks a dagger in my neck—I would not just hand over the relic to you. Crom! Such a pearl, even without the legends that embellish it, would fetch a king's hoard of gold. And for all I know, that is your game, Sivitri. Perhaps you seek it for yourself—for wealth, or maybe for its powers. For if you know the secret name, what would stop you from usurping your ruler?"

"Gold?" Sivitri asked indignantly. "Gold! Is that all that can move you, barbar? Your heart is as cold as the snowy hills of your Cimmeria. I am not surprised, but I thought—"

"Thought what? That you could dupe me again—"

Sivitri interrupted. "No motive of profit compelled you to save me from the *asshuri* jailer, before you knew my hidden purpose. And you could have deserted me in Varhia. I am in your debt, Conan. Those events at the Grape and Thistle were no part of my plan. So if gold is all that you seek, then you shall have it." She rose from her chair, plucked a lit taper from the candelabra, and walked stiffly toward a tapestry. "And if you believe not my tale, then take the god to Caranthes yourself. I did not presume that you would wish to journey to Hanumar, for it is common knowledge that Caranthes never departs his temple there. I wished to accompany you only to be certain that the accursed statue would reach him safely."

Conan drained the last of the wine—smacking his lips at the unexpectedly bitter aftertaste—and looked at the assortment of victuals. Though he had eaten infrequently of late, the food seemed to have lost its appeal.

Sivitri knelt to gently push the candle's base onto the floor, then rose and pulled aside the tapestry to expose the wall of stone blocks behind it. As her fingers probed the seam near the floor, she withdrew her stiletto from her boot and wedged the point into a tiny gap in the mortar. Leaving the blade embedded, she shoved her heel against the lowest stone in the floor, directly below the gap. From somewhere within the wall came the muted clank of metal, like the drawing of an immense bolt. The stone slid backward, into the wall, with a dull thud. "Follow me, then," she said, turning to face Conan, "that you may name your price for the god." She pulled her stiletto free from the seam in the stones and shoved her shoulder against the center of the wall, which soundlessly swung inward. Beyond it, a narrow, steep stairwell led upward.

Conan marveled at the craftsmanship. He had seen his share of secret doors over the years, but this was surely the work of a master builder. In a recessed area of the floor, he saw the exposed mechanism that worked the door: rods of oiled iron and cunningly fashioned wheels of metal.

Retrieving her candle from the floor, Sivitri lit a lantern that hung on a wall-hook at the base of the stair.

Intrigued but wary of treachery, Conan followed her into the gap and up the slender steps. The pungent smell of oil, which besmeared the inner edges of the false wall, washed across his nostrils. From the stale scent of the air in the niche beyond the wall, Conan surmised that this passageway had not been used for some time.

"Balvadek knew not of this 'addition' to his citadel," Sivitri commented. "Or so Narsur said when he told me of it." She paused before the seventh and final step. "Tread only upon the leftmost edge of this stone," she cautioned, pointing upward.

Conan peered at the ceiling, his brow wrinkling. Several dozen holes, each the diameter of a man's thumb, pocked the stonework there. Belike the top step triggered an arrow or spike-trap to skewer a would-be intruder.

Sivitri slid along the left wall and reached the top of the steps, with Conan close behind. The stepped passageway opened to a stone floor within a circular chamber whose shape was identical to that of a cistern, built to hold water from rainfall for use by the inhabitants within. This enclosure, however, had been roofed in to store resources of much higher value.

"The spoils of smuggling," Sivitri said dryly, gesturing toward the tall stacks of barrels with a sweep of her hand.

They lay on their sides, small oaken casks stamped with the markings and brands of the most precious vintages of Kyros and Ghaza. Eleven of them formed the bottom row, with ten above, then nine, and so on, seven rows high. Conan counted nearly sixty barrels in all. No tavern would ever see these, for their contents were the sort reserved for kings. The Cimmerian reckoned that the least precious of the barrels would fetch a hundred pieces of gold.

One cask sat on its end, in front of the stack, its lid askew. Sivitri lifted the wooden cover and plunged her hand inside. Instead of a slosh of liquid, the clink of metal sounded within. She casually took her hand out and let the coins fall from her open palm, back into the barrel.

"Bel's beard!" Conan's heart leapt into his throat when the cascading gold gleamed in the lamplight. He sauntered toward Sivitri and stared into the cask, which was two-thirds full of golden discs. Here was more wealth than many men saw in their lifetimes, a hoard of diverse sizes, shapes, and stamps from the treasuries of a score of lands. Altogether it bespoke an enterprise that spanned the western seaboard of Zingara to the distant cities beyond eastern Vendhya's steamy jungles.

"All that you and your horse can bear shall I give you, Cimmerian, if you undertake this trek to the Brass City with me and help me retrieve the Grim Grey God."

Conan growled and paused for a moment before accepting the offer. By Erlik, he had accepted greater risks for poorer reward than this! But even the richest loot was of cursed little use in Hell. He gave the matter another moment of thought. "To the Brass City, then," said Conan. "For gold and the god!" Assassins, power-mad guildmasters, and superstitions be damned, he thought. The Cimmerian would have hacked his way through every war-clan in Pictland for the rich booty here. Had he known that wine-smuggling was so lucrative a practice, he might have taken it up long ago.

Sivitri smiled thinly. "We may have little time before collectors come to take these to my mistress. Narsur told me that they arrive at irregular intervals. One of the collectors is a seer with the gift of truth-seeing—none of the operatives can steal from the hoard without her knowledge. Narsur will report to the collectors my taking of some gold, but I care not. My own life would I give to save my sister from the fate forewarned in those tablets."

"With such wealth to spare, why did she not simply hire me to fetch the god?" Conan looked away from the cask's contents to study Sivitri's thoughtful expression.

"You are a man, Cimmerian, and as I mentioned, men are but tools for her. She takes great pleasure in the using of men, when the circumstances are right. Why haggle with you, when she knows you plan to seek the god? When she learned that you intended to follow your map to the Brass City—"

"But only you and Rulvio knew this," Conan protested. "Why would you tell Jade, if you sought to keep the relic from falling into her hands?"

Sivitri shook her head. "I am sorry to say that there are those among your crew—no, not your first mate—who also knew. My mistress has a spy aboard nearly every pirate vessel afloat, be it Argossean, Barachan, or Zingaran. I was present when the spy from your *Hawk* gave his account, though at the time, she spoke not of her plan to let you find the god and have Toj slay you for it. I supposed that she would steal the map back from you. Not until later, when she made no attempt to wrest the parchment from you, did I begin to suspect her scheme. And Toj's presence here confirms it."

Although Conan saw no avoidance in Sivitri's face, he misdoubted her true motives. Even so, he was determined to journey to the Brass City, retrieve the pearl statue, and see if Sivitri might then hatch a plot against him. He believed himself safe for the nonce. The Cimmerian felt as if he stood in the becalmed center of a great hurricane, one that would bear down on him from all directions if he seized the god. Well, he would be ready for that moment, and face it with open eyes and naked steel.

"Let us retire, then," Sivitri said wearily. "It were better if we departed as daylight breaks."

They descended the steps—carefully avoiding the topmost—and reentered the Amethyst Room. Sivitri worked the secret door, a process that required her to pull on the portal and slide the floorstone into place. After several attempts, it closed with a thump.

"The bedchambers lie at the end of the hall," said Sivitri as she and Conan left the room.

"Aye, Crom knows we can use a few winks of sleep." The Cimmerian yawned and stretched, welcoming the chance to rest both his mind and body. He paused in the hallway to admire the gem set into the ornate door there. Impulsively, he decided to put the woman to a small test. "Afore we retire, I would ask but one token of your faith—that amethyst. 'Tis a token I shall keep only until I safely bear my gold through the gates of Saridis."

"Take it if you wish," she nodded, without so much as blinking. "Keep it safe, though, or another will have to be fashioned to work the door. And *gently* prize it loose from the metal fitting behind, so that we may replace it later without delay." She handed her stiletto to the Cimmerian.

Conan loosened the gem from its cleverly molded setting and popped it free. He glanced at it before tucking it into his vest, marveling that such a handsomely polished stone would serve as a mere opening device.

As if speculating on his very thoughts, Sivitri smiled. "Balvadek spared no expense. Wait until you see the Sapphire Room."

They walked along the thick rubiate carpet, moving away from the steps that led to the great hall beneath them. The muted echoes of singing faded when they reached the end of the corridor. There, another gem-garnished portal stood before them. Flanked by sconces that held flickering torches, this door bore a carving of the duke's crest, set with a half-score of winking jewels as blue as the Western Ocean on a summer's noon.

Sivitri seemed to pay these no mind, as if she were accustomed to richly bedecked surroundings. Her mannerisms, in fact, did seem to fit those of one who had grown up in a palace. For his part, Conan felt more at ease in the wilds or upon the waters. He had won or seized fortunes in his years of adventuring, but they seemed to slip away before he ever thought of settling down and building a base of his own. The Cimmerian believed that one day he might set himself up in such luxury, after amassing more wealth than he could simply wench away or lose at dice. Yet he doubted that his vanity was equal to Balvadek's, who adorned his very doors with riches enough to feed a dozen families for as many years.

"By Bel, never has a hot bath appealed to me as it does now," Sivitri said in a low voice as she opened the door and stepped into the high-ceilinged chamber beyond. A plushly furnished antechamber offered seven exits. Sivitri took the rightmost of these, an arched corridor that wound slightly upward. Gilded cressets along its walls held lamps of scented oil, and plush Vendhyan carpets lay atop the smooth stone of its floor. "The servants were told to draw hot water—enough for two, in the event that bathing is a custom observed by men of Cimmeria."

Admiring her shapely figure for what had to be the twentieth time that day, Conan grinned. He was not so fatigued or preoccupied to miss how the striped velvet clung to her curves, or how her hips swayed in her close-fitting leather breeks. And he knew enough of women to wonder if she might have more in mind than mere bathing . . . although if her words veiled such an offer, he would be surprised. Sivitri seemed to treat him with inordinate disdain, and her professed affections for Jade had caused him to wonder if she might prefer the company of women to that of men.

"Many Cimmerians bathe seldom, it is true," Conan agreed. "But

I have nothing against a good, long soak. In fact, in my travels to diverse lands, I've learned many different customs of . . . bathing."

"No doubt you are full of surprises, barbar."

They rounded the bend in the corridor, which ended in a simple curtained doorway. Conan followed her to the heavy drape, which she drew aside and stepped down into the chamber within. The humid air soaked into Conan's pores, and the muted scent of oil seemed to clear his mind. The bath was a large, recessed oval. Narsur's servants had evidently boiled the water before filling the basin, for the smooth surface of it still steamed faintly. Towels were piled nearby, upon the stone tiles.

Sivitri inhaled deeply and sighed, closing the curtain behind them. With little modesty, she turned her back to Conan, casually unbottoned her tunic, and shrugged it off. She looked over her shoulder as she unlaced her breeks, smiling as if at some secret jest. "For too long I have gone without a proper bath myself," she said, stepping out of her low boots, sliding the leather leggings down her shapely legs and kneeling to set them aside. She slid languorously into the water until her full breasts were barely submerged.

Conan quickly kicked away his sandals and doffed his dusty rags. Laughing loudly and lustily, he jumped into the basin with a splash before Sivitri willingly came into his arms.

Thirteen
Deathspeak

Tevek Thul departed from Kaetta when nightfall spread its black stain across the azure sky. He had withdrawn his dark energies from the cadaverous legions in the catacombs, and silence now ensconced the village. A breeze stirred Tevek's dark robes and wafted the ripe sweetness of death into the necromancer's nostrils. The thrill of the doom he had wrought here still lingered within him, like a serpent slithering slowly among his vitals.

Kaetta's population lay hither and thither, heaped mostly near the temple's entrance and piled high at the narrow crevice that was the village's sole exit. Not a single heart still beat within the breast of any inhabitant—indeed, many lacked hearts. Some of Tevek's macabre warriors had unwholesome appetites, and they had fallen upon the slain in a frenzy of gruesome feeding. Ibis's defiled temple had become a blood-splashed charnel house.

The maidservant, whose name he could no longer recall, lay upon the desecrated altar where he had left her. She was as lifeless and unmoving as the rest of her kin, though Tevek had fleetingly considered keeping her as a concubine. But she was unfit for one of Tevek's station, and when he needed more cold flesh to satisfy his appetites, he would find it elsewhere. No, these foolish sheep were fit for naught but sustaining the vultures and worms that would feast here soon enough.

Tevek paid the slain no mind as he hastened away from the temple. He rubbed his dry lips together and paused before the jumble of corpses that clogged the crevice. Panicked villagers had jammed the narrow passageway, crowding and crushing each other in their haste to flee from Tevek's shuffling, shambling horde. Expending a small measure of necromantic essence, he animated the intact bodies and commanded them to clear the path.

While his silent minions finished untying the knot of dead flesh that blocked his way, Tevek turned for a last look at the devastation his necromancy had wrought. The Black Ring's power fascinated him, and he longed to evoke it again. But he realized that its dark whispering had enticed him to drink too deeply from its well of power. Like a mercenary squandering his pay in one colossal debauch, Tevek had channeled too much of his energy into the ring. The bronze tablet had not warned him that the ring hungered to perpetrate evil. It would renew itself in time, but now it seemed sluggish, like a glutted serpent digesting a meal of excessive proportions.

No matter. Trevek would not reach the Brass City until nightfall tomorrow, and he would not have need of the ring until then. A sliver of annoyance lingered in his thoughts when he considered that his deeds here had distracted him from his main purpose. He would be more cautious when he used the ring again—he would bend it to do his bidding, and heed none of its cajolery.

Letting the bodies of his crew thump to the ground, Tevek strode through the besmeared stone passageway and descended the slope that circled the dead village. Hovering across the sand would take too much sorcerous energy, so he resorted to walking. He relaxed his mind and lapsed into a meandering stream of thought: what awaited him in the City of Brass, what fate Thoth-Amon planned for him, and how to more swiftly accomplish his lifetime longing for vengeance.

So it was that he scarcely noticed the passing of time until a dim wrinkle of dawn appeared on the sky's dark face.

Blinking at this unwelcome intrusion of light, Tevek stopped to survey his surroundings. He stood upon the crest of a tall dune that debouched into a vast hollow, as if a god had scooped an immense handful of sand from the desert. He squinted into this wind-swept bowl and squeezed shut his eyes when a reflection struck them . . . that searing first ray of sun had found something other than sand.

Somehow his mind had guided his feet, for not too distant was the landmark he sought. Its brass dome glittered in the encroaching sunlight, and though its brightness pained him, Tevek let his gaze linger for another moment. Here was the Nithian desert then, hiding the Brass City for eons beneath shifting veils of sand. He sensed a strange taint in the air here, a pestilence that seemed to hover invisibly above the sand. The withering disease, spoken of in the rumors of Nithia, was real. Tevek did not concern himself with it, for his powers protected him from even the worst of plagues.

Traveling beneath the sun's burning glare was unthinkable, but Tevek could not bear to await the coming of night. He tore a dark strip from his robe's dusty hem and knotted it over his eyes, leaving but a parchment-thin slit for visibility. Then he drew his hood tightly about his face and cast his necromantic sight as deeply as he could into the sand ahead.

Later, when the hateful sun burned high above him, Tevek's subterranean search encountered the first of the Brass City's long-dead inhabitants. Emanations from the remains told him that the Nithians had died violently and suddenly. Even so, the bones were nearly devoid of the spiritual echo that lingers long after a soul is wrenched, screaming, from its body. With intense concentration, he listened to that echo. All he could hear was a terrified whisper that sounded like "Jackal."

As he stepped closer to the ancient brass spire, he divined the depth of the sand at which the bones lay. And he heard thousands of ghostly echoes from within that depth.

They had all been slain. Like their ancient ancestors from Atlantis, these people had drowned—but in a sea of blood, not of water. Someone had butchered them like cattle. How interesting.

Tevek grew weary of their incessant, albeit muted, mourning and shut his mind to it. He was troubled by the realization that in all the murmurs he heard, the sole emotion expressed was that of sorrow. At the moment of death, no trace of fear, hatred, or vengeance had entered the thoughts of the slain—not even among the very young in their midst. Never had the necromancer visited an ossuary or sepulcher where such feelings did not fester within the bones interred therein. These had been true believers of Ibis, secure even in death, taking comfort in the knowledge that no Hell awaited them. Their god would care for them in the hereafter.

Fools. Ibis had let them die. But the powerful convictions of these fools set them apart from the sheep in Kaetta, who had merely professed to worship Ibis. They had mouthed prayers, sung hymns, and paid obeisance—all superficial, and no amount of gilding could ever turn lead into gold. They had died in fear, some in rage, others with revenge their foremost desire. None with sorrow—not even the priests of Kaetta. But these Nithians had been faithful.

Tevek paid no more mind to the decayed residents of Nithia and instead turned his thoughts to the next task at hand. Only the spire rose above the sand. What he sought lay buried deeply. He had not realized that only little of the city had been exposed. Here was so daunting a labor that a hundred men might spend a day just clearing the sand from the tower beneath the brass spire. Tevek, however, would simply tap into the unusual resources at his command. What a hundred men could do in a day, a thousand might accomplish in a single turn of the glass. And thousands of skeletal laborers awaited Tevek's orders. That they lay far below the surface mattered little to the necromancer—his irrestible summons would awaken the dead in droves and force them to claw their way out of their graves. This time, however, he would avoid the Thanatosian necromancy that he had used in Kaetta. A less taxing spell would do to summon the dead for a simple but time-consuming task.

The trip across the desert had given him only a short time to regenerate his energies, but he was eager to press on with his purpose. The Black Ring again pulsed with power, ready to effuse at his command. Inhaling deeply as he gathered his willpower, Tevek again opened himself to the flood of spectral sighing that emanated from Nithia's deceased. The fingers of his mind reached down to one and brushed it lightly, to rouse the bones from a centuries-long torpor.

It did not stir.

Brow furrowing in consternation, Tevek tightened his necromantic grip on the reluctant corpse, shaking it and calling loudly to it.

Again it ignored him, its only response the sibilant sadness that he now found even more maddening. So accustomed was Tevek to the dead rising instantly at his command that he was taken aback. His frustration grew when he tried to raise another who ignored his call—even with the Black Ring's power added to his own. He suspected that their very beliefs locked the residue of their spirits away from his necromancy.

This unexpected development posed a problem most vexing. Even with the Black Ring, Tevek knew none of the sort of spells that raise wind or move and shape the earth. Such sorceries originated from schools of magic foreign to his own. He could return to Kaetta and recruit his laborers from the fallen there, at a cost of time that he could ill afford to spend. No, he decided, that would be a last resort. He would instead sift through the slain below, and survey a wider area than that which he had already scanned. Briefly did he consider that the sun itself might be thwarting his efforts, for certainly its radiance impeded his ability to concentrate. But no light reached where his would-be minions lay, so he misdoubted this as a cause of failure.

He hurried toward the spire, which he presumed to be the center of the Brass City. Here would he begin the search anew. Drawing in a deep breath of the hot, dry air, Tevek thrust his thoughts downward.

Ah! Here, at least, the deceased did not exude that irksome lassitude. In fact . . . here he discovered something quite interesting. His necromantic gaze was *pulled* toward the skeleton of a man who must have been quite imposing in life. He was tall and thick-boned, a giant to be sure, but what intrigued Tevek more was the unquenched rage that yet seethed within the decayed corpse. That rage must once have burned like the sun itself to retain such vigor. Here was one whom Tevek could use. This one had succumbed to something slow and painful—not to wounds of battle, but perhaps to suffocation. Seldom did the necromancer encounter such a powerful, radiant aura surrounding one so long demised. And when he called, the bones answered eagerly and began the painfully slow process of self-excavation.

Others also heeded his summons. One by one he awakened them, though none were so empowered as the first. Soon he assembled enough for his purposes. Many registered anger, others fear, but all were malleable to his touch.

Tevek knew from experience that they would not emerge from the sand until well into night. Sand was a strangely confining substance, compared even to hard-packed dirt. A corpse freeing itself from the latter would pull down clumps of dirt and push itself upward. In sand, the method more resembled that of swimming upstream, against stubborn currents. But Tevek would wait. He moved into the small shadow now cast by the spire and, to pass the time, continued to pick at the bodies below.

Almost all of those directly beneath the brass-topped tower had died of the same cause, and he was now certain that it had been asphyxiation. Yet there were several exceptions. Could he speculate upon what had happened below, so many centuries past? Not yet, he realized. Five of the slain lacked any essence whatsoever. These had quite possibly died of beheading, and they evidently met death fearlessly and at peace with themselves. From them, he would learn nothing. But within a sixth headless one he found lingering traces of fear—mingled with regret. This Nithian might reveal something to him, in time. It was a matter he would attempt to probe later, after the temple was cleared of sand.

While his undead slaves wriggled upward, Tevek raised others, stopping only when the count reached some three hundred. Then he rested for a span, thankful that the sun would soon sink below the horizon. Its retreating heat drew but little sweat from him. No, the physical discomfort of the sun was secondary to its intrusive light. How he hated its glare! He fumbled with the dusty rag tied about his head and closed the thin gap to shade his eyes completely. For a turn or two, he rested blindly in shadow, half asleep.

A loud rustle stirred him. Pulling up on the cloth strip so that he could see, he was gratified to find that the sun had fled the sky and given way to the more tolerable moon. In its pale glow he saw the giant, who had at last broken free of his sandy prison. He stood but a few paces away, silently awaiting Tevek's next directive. The necromancer observed an unusual facet of the giant's appearance. The bony fingers of his right hand were clenched into a fist; in his left he held a massive sword, its blade tarnished black by the passage of time. The weapon must have been in hand when he died, for the bones yet grasped its hilt. Iron latches held his burnished breastplate in place around his broad rib cage.

Bones of this extreme an age were often fragile and loose, bound together solely by the necromantic energy that Tevek channeled. That energy was not always sufficient to support such burdens as were laden upon this giant, but the power of the Black Ring supplemented the surprising amount of residual force within the bones themselves.

The armored skeleton somehow conveyed a distinct impression of . . . *impatience.* Tevek, in his long experience, had never seen this kind of display. He would soon know its cause, for earlier he had decided to speak with this one. In doing so, he would ultimately prolong his task, but he could not ignore the likelihood that this giant might know something of the object sought by the accursed Thoth-Amon. And such knowledge might provide Tevek with the means to escape from the Stygian who had netted him with the spell of death.

Rummaging through his robes, the necromancer assembled the few necessities required for speaking with one dead for so long. Some of the conjurative components were quite rare—a tongue cut from a virgin's mouth and dried under the moonlight upon the tombstone of a murderer—but others were simple, such as the oil-soaked bone-dust sprinkled upon the tongue before he placed it into the tiny iron cup and set it afire. He muttered the phrases memorized from the blood-inked pages within a tome of ancient Pythonian necromancy. Then he commanded the giant to approach. Smoke from the cup curled upward like an airy eel and sought the giant's grimacing, hollow-socketed skull.

"Speak, ancient one," commanded Tevek.

The huge, crooked-toothed jaw did not move.

Tevek nodded, reprimanding himself for committing a neophyte's blunder. This fellow knew no Stygian, for if the histories had it right, the last of the Nithians had perished near the end of the Acheronian era. Some of the most powerful tomes of sorcery dated to those times, so Tevek was of necessity well-versed in the languages of that period. "By what name are you called?" he asked haltingly, for seldom had he needed to speak in the awkward tongue of Acheron.

"The Jackal," came the response, hollow and distorted, as if its speaker stood at the bottom of a deep pit.

"From where come you?"

"Tartarus."

Tartarus—the very seat of the Acheronian empire! Did Tevek hear bitterness in the voice? This Jackal's tones were not as flat as those of the other dead with whom Tevek had spoken. "What name was given to the place where you were born?"

"Pyrrophlagalon."

The City of Burning Souls—the very black heart of Acheron! Were he not so pressed for time, Tevek would have questioned this Jackal at length for lore of that lost capital. Little was known of Acheron's cities, most of which had been burned, nay—*razed*—when the empire fell. "What station held you in Pyrrophlagalon?"

"Supreme Warlord of the Imperial Legions."

Tevek could not miss the tone of that voice, proud and arrogant even in death. But the answer did not jibe with the historical accounts, not those familiar to the necromancer. The Accords of Acheron listed the names of Acheron's warlords, and the only one distinguished as "Supreme" had been Dhurkhan Blackblade, brother of the dread sorcerer Xaltotun. Blackblade had vanished with many of his warriors while on a campaign of eastward expansion. His final resting place had remained a mystery—until now, perhaps.

"By what names were your brother and father called?"

"Xaltotun, my brother. Ixion, our father."

Ixion . . . here was lore sought after by many a scholar, for the name of that most evil of tyrants had been stricken from every scroll, every tablet. That name was the foulest curse to any worshiper of Mitra. To history, the father of Xaltotun had been known only by the name "Devourer."

"Why came you to Nithia?"

"To ensure the eternal supremacy of Acheron."

The evasive response momentarily irked Tevek. The deathspeak enchantment did not always elicit a response, but neither could its subject lie outright. Even so, avoidance of questions was not altogether uncommon. "And what object within Nithia sought you, then?"

"The Grim Grey God."

Had the bony grip on the sword tightened? Tevek could not be certain. He would study Blackblade later, at his leisure—after he acquired the key to freedom from Thoth-Amon's death-spell. "And we shall find the god together, Blackblade," muttered Tevek. As he spoke, more skeletons emerged from the sand, rustling and creaking.

There was work to be done before Tevek continued his inquisition. He derived some satisfaction from subjugating the Supreme

Warlord of Acheron, and he deemed it fitting to raise the ancient enemies of Ibis from the dust to aid him in his quest for vengeance. One by one these bony minions extricated themselves from the desert grave. Tevek commanded them to assemble in a single file behind their former leader.

Most of these Acheronians wore breastplates, as did Blackblade. Some wore shields upon their backs, held there by chains of hammered bronze. This armor would serve well to aid in the excavation of the tower. The necromancer ordered the lot to remove these makeshift tools and begin scooping away the sand. He could only guess at how long the digging of this immense pit would take, but at least his workers never tired, and the simple spell he had woven would keep them at their task until he bade them stop.

Before long, they exposed a span of white marble, where the brass spire ended. The scene would have unnerved anyone but a necromancer—hundreds of the walking dead, scooping sand into their shields or breastplates, hauling it to a distance carefully measured by their taskmaster, dumping it and returning for more.

Tevek commanded Blackblade to drop his sword and dig, but the ancient giant did not obey. This perturbed the necromancer. Suspecting that some spell yet enchanted that exotic weapon, he gave the order again, this time adding a burst of power from the Black Ring.

Knuckle by knuckle, the fingers lifted from the hilt. Tevek felt a tangible resistance, but he overcame it eventually. He next willed Blackblade to unfasten the breastplate before realizing the futility of *that* directive. The latches that held it in place had been riveted there. The man must have slept in his armor. The necromancer simply dismissed the idea of including Blackblade in the labor. In fact, here was an ideal time to learn what he could of the giant's tale.

The tongue yet smoldered within the cup, and while it did so, he could interrogate this Jackal. "Take up your blade again," he said, his tone that of a magnanimous lord granting a boon to a serf. Tevek moved away from the spire with the giant in tow, repositioned the smoking cup, and seated himself atop a mound of sand. "Now, Dhurkhan Blackblade," he began. "Tell me, how came you to Nithia . . . and what were your plans once you seized the Grim Grey God?"

As he heard the details of Blackblade's bloody deeds of long ago, he posed many other questions. While the moon traveled across the dark sky, illuminating the strange events taking place below, the necromancer listened to a tale recorded in no writings, a tale known to no living sage.

And in the hours before dawn, an ancient and diabolical scheme of vengeance was born anew.

Fourteen
Desert of the Damned

By Erlik and Zandru—look you yonder!" Conan exclaimed, shifting in his saddle and pointing toward the desert's eastern horizon. There, above a rocky plateau, vultures flapped, first circling the cliffs before diving behind them. None flew away from the plateau—rather, more seemed to be gathering there. Their dull black forms filled the sky above that sloping hill. The Cimmerian knew at once what must have transpired there to draw so many carrion birds. This was neither a dead beast, nor a merchant caravan slain by brigands. A flock of such size bespoke a recent battle in which hundreds—perhaps even thousands—must have perished.

"What in Mitra's name . . ." Sivitri started, staring at the massed scavengers.

"Mitra had no hand in that. 'Tis the work of men . . . of many men, to judge by the drawing of so many carrion-fowl. But for what would so many fools fight? I know less of this barren region than of the western part of Shem, but naught is about save sand and rock. Although . . . when I was among the *kozaki*, some of them spoke of

148

mining settlements in eastern Shem. And this road that we happened upon seems to lead toward the area."

Sivitri nodded. "Just so. One of the thieves' guilds—in Khoraja, north and east of here—traffics in precious ores stolen from the merchants who travel through here."

"And their trade road leads into the thick of those feasting vultures. Crom!" Conan brought his horse to a halt and pulled the map from his vest. Smoothing its sweat-stained parchment, he studied their surroundings. "If I read this aright, the Brass City lies not far from here. Another day's ride at most."

"Can we not turn from the road and avoid this place of death?"

Conan, who had been considering just that option, readjusted his sweat-soaked headdress and dug his heels into the flanks of his horse until the beast resumed its canter. "No," he said finally. "I would as soon not delay our search for the god, but if the army responsible for *that* is still at large, better to know sooner than later. Let us see what transpired ere we press on."

"What say you that we make camp in a few turns?" Sivitri suggested. "I know not what has made my body so sore—yesterday's ride with the *asshuri*, last night's . . . bath, or this cursed cheap saddle."

Conan grinned. For his part, he had found the bath invigorating, though it had left them with less time for sleep. When he awakened at sunrise, with Sivitri curled up beside him, many aches that he had felt so keenly all day had fled from his limbs in the night. The barbarian's wolfish vitality had ever been such that he recovered from wounds or weariness with little rest—especially if he was driven by a purpose. Today, he was eager to seize the god-bauble, collect his reward, and return to Messantia at full gallop. Entanglement in the webs of thieves and assassins put a man's nerves on edge. Conan preferred the company of simpler rogues, like those of his *Hawk*. And Rulvio, though honest enough for a seafaring rogue, would not wait forever for his return.

"Well, Conan?" Sivitri asked.

Lost in his thoughts, Conan had forgotten to consider Sivitri's suggestion. "Camp? Nay, not until the stars shine. The moon will be bright enough to light our way, and the best time to travel through this desert will be under the night sky."

"Our horses cannot go all day and all night," she argued. "Know you of any springs or any oasis that lies ahead? Though we brought water, it were better to conserve when we can."

"No man knows the deserts of eastern Shem—or western Turan, as some call it, depending upon the monarch to whom they swear fealty. When I rode among my *kozaki* as chief, the Shemitish claim seemed stronger. Most nomads and raiders alike shun this stretch of desert. And if you care to listen, they'll blab legends of curses and hauntings that set your teeth on edge. Such tales are as common as grains of sand hereabouts—and some might even be true. Only foreigners and a few hardy traders frequent this waste. By Crom, I never gave thought to trudging here until I came by the map to the Brass City."

Sivitri watched the circling vultures and considered Conan's words. " 'Tis certain this ribbon of road leads *somewhere*. Mayhap we shall find water beyond the rocks of yon plateau."

"Water—aye, that we might. But I doubt not that much more than water awaits us there. Wrap a cloth around your face and breathe no open air when we near that grisly feast . . . the smell alone could tie your stomach in knots. Be advised to look away when we approach, unless you have seen a field of carnage. Vultures are sloppy eaters." He grinned wolfishly.

"Like you, I have broken bread at death's table on more than one occasion. A warrior pays no mind to the stink or the aspect of carrion."

Their conversation dwindled as their mounts trotted along the road, which sloped gradually upward. The afternoon sun continued to pound the dunes and suck every morsel of moisture from the air. Soon, the smell of baked horsehair and dry dust gave way to an odor of increasing pungency. They neared a cleft in the rocks, through which the road led. Here the flapping and rustling of wings and the cawing of squabbling vultures became loud.

When their horses' hooves brought them into the cleft, the carrion-stench flowed into their nostrils like a reeking wave. Sivitri coughed and raised a hand to her mouth, her face paling in spite of her earlier bold words about death. The road had narrowed to a path, flanked on both sides by steep cliffs of stone. The Cimmerian admired the effectiveness of this natural fortification; anyone approaching the plateau was forced to follow this pass, which a small band of men could easily defend.

Conan proceeded carefully around a bend in the path. "Zandru's bones," he muttered. Several paces ahead, where the path ended and opened onto the plateau, he counted at least a score of slain men. Vultures squawked in annoyance at the interruption of their feast, flapping away from a heap of sprawling corpses. The pile was half the height of a man, a tangle of chewed limbs and gutted bodies. Empty sockets gaped lifelessly from bloodied faces, the eyes torn out by scavenging beaks. Much of the flesh had been stripped away, exposing patches of bone here and there among the fallen. Flies, not as shy as the carrion-fowl, swarmed around the mound of the dead.

Under the hot afternoon sky, the overpowering reek of rot was more than even Conan could stomach. He took a rag from his saddlebag and knotted it snugly in place to cover his mouth and nose. Sivitri hastily did likewise. They slowed their horses and stared with morbid curiosity at the carcasses.

"Who were they—and how did they die?" Sivitri asked, her voice somewhat muffled by the cloth.

"Shemites they were, though swarthier. Dead for no more than a day, else the maggots would writhe among them. Some carried weapons and wore leather jerkins," observed Conan, dismounting for a closer look at the grisly remains. "Strange," he murmured. He slid out his sword and used it to flip a corpse onto its back.

"What?" demanded Sivitri, who remained upon her horse. She rubbed at her neck and yawned, as if bone-tired already.

To Conan, she seemed a trifle wan; perhaps mild sunstroke was setting in. But the ride had not been unbearably hot, certainly cooler than some Conan had endured. Of course, she was not accustomed to this sort of travel. He would keep an eye on her for signs of any serious illness, he decided, then turned his attention back to the mound of the dead. "The symbols—three triangles within a circle— etched upon these jerkins," he replied absently as he separated more of the dead and studied them.

"Most warriors, unless they be mercenaries, adorn themselves with devices of one sort or another. What of it?"

"I have seen their like nowhere south of the Nemedian capital," Conan answered. "If I have it aright, these folk were worshipers of Ibis."

"Quite so, young man." The smooth tones seemed to come from nowhere.

"Crom!" Conan jumped backward, sword upraised.

151

Sivitri hissed in surprise, whipped her blade from its scabbard and held it at ready, scanning the pass behind them.

Conan then noticed that he stood in the elongated shadow of a man . . . one who stood above and behind him. He spun and looked up, to the top of the rocks. The cliffs were not so steep here, where the pass ended.

There stooped a thin old man clad in a long-sleeved tunic and breeches of dazzling white silk. His thin, silvery beard sprouted from his wrinkled face and swept down to the pale leather straps of his sandals, to curl slightly upward. In a knobby fist he clasped a tapering staff, its wood the color of alabaster. His belt was of bleached, braided cord, its clasp of flat silver fashioned into a symbol like that emblazoned upon the jerkins of the slain. The clasp was the only bit of ornamentation among his plain garments.

"Crom?" The old man repeated Conan's epithet, shaking his head. He tapped his staff against the ground and vanished.

Conan whirled and scanned the tops of the rocks, the face of the sloping cliff, and the bend of the path behind him, finding nothing.

"Gone!" Sivitri flashed him a look of puzzlement ad shrugged her shoulders. "How? It cannot be!"

"Quite so—again," came the voice. This time, the wizened stranger stood at the end of the pathway, where it led out to the plateau. "Weigh not so heavily the evidence gathered by your eyes—too easily can they be deceived." He shuffled toward them and stopped a sword's length from the edge of the carrion-pile.

Conan kept his sword in hand but did not raise it. A sudden quiet settled over the pass, and the Cimmerian only then realized that the flies had stopped buzzing. He glanced down at the gruesome heap, his scalp-hairs prickling. The flies lay still upon the ground. "Crom! Whence—"

Dozens of new wrinkles appeared on the bearded face as the old man smiled. But his brow remained furrowed, as if in sadness, or perplexity. "Not Crom, young man, no indeed, not I! In the halls of mist beneath his mountain of grey stone does he brood, never to venture into this realm. But how like him are you men of Cimmeria—how hardened your thews, your minds—your souls." He sighed.

Sivitri swung her legs from her saddle. She mopped at her brow and sauntered over to Conan's side. "You have a face like that of Caran—oh, it must be the heat, for it could not be him. Enough of your rambling, old one! State your name and your purpose, or, if you be a spirit, disappear and trouble us no more. We have an urgent errand that is no concern of yours."

"No spirit am I . . . naught but tired flesh and old blood, which, as a whole, form the man known as Caranthes, priest of Ibis."

Conan could not conceal the doubt in his tone. "Caranthes? Come you hence from your temple in faraway Hanumar, then? Or do you deceive us with some priestly mummery?"

"Both, you might say. For as I stand here at the gate of Kaetta, I stand within the Seventh Ring of Prayer upon the roof of the temple in Hanumar, bathed in the bright sunlight there. It sits ill with me to involve others in this matter, but time is short, and no portent forewarned us of the fate that may soon grasp us all. Holy Ibis, roused from a long and deep slumber by the dying screams of his devotees, awakened me. He could not stop this carnage, for his temple here had been too thoroughly desecrated. He came unto me in a dream and bade me to spiritwalk here, where dire and blasphemous work has been wrought within the sphere of our sister temple."

Conan could not deny the benevolent radiance he felt within this man's presence, though he knew not if the man were holy priest or foul sorcerer. "Spiritwalk?" he asked dubiously. "Men say that ghosts cast no shadow, and I stood in yours not long ago."

"As I said before, your eyes can mislead you. You saw the shadow because you believed I stood atop the rock. But I urge you, spend not the few coins of daylight that remain to us in idle debate with me. When the sun sets, I perforce return to Hanumar—there to stay until sunrise next."

An ache, brought on by the appearance of this strange priest, had begun to develop within Conan's skull. He rubbed at his face and then met Caranthes' piercing gaze, whereupon he was at once startled by the contrast between the priest's eyes. The right glowed like amber in bright torchlight, the left gleamed with blue as intense as the cold waters of the northern Vilayet Sea. This brought to Conan's mind the rumors he had heard long ago in Numalia—that Caranthes had been born with one blue and one orange eye, a phenomenon that had designated the priests of Ibis for as long as men could recall.

"Though I know not why, I believe you really are Caranthes. You must know that we had naught to do with this slaughter," Conan said, indicating the dead with a sweep of his blade.

"We but wished to passed through," added Sivitri. "Bel! You really do look like Caranthes."

"I assure you that I am. And that," Caranthes said with a nod, "that is why your 'urgent errand' concerns me, despite your claim to the contrary. I would like to say that Holy Ibis guided you to this place, but no priest of Ibis has ever spoken falsely. Nor is it the will of your gods—the concerns of Ibis are far removed from those of reclusive Crom." He craned his head toward Sivitri. "And the motives of whimsical Bel seldom parallel those of the One True Sun God." He glanced upward, pausing. "No. It is of your own free will that you come, and if no prophecy of Ibis speaks of you . . . then none of accursed Set names you either. Therein lies our advantage, for we can surprise those who——"

"Half a moment, Caranthes," objected Conan. "*Our* advantage? Whom are *we* to surprise, and why? Have you come for vengeance against the slayers who did this deed here?"

Caranthes took a step backward. "Vengeance is neither motive nor purpose for a follower of Holy Ibis. Never have we sought it." His words came slowly, full of sorrow. "I mourn those who perished here, but in death they may have fulfilled their purpose, and they now dwell in peace and light. Had the evildoer not revealed himself to Holy Ibis by wreaking this slaughter, we might have been too late to stop the fingers of evil from clasping the god and twisting it to foul deeds.

"Nay, Cimmerian. I come to stop what must be stopped, to shield the candle of goodness from the dark gust that would extinguish its flame forever. While I dreamed, Holy Ibis revealed to me an image from the past, of a place thought lost forever to us . . . gleaming spires of brass, smooth walls of marble. Centuries ago, before the rise of Acheron, my ancestors worshiped Holy Ibis within a temple of such splendor that none today can claim. Two purposes did it serve—as a place of prayer, and as a vault in which an object of ancient power was hidden."

"The Grim Grey God," Conan said with a scowl.

Sivitri glared at him. "Will you not let him finish, barbar? Bel!"

Caranthes ignored her outburst. "In Nithia, which means City of Brass, where the Seven Fountains of Ibis once flowed, the Priest-King Solnarus became the last of my order to hold that title. For he perished there with all Nithians save one—his own son, whom he had secretly sent away, knowing that the doom of Nithia was nigh. His son founded the lesser temple in Hanumar, where I stand today.

"Never did Solnarus's son commit Nithia's whereabouts to scroll or tablet, nor did he speak of the Brass City to his heirs. The dead stir not when they are forgotten by the living, or so we believe. But other forces, as ancient as Ibis himself, conspired to make known again the burial ground of my ancestors.

"Holy Ibis disclosed to me the location of Nithia. I was warned that the site is known to another: Set's most evil disciple, vile Thoth-Amon."

"Thoth-Amon!" Conan growled, tightening his grip around his sword's hilt. "There's a name I hoped never to hear again. What has that motherless serpent-spawn to do with this?"

"Nothing, if you reach the Brass City in time," said Caranthes, his orange eye flickering. "Though Ibis spoke not of how Kaetta fell, 'tis my suspicion that we look upon the hideous handiwork of that sorcerer. The taint of his Black Ring lingers here."

"True enough," Conan agreed. He put a hand on Sivitri's arm. "See here the evidence. Some of the bodies wear neither weapons nor armor, and look at this one." He nudged it with the toe of his sandal.

Sivitri leaned to stare at remains that were utterly bare of flesh. "The vultures may have picked it clean," she said, as if to convince herself. "But it lay beneath the others—"

"Aye, that it did. The flesh was long gone from these bones—it rotted away, it was not eaten by vultures." With the tip of his sword, Conan pointed to the corpse's bony fingers, the knuckles of which were wrapped around the hilt of a bloodied scimitar. "This may be the work of Thoth-Amon. These people did not perish in battle with desert raiders."

Caranthes smoothed his beard. *"To Kaetta will come those who seek Nithia,* Holy Ibis told me. *Those who know the way. And if their feet tread upon the sands of the Nithian desert before sunset, they shall bring about the death of the defiler of Kaetta, and to their care will the fate of the Grim Grey God be entrusted."*

"Sunset?" Conan pointed toward the rubiate sun. "Why, your tale whiled away a half-turn of the glass already. If your foretelling be true, we must gallop from here without delay. Crom and Badb! If Thoth-Amon wishes to crush us, we shall be hard-pressed to stop him. With steel, we can lay low any foe of flesh and blood, but to face that devil's spawn armed only with swords and a prophecy from your dream . . . have you aught else to offer?"

"Thoth-Amon is flesh and blood, doubt it not."

"Wait . . . Caranthes," Sivitri interrupted. "We must know more about the Grim Grey God. Why does the Stygian sorcerer seek it? From what I hear of his dealings, treasures move him not. He places value on that which others might deem worthless."

"The relic has powers which, by comparison, would render his Black Ring a child's toy. Quite fortunate are we that the complete name of the pearl god was buried with the fall of Acheron. I know three of its names, enough to awaken it, but it can be destroyed only by speaking all six of its names in reverse. The other three names were inscribed within tomes that vanished when Acheron fell. These are rumored to exist, though I have not seen them. But Thoth-Amon is too dangerous, too cunning. If the statue falls into his hands, he might one day divine its true name, awaken the forces of Chaos, and begin anew the god-war that sank Atlantis and nearly took the rest of the world with it."

"So it is no mere giant pearl after all," murmured Sivitri.

"Quite so," Caranthes said. He shifted his staff to his left hand and flexed the gnarled fingers that had held it. "I would venture to say that you knew—or guessed—that it was more than a treasure. But I cannot coerce you to retrieve it. You must choose to do this thing of your own volition, for whatever motives you may have, be they base or noble. If you dare not face the dark disciple of accursed Set, then get you from this place of death and return to whence you came."

The throbbing of Conan's headache had trebled. To confront Thoth-Amon surely meant taking the short road to Hell, but if there was a chance . . . if the god Ibis had truly foretold of that fiend's death . . . well, to a Cimmerian, vengeance was both motive *and* purpose. If he could eliminate that damnable Stygian and profit from so doing, then why not? "So if we hasten, then the relic will be entrusted to our care. Expect you that we shall deliver it to you afterward?"

Caranthes slowly shook his head. " 'Tis unclear to me. If the god was not safe in Nithia, it would not be safe in Hanumar. This matter must I meditate upon, and at sunset shall I confer with those of our order. Much may depend upon events that have yet to transpire."

Sivitri sheathed her sword. "Tomorrow, you will again . . . spirit-walk and appear before us?"

"If Holy Ibis empowers me to appear once more, I shall return."

"Not too soon tomorrow, if you please," Conan said. "Slaying a wizard and searching a lost city for a relic sounds to me like a full night's work. Into the saddle, then, and on to Nithia." He wiped his sword against the sole of a sandal to clean it of stains, slammed it into his belt, and bounded onto his mount.

Caranthes held up his hand. "A final question before you go—what are your names?"

"Conan of Cimmeria."

"Kyla—" Sivitri began, then paused for a moment. "Sivitri, of Zamora."

A frown flickered across Caranthes' face—disappointment? But it was swiftly replaced with a warm smile. "Well met, Conan and Sivitri. May Holy Ibis watch over both of you, my young friends. You must turn back and go around the plateau, for no road leads out of Kaetta save the one beneath the hooves of your horses."

Conan and Sivitri exchanged glances and took up their reins, steering their mounts around. Caranthes waved at them, a grave expression on his aged face. Neither Cimmerian nor Zamorian spoke until they were halfway through the pass.

"Believe you that Caranthes actually appeared before us, then?" Sivitri began.

"What matters it? Were that illusion or not, my plan has not changed." Conan was troubled by a strange sensation that he was being watched. On impulse, he scanned the tops of the cliffs that flanked the road, then glanced backward. He shrugged the feeling from his shoulders, deeming it an aftereffect of the strange encounter farther back.

"What if it were a trick played upon us by another, to cause a delay? He went on for some time, claiming urgency, then bade us to go *around* the plateau—further slowing our departure."

"Perhaps," Conan said amiably.

"And this talk of Thoth-Amon. He is no stranger to our guilds—many times has my mistress procured the odd item for him, for he is free enough with gold when he seeks something and has no time to obtain it himself. Our information places him in the Oasis at Khajar, from which he has not stirred in some time. A constant, if distant, watch is kept by agents of our Stygian guild, and last I heard, he was in the midst of some unfathomable conjuration expected to occupy him for years."

Conan swigged from his waterskin. "If you knew of him . . . suffice it to say that his sorcerous arm has a long reach. Distance means nothing to that Stygian devil. Those who whisper of him say that he works his wizardly mischief without leaving his lair."

"You act as if you have run afoul of him before. Tell me, what would Thoth-Amon, who sways the fate of nations, have to do with a barbarian freebooter?"

"Nothing—and I would have it remain so. Only a slack-wit embroils himself in the affairs of Stygian sorcerers. But as a youth, I abided for a time in Nemedia. There was an occasion when a foppish fool of a Numalian hired me to borrow a certain object from a nobleman—without telling that nobleman, mind you. When the blasted watchman caught me at my work, my neck nearly made its way into a Nemedian noose. Whilst making my escape, I spoiled a plot of Thoth-Amon's and slew a minion spawned in Set's blackest breeding pit." He shivered at the memory of the horror he had witnessed before taking to his heels. He hoped never again to encounter a beast like that, a thing with a human head of flawless beauty that sat atop the shimmering coils of a serpent.

"So you find nothing suspicious in that Caranthes himself would take notice of us and so handily knit a cloth of enticement?" Sivitri pushed a stray lock of hair aside and raised an eyebrow. "Did it not occur to you that we may have seen an illusion conjured by some mage—perhaps even Thoth-Amon himself—one who sought to turn us away? Most would flee at the mere mention of Thoth-Amon's name."

Conan massaged his temples with his free hand in a futile attempt to stave off the growing ache within his head. "Crom, woman! You see hidden purposes and deceitful plots everywhere."

"Because they *are* everywhere. If you knew a tenth of the schemes that I have—"

"I'll not cloud my thoughts with *ifs*," Conan grumbled. "Let Thoth-Amon and every bald-pated priest of Set lie in wait for us at Nithia! We shall feed them a feast of steel and send them to Hell ere they overwhelm us. As for Caranthes, perhaps you can clean out his coffers by offering the statue to him. As I see it, we lose nothing by making for the Brass City at full trot. Keep one hand on your reins, the other on your saddle horn, and follow me." Conan dug his heels into the flanks of his stallion and spurred it to a trot, then to a gallop.

A cloud of dust billowed behind the pair as they raced toward the uncertain future that awaited them in the dunes of Nithia.

Fifteen
Excavation

Toj slid down the scarp and brushed the thick layer of dust from his indigo cloak. He stood for a moment in the shade afforded by the cliff in the narrow pass and let a measure of the sun's heat abate from his body. He had been fortunate that Conan and the woman—Sivitri was her true name, he now knew—had slowed their horses while following the road through the rocky wall that ringed this desert plateau.

Tracking them from Saridis had been no easy task. The dunes has provided little cover, forcing him to follow at a greater distance than he would have preferred. Fortunate was he that they had kept to the trade roads, where their hoofprints were not too difficult to discern. But he had foregone a few nights of sleep to keep up with them; his horse was apparently inferior to theirs, and the tedious task of ascertaining their route had required him to stop on several occasions. Only after nightfall, when his quarry stopped for rest, did he draw near enough to actually see them. Then he would settle in until sunrise.

The assassin yawned and stretched, flexing his limbs. Earlier, he had watched them enter the cleft in the rocks at the base of the plateau. Then he had taken a chance and closed the distance, making for the cliffs at full gallop. The risk of being seen had weighed not so heavily as that of losing them in the pass. Even so, he had deemed it folly to actually ride into that gap after them, and instead, he had concealed his horse in an outcropping near the mouth of the pass and climbed to the low clifftop.

While the Cimmerian and the woman had cantered up the narrowing path, Toj had run along the high road above them. The dirt encrusting his garments helped him to blend with his surroundings. To avoid being seen, he had followed them by ear and did not risk a glance into the pass. When he came close enough to overhear Conan and Sivitri speaking, he had slunk toward the edge of the cliff, to lie unmoving in a suitable position of espial.

The quaint priest's appearance had amazed him as much as it had seemed to startle the pair below. Listening with fascination, Toj had at once understood Jade's lust for the Grim Grey God. Small wonder that she had gone to such extremes to obtain it—to Jade, the Red Asp had been a mere token compared to a relic of such purport. The assassin had little use for baubles or treasures of history, save those that furthered his profession. He had risen to a comfortable station in life, one that provided him with ample opportunity to indulge in his pastime of choice: killing. Why relinquish his freedom to dabble in the affairs of empire?

The presence of Sivitri here was both interesting and unexpected. He knew of her by name only; she ranked high within Jade's operation. Some claimed that she was Jade's sister, though none knew for certain save perhaps Jade or Sivitri herself. He was glad now that no opportunity to slay her out of hand had yet presented itself, since Sivitri would provide him with a measure of insurance that Jade would rid him of the *kalb* beetle once the god was delivered. Yes, Sivitri would be an ideal hostage.

Wrinkling his nostrils, Toj studied the bodies in the pass with professional curiosity. The smell must be strong indeed to penetrate the *unjjaj* ointment he had daubed on his upper lip when he had first met the odor rising from the pass to the plateau. His ointment had proven useful in many situations past, where one could not risk impairment or distraction by the effluvium of certain surroundings.

Conan was right. Many of these soldiers had only recently met their end. The vultures had made a mess of the cadavers, but Toj's expert eye soon divined a few peculiar aspects unique to those who had worn the leather jerkins. The throats of many of them had been mauled. Traces of four parallel scratches were visible at the edges of the wounds, marks of a size that human fingers made. In one torn jugular, Toj saw a protruding finger-bone.

More peculiar than this were the few skeletons with fully desiccated flesh. Their ribs, limbs, and skulls bore fresh white chips and scratches, as if the soldiers had hacked at them with their blades. One bony hand grasped a bloodied scimitar. On the limbs of another jumbled skeleton, Toj saw the tattered wrappings of dull grey cloth . . . like that of an aged burial shroud.

Now he understood the banter about sorcerers and the mention of Thoth-Amon. Here was one explanation: A practitioner of dark arts had imbued these bones with the power to deal death. He found this an interesting way to slay. The shock of facing a foe who had been raised from the grave might freeze the victim with fear. The animated dead, supposed Toj, would be as obedient as any weapons of murder—which were as effective as the wielder. In this case, quite effective.

Toj, however, could ill afford further admiration of this handiwork. He had let Conan and Sivitri gain enough ground, and sunset would come soon. As he sprinted through the pass, he realized that he might have opportunity to pit himself against the sorcerer. For if the priest had spoken truly, and if the Cimmerian did not reach the Brass City by sunset, then that sorcerer might seize the god-relic.

Only once in his long career had the assassin been called upon to dispose of a wizard. Gajaq the Red, cruel seer of the Zamboulan Khan, had made enemies of many men—so many that he had summoned a demonic bodyguard to watch over him night and day and to thwart all attacks on his person. As proof against poison, he cast spells of purification upon his food and water. Toj had spied upon one of the demon-binding rites performed by Gajaq in his tower. When the decadent seer and his guardian had left the chamber, Toj had cut a razor-thin line into the protective circle painted in blood upon the floor.

Gajaq had died rather violently when he next stood within his circle and tried to bind another demon to do his bidding. The simple cut had wrecked the circle's properties, and the demonic bodyguard had been unable to stop one of his own kind. Toj remembered that event well; never had he seen a man's head crushed so forcefully that both eyes had popped from their sockets, flown through the air, and splattered against the wall. Spellcasters were indeed fallible— mere flesh and blood beneath their veneer of magic. If circumstances dictated that Toj slay another sorcerer, he would find a way. He would obtain the Grim Grey God and bring it to Jade at once, before the *kalb* beetle finished its crawl through his vitals.

As for Conan, whether the Cimmerian succeeded or failed mattered not to Toj. Be it barbarian or mage who first laid hands upon the pearl god, only Toj would leave the Nithian desert alive.

Tevek Thul paced the rim of the pit that had widened and deepened all too slowly as the day turned to night. Tevek's skeletal slaves had labored tirelessly, uncovering the tower completely as they lifted the lid from the coffin of sand wherein the Nithian temple had lain. The process was taking far longer than he had anticipated. The delay bothered him little at first, for he had been engaged in the questioning of the dead Blackblade, once Acheron's Supreme Warlord.

Eventually, when the last of the smoldering tongue had turned to pale ash in the cup, Blackblade had lapsed into silence as the deathspeak conjuration wore off. Tevek lacked another tongue with which to renew the spell, but already he had gleaned invaluable knowledge from the dead man. So he had stood beside the giant Blackblade and watched the excavation progress. As the hole in the sand widened, he had circled it, always with the sword-wielding Acheronian warlord at his side.

The brass spire rose from one corner of the broad marble roof, now entirely cleared of sand. The building laid bare was square in shape, and broad enough for a dozen men to lie head to toe along each side. The roof had not been built entirely from marble. Crystalline skylights made up much of its surface, though most of these were broken. Fragments of the translucent panes were still attached to the edges of the frames, where they gleamed like glass daggers in the waning sunlight.

Impatient with the slowness of his workers, Tevek searched his memory for any spells that might help to further move the mass of sand. The loss of time pained him, and he thought too often of Thoth-Amon's spell of death—of the spirit-candle that burned shorter with every turn of the glass. Thoth-Amon would doubtless have made short work of this excavation, but Tevek's repertoire simply lacked any sort of spell to move earth. He had devoted his time almost exclusively to a study of the dead, of the spirit world, to gain power that would serve his lifetime goal of vengeance against the Khyfans. What he had done yesterday at the desert village of Kaetta would seem merciful in comparison to his plans for the offspring of those who had murdered his ancestors.

Tevek frowned and stopped his pacing. There was no better way to clear away the sand. He could not afford to exhaust himself again by channeling power into the Black Ring. And the Acheronian soldiers that now served him were moving with as much speed as Tevek could squeeze from them, and he would simply have to wait for them to finish. To while away the time, he extended his necromantic sight into the partially bared temple and probed for any emanations from the god therein. Blackblade had confirmed the relic's presence there—indeed, the warlord had held it in his hands before the Priest-King's spell had buried Nithia. But it was too large for him to hold onto and, at the same time, dig himself free of the sand.

As Tevek concentrated, his mind brushed against the five headless dead who lacked any essence. They were of no interest to him, but the sixth body . . . fear yet lingered within it, where Tevek had detected it before. Five of the Nithians' minds were closed to his, their ears deaf to his whispers. Now would he work on this sixth one, picking at the scab of woe upon its spirit until he could probe the wound beneath. A pity that he had no spare tongue for the deathspeak spell. This Nithian might have much to say. Of course, there were other ways to extract secrets from this headless one.

Tevek walked down the sloping, sandy wall of the pit and hauled himself up onto the roof of the temple. He sat cross-legged upon the marble, cast back the cowl of his robe, and closed his eyes to seal them from the sun's waning rays. Then he thrust the whole force of his mind, daggerlike, into the spirit of the Nithian who had died in fear. *AWAKEN*, he urged soundlessly, as the dead one's essence tried vainly to pull away from him. *RISE UP!*

Sluggishly, the Nithian obeyed. Tevek fed his summons with a measure of power from the Black Ring. The dead one's spirit thrashed, as slippery as a fish in the fingers of Tevek's grasping mind. But the fish had been speared, and soon its struggling abated. *FROM THE SAND I SUMMON THEE,* he commanded. The skeletal limbs below responded to his call; he felt the reluctant resurgence of life into the bones, and with it, the return of pain and trepidation. But the Nithian continued to resist him. The Acheronian soldiers—all save Blackblade—required almost no conscious thought for Tevek to control them. Not so this fear-wracked spirit.

The necromancer continued his goading, determined to bind these bones to his will. Finally, the decayed body emerged from one of the roof's shattered skylights. Tevek opened his eyes and blinked. During the slow summoning, the sun had dipped closer to the western horizon. Nightfall would come within a turn or two of the glass. He welcomed its coming, for his powers had doubtless been hindered all day by the hateful sun.

Tevek at once saw part of the reason for his subject's slow upward progress. The upper torso had been severed, the rib cage and spine shattered. The missing arms would present a further problem. Without them, the corpse was of little use to the necromancer, whose intent had been to furnish the dead one with a stick of charcoal and force it to inscribe the events just prior to its death. For now, it would wait until the sand was cleared from within the temple.

The ravaged skeleton fell into a heap of bones when Tevek released his grip on the spiritual residue lurking within. He cast forward his cowl and rose to his feet, brushing sand from his robes. While Tevek had occupied himself with the summoning, the excavators had made a measure of progress. Much of the sand obscuring one wall of the structure had been taken away, and the top of the temple entrance would soon be visible.

A strange pain struck Tevek suddenly, nearly doubling him over. The ache came from within him . . . the curse that had afflicted the Zamorian smuggler, Harrab! He chided himself for his lapse of memory regarding Solnarus's warding. He had assumed that the disease would not affect one possessed of his immunities. But it was strong. Even so, for a mage of Tevek's skill, the enchantment could be avoided, unless it progressed too far. Fortunately, his body had furnished him with ample warning.

From a pouch containing numerous tiny phials of bone, Tevek selected one marked with a special rune. He shook grey powder onto his finger, held his hand up and out and began to turn in circles as he lowered his hand. A spiraling tendril of green mist soon surrounded him. It contracted slowly, like a vaporous python, and melted into his skin. Tevek endured the burning sting of that contact, and soon the sensation faded. Then the mist was gone, and with it, the ache brought on by Solnarus's curse.

Tevek walked toward the wall where the entrance to the temple would soon be accessible. When the sand was cleared from within, the god-relic would be his. He glanced westward, where the huge form of Dhurkhan Blackblade loomed at the edge of the pit. The Acheronian would play a central role in the revenge that Tevek had planned for the Khyfans. In his mind's eye, the necromancer could already see the blood of the Ibis-worshiping scum flowing into their streets as Tevek unleashed Blackblade upon them, at the head of an army of the dead that would outnumber the living army of mighty Aquilonia.

But first he would deal with Thoth-Amon. When he freed himself from the Stygian's coils, never again would he be taken by surprise and subjected to another geas. Prince of Magicians? That menial of Set's might wield power and hold such a title now, but even he would one day bow before another.

Soon all would acknowledge Tevek Thul—wielder not only of the mighty Black Ring, but of the ultimate power that was the Grim Grey God—as King of Magicians. And after the Khyfans had suffered the brunt of his wrath, Tevek would find others to punish. Every descendant—every branch that had sprouted from their family tree—must face the ultimate punishment for the sins of their fathers.

For that matter, thought Tevek, did not all people of the Hyborian lands share ancestry with the Khyfans? Indeed, should he not penalize all of those who lived north of the River Styx and west of the Turanian desert? Only then could he cleanse every drop of blood that stained Dûmâhk's honor.

None would stand before his legions. Countless dead would march before him, summoned forth by necromantic rites that tapped the Black Ring's awesome energies, and they would sweep across mountain, plain, and forest . . . a pestilence of blood and bone that would litter the continent with rotting cadavers.

A campaign of such vengeance was more than a lifetime's work, but time would soon mean nothing to Tevek Thul. What mattered the passage of years to one with the god-relic's powers at his command?

Below, the Acheronian soldiers filled their shields with sand from the top of the temple's entrance.

Soon, thought Tevek. He crossed the marble roof and carefully descended the steep bank of sand, circling the temple to stand near the entrance. *Soon.*

In the shadows beneath his hood, the rictus upon Tevek's cadaverous face was untouched by any of the waning warmth from the slowly setting sun.

Sixteen
The Serpent Awakens

Hot and dry was the wind that rustled the leaves of the palms, rippled across the dark pool, and whispered past the walls of the stone edifice that rose from the Oasis of Khajar. It swept past the rune-covered columns in the long hall within and gently stirred the hem of Thoth-Amon's robe. On the floor near his sandaled feet, a deadly emperor scorpion scuttled. Its bronze-hued body was nearly as long as the Stygian's foot. Its claws brushed against dusky skin, its carapace an angry red in the hall's eerie glow. The stinger-tipped tail bobbed but did not strike, and the desert predator moved on.

The sorcerer sat inanimate upon his throne, feeling neither wind nor warmth. He did not stir or flinch at the questing touch of the scorpion. His full attention was directed elsewhere, and the grim set of his jaw belied the turmoil that raged within his mind. He stared forward, his eyes hazy pools of blackness. They focused now on events transpiring in a place far north and east of his oasis.

A scaly snout emerged from a crevice in the wall, forked tongue probing, slitted eyes glimmering. As the serpent slithered forward, its head flattened into a hood and its fanged mouth opened wide. The scorpion took no notice of the doom that approached it. It thrashed and died moments later, pierced by those envenomed scimitars. Had the cobra been like others of its kind, it would have then eaten its prey, but instead, it slithered past, arranging its coils on the stones before Thoth-Amon's throne.

Its shiny form began to swell, its hood widening and stretching until it loomed above the motionless Stygian. The body was now as thick as a man's waist, the menacing eyes as large as hens' eggs. A crimson tongue flicked at the air when the mouth opened. "Hear me, mine servant," it hissed is the harsh tongue of archaic Stygian, its voice rustling like dead, windblown leaves across cold stone.

The hazy cast in Thoth-Amon's eyes cleared, and pupils slowly reappeared in his inky orbs. If he was startled by the menacing apparition before him, he gave no sign, save perhaps the clenching of fingers upon the stone armrests of his throne. But visitations were rare, and this sudden appearance gnawed at his mind. He could not help but connect it with the imminent doings in the Nithian desert, where he had been projecting his *ka*. Tevek Thul had been most efficient in the fulfillment of his errand. "Father Set, my Master." He bowed his head in obeisance. "What service can thy unworthy minion proffer to thee?"

"Thou hast served me well and faithfully, hast thou not?"

Thoth-Amon shook his head. "Never shall I rest, my Master, until thy plans to banish accursed Mitra have come about."

"For thy deeds have I awarded thee with dark might, and prolonged thy mortal life beyond that of they kind." The sibilant voice rose in pitch, suddenly angry. "Yet thou wouldst seek more! Thinkest thou, in the blackest depths of thy thoughts, that thou canst hide aught from thy Lord?"

Thoth-Amon shifted uncomfortably upon his throne of stone. The unfamiliar sensation that traveled down his spine was *fear* . . . he had displeased Set. "I beg of thee, my Master, tell me: What hath this unworthy one done to wrong thee?"

"Thy hunger for more power may demise thee, greedy one. Shouldst thou seek, in thy ignorance of its nature, to bend the Grim Grey God to thy purposes, it shall consume thee. Why didst thou not consult first with thy Master before thou undertook an operancy of such portent?"

"Dread Lord, I but wished to further thy causes, to which my life hath ever been devoted."

The slitted orbs of the serpent flashed. "What knowest thou of purpose? Dost thou presume thyself to be a god? I am God and Master to thee, and it is I who shall determine thy purpose! Ever have I designated the sorceries to be executed by thee, and therein thou servest me best. Thy greed hath distracted thee from a more urgent task."

Thoth-Amon decided that further attempts to explain his actions would only prolong this visitation. And no man, not even the Stygian Prince of Sorcerers, wished to remain long in the presence of one of the Serpent-God's apparitions. Besides, he could not deny that Tevek's appearance had disrupted a laborious and time-consuming magical operation that had been underway for some time. Though he had tried to resume it immediately after Tevek's departure, the ritual in progress had failed outright. Thoth-Amon would start it anew, but the necromancer's interruption had caused a delay of years, for the spell could not be woven again until the stars positioned themselves appropriately.

"Wasted hath thine efforts been, by all reckoning. The Grim Grey God is naught but a lump of inanimate matter to one ignorant of its true name. And no scroll, tablet, or tome contains the six parts of its *true* name. For the name of Chaos, by its very nature, defies the ordered methods that mortals hath devised to record such details. Nay, only three of its parts can be uttered, and these are known to none but the high priests of Nithia and one lone-dead warlord of Acheron, who was swallowed in the same storm of sand that buried the Grim Grey God. Even thy Master knows not the other three names."

Thoth-Amon was taken aback by this admission. His prized *Acheronian Arcana*, though half-charred, noted three of the god's names. The work was Xaltotun's own, stolen from him at Thoth-Amon's bidding by the powerful Guildmaster of Thieves in Messantia. Its writings were unique and potent, if at times indecipherable.

The other three names of the relic he had hoped to learn from Set himself.

The serpent stirred again. "Further, the doings wrought by *thy* pawn in the lifeless land of Nithia hath awakened he who was once my bane—back in the dawn of thy kind, when thy ancestors were but mewling things that wriggled in the primeval mud. I speak not of accursed Mitra, but of one more ancient, more apt to thwart our purpose."

"Not *Ibis*—may thy coils crush him into oblivion," Thoth-Amon muttered.

"The same," hissed the Serpent-God. "And thou knowest what thine own errant minion has done to rouse him."

As he reviewed Tevek's actions in the Brass City, Thoth-Amon rued his ill decision to equip the necromancer with his ring and send him on a quest. He had considered Ibis to be reclusive—his followers scattered and far less numerous than those of the more popular Mitra. And no record existed of intervention by Ibis. Many thought the god false; scholars speculated that Ibis had fallen in the god-wars of Atlantean times. Since the fall of Nithia centuries ago, the worship of Ibis had waned. Few would bend a knee to a god who allowed his followers to be slaughtered wholesale. Aside from sundry scattered groups, the only worshipers left had hidden themselves in faraway Hanumar.

This remnant was attended by Caranthes, one of the few priests of Ibis who, over the centuries of rivalry, had escaped assassination by agents of Set. Even Thoth-Amon's own plot to murder him had failed. After that attempt, Caranthes had not dared to leave his ivory-inlaid chambers.

Of course, Thoth-Amon had not looked in on Tevek until the necromancer had reached the Brass City. Perhaps he had done something amiss before his arrival there. "Other matters occupied me, Master," he replied after the long pause. "I heeded not the minion's deeds until he arrived in ruined Nithia."

"Then heed them now," the voice rasped, like a dagger against a sharpening-stone. The serpent's mouth yawned open, throat gaping like a corridor to Hell. A sickly mist billowed forth, bile-colored and as rank as the odor of a charnel-house. It coalesced into a sphere of diameter equal to Thoth-Amon's height. The hue faded, and figures became visible within. "Learn the folly of thy pawn, witness the events that awakened the sleeping titan."

The Stygian mage watched with interest, noting the shapes that moved within the mist-globe's confines. The orb was not a scrying sphere, but rather, a mirror into the past. He witnessed the arrival of Tevek at Kaetta, and immediately identified the symbols upon the structure there. "Another temple of Ibis? None were known to exist but Caranthes' hovel in Hanumar—"

"Verily, that is the last one—*now*. Observe what became of the other, a fate brought about by the power of thy Black Ring, and therefore a fate brought about by my power."

A silent Thoth-Amon looked into the sphere, his eyes flat and expressionless as he gazed upon the carnage in the catacombs, in the corridors of the temple, and in the sanctuary, where Tevek had taken the slain woman upon the very altar of Ibis. "A thorough desecration," he commented, after the visions became hazy and indistinct. "But ill-timed and utterly lacking in subtlety."

The mist dispersed and flowed back into the serpent's maw. "Therein lies thy problem," the apparition hissed. "For now hast thy pawn made his presence known to Caranthes. Doubt not that Caranthes has enlisted agents who now compete with your minion for possession of the Grim Grey God."

"They could not know its true name either," mused Thoth-Amon. "I have the only copy of the *Acheronian Arcana*, and it is steeped with curses of death for any who look upon it, if they worship Mitra or Ibis. Shall I destroy my minion, then, and let them seize the god?"

"I care not if thy minion lives or dies, but as for the god, it were best kept from the clutches of Caranthes. Should he or his line ever divine the true name, the power of the relic could crush thee into dust. Furthermore, thy foolish greed hath prompted thee to part with thy ring—my gift to thee. If thy minion falls, the ring may be taken."

Idly, Thoth-Amon stared at his bare ring-finger. "The Black Ring is steeped in sorceries that would blast the soul of Caranthes and his lackeys. Let him find the god! I shall recover it from the smoking puddle of ooze that was once his flesh and bones."

"Dost thou think him fool enough to touch it? He hath the means to circumvent thy wardings. Though Caranthes be a pathetic, misguided sheep, he hath the ear of the god whom thy miscreant hath aroused. His god may grant him the power to destroy thy ring. By so doing, he may damage me, for a fraction of my power is locked within that ring. Do whatever thou must to prevent such an outcome! Retake thy ring and keep the Grim Grey God from Caranthes, or thy Master will be most ... displeased." The forked tongue flicked between curving fangs. "Thou art not above punishment."

Thoth-Amon's jaw tightened. He clasped his hands, elbows resting on the arms of his throne, forefingers tapping against each other. "Doubt me not, Dread Lord. No harm shall befall the ring."

Slowly, the immense cobra shrank until it returned to its normal form. The hood flattened, and the serpent slithered into the gap from whence it came. Thoth-Amon then glanced down at the emperor scorpion. It lay upon its back, its stinger-tipped tail pinned beneath it, its limbs curled inward in death.

Thou art not above punishment.

The Stygian mage rose from his throne and kicked aside the scorpion's body. It was Tevek who would be punished, for the Taper of Death continued to burn down, and Thoth-Amon had no intention of stopping that death-spell. If any others dared to interfere, he would scatter them like dust in the wind. As for Caranthes, that meddlesome miscreant would soon babble no more prayers to Ibis. If the pathetic priest dared to venture forth from his sanctuary, Thoth-Amon would rip out his soul and feed it to the demonic denizens in Hell's blackest pits. No more would the old fool trouble him.

Urgency necessitated a potent sorcery: the rite of translocation. No other method would take him sooner to Nithia. Thoth-Amon hastened to the hidden chamber below his great hall, where the rarest of his spellcasting components and magical implements were stored.

"A tempest of doom comes soon to Nithia," he muttered, his sibilant tones slithering across the stones. "None shall be spared."

Seventeen
The Red Asp Strikes

The sun sagged into the horizon, a dull, orange globe that painted the Nithian desert in twilight hues of copper and gold. It shone on the brass spire that topped a tower of white marble and cast a long, tapering shadow across the broad, broken roof of a stone building.

"The Brass City," Conan rasped, his throat dry from hours of hard riding across the arid, dusty desert. He and Sivitri sat atop their weary steeds. They had reined in near the crest of a tall dune, one of several that ringed the sand-covered city. He rubbed at his dry eyes and stared again at the strange scene in the distance.

Sivitri hunched forward in her saddle. "Bel! There, at the base of that building, where much of the sand has been cleared away." She squinted into the long shadow cast by the tower, trying to discern the shapes that lay upon the darkened ground. "More of the slain, like those we saw upon the plateau today."

Conan swept the dunes nearby with a probing gaze, then studied the prone forms of those lying before the wall. "Perhaps two hundred, maybe more. 'Tis difficult to count from here. But who were they? I see no sign of a camp, and no horses or camels." He frowned. "That is to say, no sign that we can see from so far away. I would move closer, but this cursed desert denies us concealment. If Thoth-Amon is here, he could easily see our approach."

"Even now we may be within his sight," Sivitri cautioned, guiding her horse back behind the tall dune and dismounting.

"Aye." Conan inwardly cursed his carelessness and swung himself out of the saddle. He led his mount over to hers, tying their reins together. From there he crawled forward and lay flat, peering over the edge of the dune from his prone position.

Sivitri sighed and wiped at the sweat that dripped from her brow and shone on her face and neck. "You must have the skin of a Zamorian lizard. I itch all over from the sand and dust. I shall be glad to bear away the god-statue and return to the baths at Saridis for a long soak."

Conan made no comment. In past exploits, he had traversed deserts far worse than that of Nithia. These dusty dunes were milder than the hot, stinging sands of the windswept Shan-e-Sorkh in the great Eastern Desert, or the blistering terrain of the Wuhuan Desert in southern Hyrkania, which could turn a man into a dry scrap of leather. Nonetheless, he shared Sivitri's sentiment. Of late he had become accustomed to the sea's humid air, which did not parch one's throat or burn one's eyes.

Sivitri crouched beside the Cimmerian. "Do you see that shield?" She pointed. "There, the one that lies far from the bodies, much closer to us. Its rim is fashioned like a serpent that circles the shield."

"Stygian," Conan nodded. "Its shape likens it to those used by the Stygian army in Luxur, who bear shields of iron and bronze. But these are copper and bronze."

"They must be Thoth-Amon's men," she said, lowering her voice to a whisper. "Where do you suppose *he* is?"

The Cimmerian pondered for a moment before answering. "He may not be here. I have heard tales of his schemes, and it seems he prefers to work his dark sorceries from afar. But we cannot be sure. Perhaps even now he lurks in his oasis, watching us by means of his foul sorceries, though I would doubt it. This site bears signs of a massive excavation—see the ribbon of tracks that leads to those piles of sand and dirt over there? The impressions in the sand are deep, as if those who made them were heavily laden. Nay, I think that Thoth-Amon may have been here already. Whoever dug this up wanted something inside that building." Conan propped himself upon his elbows.

Sivitri trembled as if chilled to the bone, in spite of the air's warmth. "Let us hope that he has not found it yet. Surely the god was buried deeply, and Caranthes said that if we reached the Brass City before sunset, we could thwart Thoth-Amon's plan. Bel! Look at how much digging has been done. If indeed the god-relic is within that structure, we are also fortunate that those men did the digging! I know not what we would have done, had we arrived here first."

Conan shrugged. " 'The best of treasures are buried deepest,' as the old Zamboulan looters' saying goes. I would have tried to enter through that brass-spired tower. If this building had been buried by one of the sandstorms that come upon these places so suddenly, the inside may not be filled. But the roof does seem to have caved in— Crom!" he hissed suddenly, eyes narrowing.

"What?" Sivitri glanced at the dunes around them. "What do you see?"

"Surely this was Thoth-Amon's work," he mumbled, jabbing a finger toward the figures that sprawled in the distant tower's shadow. "Look there, at the one who lies partly outside of the shadows. Of more import is what you will *not* see—flesh and blood."

"Bel's beard," she whispered. "Did the serpent-mage summon the dead to perform this labor?"

Conan felt his scalp prickle at the sight. There it was, the body stretched out on the sand, ivory bones and grinning skull revealed in the sun's waning light. A large shield lay beside it, heaped high with a conical mound of sand and dirt. Draped across its bony torso was a baldric of bronze links, fastened to a tarnished copper scabbard. The hilt of a sword jutted from it.

"This place has an ill feel to it," Sivitri noted, crossing her arms. "Perhaps it is the taint of these dead. The king's cemetery at Arenjun felt much the same to me, when I once wandered through it. Does not the air itself seem heavy here? It burdens my lungs to breathe it."

Conan rose to a crouch and brushed sand from his hands. "Taint or no, we must move on now, before the sun sets, and learn what lies within that building. Thoth-Amon may have raised an army of the dead and marched them from Stygia to here . . . how could warriors of Stygia otherwise have come to this desert? That sorcerous dog must have known that uncovering the statue would be a great labor.

Crom, what a sight—an army of the dead, digging at the dunes to uncover the ruins."

"Perhaps they marched first to that village on the plateau, to massacre and desecrate as we saw."

"It matters not," said Conan. "They seem to have served their purpose, for there they lie—unless this is a trap," he added. "We shall be wary of those things as we move inward."

"If Thoth-Amon is here, how do we defeat him?" Sivitri asked as she slid her slender longsword from its scabbard.

Conan drew his sword, eyes gleaming with ferocity as he stared at its glittering blade. "Steel," he said. "With steel and strength shall we pull the fangs from that Stygian serpent. Whatever else he may be, he is flesh and blood. But if we face him, look not into his eyes, lest they blast your soul. I have learned the hard way that much of the wizardly weavings of men such as he is but an illusion—believe their wiles not, turn your face away, and close your ears to their chants."

"Steel," she repeated, as if to convince herself. "Were Toj here, the assassin's skills would prove quite useful. Oh, I doubt not that you have beaten sorcery with steel and strength, Cimmerian. A pride of angry lions could not match your spirit in battle. But I fear we are outmatched, unless Caranthes spoke truly, and the gods somehow grant us a boon."

"As indeed they have," came the soft, Turanian-accented voice from behind them.

Equally startled, Conan and Sivitri jumped upward.

"Crom's devils!" the Cimmerian bellowed, whirling, his sword upraised to strike.

"Toj!" cried Sivitri. She stepped backward and dropped into a fighting stance.

"Back away, dog," the Cimmerian rumbled. "You may have saved my skin back in Saridis, but if you raise a hand against us here, I'll spit your black heart on my blade and—"

"Save your threats," Toj said, his voice smooth and oily. He stretched out his hands and opened them to show that they were empty. "We share a common goal—at least for the nonce. After some thought, I deem it wise for us to join forces. Thoth-Amon will be no easy mark for you, and even I may find him a challenge."

Conan's eyes narrowed. It irked him that the assassin had crept up behind them so readily. A woodland-born Pictish scout could not have surprised him so. The man had rubbed his indigo cloak with dust and soil so that it blended well with the desert terrain. The Cimmerian glanced at Toj's soft, low boots, and noted that the man's attire had been crafted for stealth. He wore no metal openly, nor anything that would click or rustle—just soft cloth. This Turanian's armor was his incredible speed and dexterity, which Conan had seen in action. If Toj could not surprise Thoth-Amon, then no man could.

"So silent, Conan? Have you no witty rejoinder for me? And you, Sivitri—'tis strange to find you in the company of a man at all, especially that of this witless, oafish hulk of flesh. What would Jade say, I wonder?"

"Murdering swine," Sivitri spat. "You would not dare speak to her of my doings. She would not believe you if you did." A flicker of doubt in her expression colored her bold words.

"Would you wager your life on that? I think not."

"We need no help from an arrogant throat-slitter like you, Zamboulan scum," Conan retorted. Bitter sarcasm crept into his tone. "And one of your immeasurable skills can surely dispatch a whelp like Thoth-Amon without so much as breaking a sweat. What help could we offer?"

"You may be right, Cimmerian. I am of a mind to slip inside the tower there, slay the mage, and flee with the god. Then you and Sivitri would give chase, and I would be forced to kill you both."

"Try it," snarled Conan, tossing Balvadek's hilt deftly from one hand to the other.

"In time, Cimmerian, in time. Hear me out first, then decide. I am merely—" he flinched, as if suddenly in pain, and drew in a sharp breath. His hand lifted briefly to his chest.

Conan suspected that this display was a ploy to cover a sudden attack. He stepped forward, raising his arm to strike.

Toj took two swift steps backward. He blinked and, again, slowly extended an open palm. "I am merely trying to save myself some time. You, Cimmerian, are a blunt but useful tool. With your cooperation, I can sooner wrest the prize away from Thoth-Amon. Then you can try to take it from me. And you, Sivitri, you must not die here. My life may depend on yours. I revealed my presence mainly to detain you—no farther will I suffer you to go."

Sivitri raised a quizzical eyebrow, while Conan, still tensed to spring, looked on suspiciously.

"Jade provided me with a certain incentive for returning the statue to her," Toj continued. "The twinge I felt just now was a reminder of it."

"A *curse*?" Sivitri asked. "She is no witch! And tell me not that she poisoned you. Toj Akkhari could bed down among a nest of cobras and take no harm from their bites. No herb or venom exists that your antidotes cannot counter."

"True enough. But against the *kalb* beetle, I can do nothing. She inflicted one upon me when we last met. Already it has burrowed deep inside me, seeking my heart—I can feel the sharp pain in my chest that heralds its coming. Only Jade has the means to stop it, and she has promised to do so if I bring the god to her."

"The *kalb* beetle? Yes, one of her most persuasive tactics. And you misdoubt her word, it seems." Sivitri's voice was dry, her tone skeptical.

"I merely do not wish to . . . disappear, as so many of her *male* hirelings have done in the past."

Conan flashed a knowing glance at Sivitri, quickly returning his attention to Toj.

"Why would I interfere with Jade's intent?" Sivitri demanded. "You are less to me than the scum in Shadizar's gutters. Few men deserve to die more than you!"

Toj shrugged. "You would interfere to save yourself," he said with surety. "Though inutile against me, poison can be quite effective against others. It has already gone to work within you, Sivitri. Have you not felt the chills, the effort of breathing? In the wine you drank at Saridis—"

"Crom," Conan muttered. "We shared it."

"So you did," Toj commented. "But the poison became active only when mixed with the potion I added to Sivitri's waterskin. You, Cimmerian, must remain healthy . . . whereas the woman will serve me well enough in a sickness. I will hide you away, Sivitri, in a place known only to me, ere I return to Jade. You *and* the idol. Only when Jade rids me of the *kalb* beetle will I tell here where you are. Fret not—an antidote to the poison does exist. I carry upon me all the necessary herbs and oils, though only I know how to mix them."

"Swine! Filth!" sputtered Sivitri. "May Derketo further shrivel your tiny manhood!" She lunged forward with a burst of frenzied slashes, but Toj deftly kicked her sword-arm and spun away her blade.

Conan feinted, deliberately drawing another kick from Toj. When the assassin's foot lashed out, he seized it and jerked Toj off balance.

"Fools!" Toj hissed, as he rolled and kicked free of Conan's grasp. He slipped a hand into a sleeve and withdrew it, simultaneously blocking Conan's brutal sword-stroke by again kicking the Cimmerian's arm. "You need me, dog," he panted as he leapt to his feet, brandishing a menacing dagger with a crimson blade. "Attack me again and feel the sting of my Red Asp, which brings instant death."

There was a moment's pause as Conan glared at Toj. Did the wily Turanian truly possess an antidote to his poison? Conan could not send him to Gehanna without knowing for certain. He was not oath-bound to save Sivitri, but it was not in him to simply let a woman die after he had shared a bed with her.

The assassin held his ground, his eyes shifting back and forth between Conan and Sivitri. He stood in an expert knife-thrower's stance, ready to hurl his deadly dagger at whoever dared to strike.

Sivitri groaned and sank to one knee beside her fallen sword. She wiped at her brow and shivered again.

Conan spoke slowly. "Mix the antidote now, and tell me the rest of your plan. When I see that she is recovering, we go together into the ruins."

"We . . . together?" Toj shook his head. "That is not my plan. You must go alone . . . straight into the midst of those skeletons, where he can see you. Thoth-Amon will surely oppose your approach—but he will not be aware of *me*. Once you distract him, I will creep forth, into the structure, and bury my Red Asp into his back. What happens to the god afterward is between you and me. So, do you agree, Cimmerian?"

"Mix the potion," Conan grumbled, lowering his sword. "By Crom and Badb, I deliver this oath: If you take the statue and do not surrender it to me, you will die by my steel. Now to it, man, before dusk ends. Night is the Stygian's ally."

"And mine." Toj slipped the incarnadine dagger back into its heavy cloth wrappings, held in place by a strap across his chest. He smiled thinly and began to rummage through his gear. His Golden Lotus could easily have neutralized the poison, but he had no intention of giving the woman a true cure. He opened a jar of thick, pale-green ointment and daubed a careful measure into the lid. From a pouch he took a small, reddish-brown leaf and crumbled it into power, smearing it into the ointment to form a paste. He then loosened his robes, showing a broad cloth belt around his waist, fitted with several loops to house some half-dozen crystal phials. Selecting one, he removed its tiny cork and shook several oily pink drops into the paste, blending it for a few moments.

Sivitri wiped at her pale, sweat-drenched face. She had neither risen nor retrieved her sword.

"Here," Toj said, extending the lid to her. He turned his face toward Conan, fixing him with a cold stare. "No man can defeat me in combat, Cimmerian. You would be a fool to attempt—ah, Bel!" He flinched in apparent pain.

Sivitri's hand had darted away from the lid, toward the hilt of the dagger that jutted from Toj's robes. She angled the blade into his breast, shoving hard so that its point pierced the cloth wrappings and shirt beneath, to slide into flesh.

Conan's jaw dropped in astonishment.

The assassin gurgled and toppled, clawing at the spreading stain that soaked his tunic. He froze instantly in that pose, the glaze of death in his eyes.

Sivitri withdrew her hand from Toj's robes, her fingers wrapped around the hilt of the assassin's Red Asp dagger. She spat into the mage's pale, still face. "Perhaps no *man* could have defeated you," she said, opening her other hand, which held the jar-lid that Toj had proffered. "But where a man fails, a woman may succeed." She dabbed her finger into the paste, lifted out the potion and swallowed it with a grimace.

"Good riddance," Conan grunted. He rolled Toj onto his back and knelt to feel his neck for a pulse. Scarcely had his fingers brushed the Turanian's skin when he snatched back his hand and mumbled an oath.

"The Red Asp's bite is that of icy death," Sivitri said, smacking her lips. "Had Toj not fallen for my ruse, it might have been you who felt its chilling effect. I know not how Toj came to possess it, for last I knew, the dagger had been stolen from a temple in Luxur and moved to a Messantian guild." She dropped the empty lid and rubbed at her temples.

Conan eyed the weapon suspiciously. "Luxur? No doubt a weapon of such unnatural potency is surely befouled with some Stygian death-spells," he said. "Well, it proved to be Toj's bane. At least we are free of him now! Yet still we must deal with the sorcerer—with daylight all but fled." Conan extended a hand to Sivitri. "Can you go on?"

Sivitri sighed as Conan pulled her to her feet, then she sank back to the sand. "Not yet," she winced. "By the morrow, I may recover, if that vile-tasting antidote subdues Toj's poison quickly enough."

"His plan might have worked," mused Conan. "That Red Asp—though as dangerous to wielder as to foe—seems a handy weapon for wizard-killing. I have half a mind to stick it into Thoth-Amon's gizzard."

"And if he slips away with the relic before we reach him, Conan—what then? I could not ride, with my head afire with fever."

"Crom, woman! With you it is always 'what if.' A man must do what his guts or his heart tell him to do, and consequences be damned! I'll not darken my thoughts with 'what ifs.' You rest here and recover," he said, bending down to take the rubiate dagger, "whilst I prove the worthiness of Toj's plan. I've a bargain to seal with you, and no Stygian swine can turn me away when a roomful of gold awaits me. There's a way to tell if Thoth-Amon still lurks within yon walls, or if naught but sand and bone haunt these ruins."

"No gold is worth dying for, Conan. And if the Stygian already has the statue, then Jade will never possess it."

"If there's dying to be done today, it's Thoth-Amon who will do it. Wait for me here until morning. And forget not the words of Caranthes, which may yet prove veritable. By sunrise, I'll be riding back to Saridis with you or I'll be in Hell!" As he spoke, he leapt into his saddle and guided his horse at full gallop toward the skeletons heaped in the shadows behind the white marble tower.

Eighteen
The Grim Grey God

Marble walls, bright as alabaster, pained Tevek's eyes as he looked upon them. The passing of centuries had not dulled their brilliance. In direct light, the inside of this temple would have burned his eyes. He had wound a strip of thin cloth around his head and cast forward his cowl to dull the whiteness. But he would have endured more to reach the prize that lay but a few paces away.

The Grim Grey God! An icy chill swept up Tevek's spine as the Jackal carefully brushed sand from the top of the pearl statue. When the Acheronian warriors had completed their labor, the necromancer had withdrawn his will from all of them except for the Jackal. Nearby stood the only other skeleton that Tevek had kept re-animated—that of the sole Nithian to hear his call and stir from the sands. He had again briefly probed the bones of six others, whose remains were scattered upon the floor before the god.

Only one of these retained any spiritual link with its corporeal form—and that one's skull was an arm's length from its neck. A strange calm radiated from it despite its apparently sudden and

183

violent death. Contact with the remnant's spirit had made Tevek queasy, and he had broken it off abruptly. Whatever happened here, in bygone centuries, was of secondary interest. The necromancer had but one priority: to retrieve the God-statue and set his plan into motion. Still, this calm Nithian would be important later. Blackblade had told him that the Nithian had been a lesser priest of Ibis, and as such, he would know three of the Grim Grey God's names. Tevek would learn those names from him soon enough.

From the arched hallway that led outside came a distant, repeated thumping. Someone approaching? No—not now! Tevek cursed softly and looked longingly at the strangely carved idol. "Wait," he said sternly to the Jackal. Then he returned his will to the dead warriors he had left sprawled outside the temple. Moments later, he was seeing through their hollow sockets.

A heavily muscled, bronze-skinned man was riding hard across the sloping dune. His sword bounced and swayed at his hip, and his jaw was set in a grim and determined expression. No desert raider, this. The man clearly knew what he was after. He had already reached the edge of the tower's shadow. The sweat-lathered horse galloped past the outermost bodies, apparently intent upon reaching the temple's gates—which had been reduced to rubble by a formidable battering ram.

The ram's immense head lay there still, a hunk of tarnished iron, shaped like the skull of a viper and attached to an iron spike that was as long as a man was tall. That spike had probably once been driven into the end of a heavy log, which in this dry waste would have crumbled to dust long ago. Tevek reasserted his will and bade four of his Acheronians to crawl stealthily toward it. The others he again awakened, commanding them to lie still—until the stranger should pass by them and fall into the trap that awaited him. This bothersome intruder would be dealt with in a short span.

Satisfied with his improvisation, Tevek measured the distance and waited impatiently.

Sivitri took a long drink from Toj's waterskin, deeming her own unsafe. She peered over the edge of the dune, into the dust that settled in the wake of Conan's steed. His courage impressed her as much as it infuriated her. He could be so bold, so honorable—and yet so coarse and callous.

Since her nightmarish youth, she had held men in utter disdain.

They were savage, egotistical creatures, and they had no use for women but slavery. Her pitiful father had permitted, nay, *condoned* some of the atrocities that the men of the palace had committed upon her body, and she had loathed him for it. Those sweaty, jeering faces still haunted her dreams at times, stirring the coals of hatred toward all males. Only by using men, by manipulating them, could she cool that heat and suppress the nightmares.

Why, then, had she given herself freely to this Cimmerian? Had this muscle-bound barbarian single-handedly unraveled a tapestry of bitterness that she had woven for nearly two decades? But she knew the answer, even as she posed the question: no. She had spent the night with him only to use him.

And in the end, he had proven no different than the others. He cared only for gold. Like all the beasts of his gender, he was incapable of love. And to think that she had almost stopped him from entering the ruins! There, the withering disease would seal his doom.

Almost. Almost had the strange Cimmerian awakened feelings in her that she thought had been forever banished. Was it the fever from Toj's poison then, that made her regret her decision to let him die? Conan had saved her freely enough—not just once, but even after she had treated him coldly. The night she had spent with him in the bath at Saridis lingered in her memory. Though his passion had been as fierce as that of a wild beast, he had not mauled or bruised her. She would never experience such a night again, for she had led him to his doom . . . all for the sake of power, to possess a talisman that would forever banish those loathsome, leering faces from her troubled sleep.

As she watched the Cimmerian's broad back, his black mane windswept behind him, she wished desperately that she could be Sivitri, the woman who loved Conan and would save him from the disease before it was too late. But she was not. Jade she was, the girl who had labored hard to master the sword, the girl whose blade had first tasted the blood of her cruel and sadistic father, a Zamorian prince, brother of Tiridates the king. Jade, the woman who had risen to a station above that of many kings—Jade, who kept her true identity hidden.

To those within her guilds, she was three other people. The woman Sivitri was one; the faceless, genderless Jade another; and when necessary, she disguised herself as a man. There were a host of others: in Messantia, Rubinia the barmaid; in Zingara, Isvara the seamstress; in Koth, Hypatia the baroness; in Nemedia, Sephir the palm-reader; in Aquilonia, Androclea the herb-merchant.

Jade she would always be. She could trust no man—not even one who had proven his reliability, like the assassin. He had lied to her about the map, forcing her to make use of the *kalb* beetle. Then, when she had later decided that she could afford no risk of failure or treachery, she had set out to follow Conan and pose as Kylanna, then as Sivitri.

Behind her, the body of Toj twitched ever so slightly. The unfocused stare shifted to the oblivious woman. The limbs were paralyzed, but the devious mind was in full motion. The woman's dagger-thrust had sunk to perhaps a finger's depth into his flesh, but it had missed his heart. The blade had pierced a bladder of that most precious of philters, the Golden Lotus. A misnomer, actually, for though its leaves were the xanthous hue of the finest Aquilonian coin, its nectar was as red as blood. Conan and the woman had doubtless mistaken it for such.

The Red Asp had surely frozen his heart for a span; there was a void in his memory where he had lost consciousness. But that scarlet nectar had seeped into the wound and gone to work swiftly, stanching the flow of blood, knitting the torn flesh, reviving his heart and warming the frozen veins within him. Soon his circulation would return, and with it, the power to deal death again. Of course, he would save that for the Cimmerian. He still needed Sivitri alive as hostage, and the false antidote he had given her would provide but a brief respite from the poison's symptoms. She would live long enough to buy him freedom from the *kalb* beetle. If only the Golden Lotus had power over that bothersome . . . *wait. Could it be?*

His thoughts paused for a moment as the realization struck him— the Red Asp had frozen him for a span; had it also frozen the beetle, perhaps destroying it? He focused on the area where the tickling sensations had plagued him, where the twinges of pain had begun to originate with worrisome frequency.

He felt nothing. True, he was numb from the cold still, but the warmth had returned first within his breast and from there, spread outward.

When he was no longer bound by that deadly affliction, he no longer needed Sivitri alive. With her back to him, she would be easy prey.

Toj's thoughts raced, jumbled by his brush with death. He decided that he would next slay the Cimmerian. Where the barbarian had gone, he could not recall. He had doubtless charged into the ruins to face the Stygian mage and retrieve the idol. Reckless nithing. If he somehow succeeded, he would return to the woman. Even if he did not come back, the withering disease would stay with him and send him to Hell.

Toj could not have foreseen a better outcome if he had schemed for days. He would in any case keep his appointment with Jade, but she would receive an unexpected surprise from the Guildmaster of Assassins.

A measure of feeling reached his arms and hands, and his fingers itched to wield the *shaken*. At this short range, he could throw them even from his awkward position without missing the mark.

Conan steered his mount cautiously through the slew of skeletal warriors, wary for any stirrings among them. He fully expected them to rise up and attack, but on horseback, he would have little difficulty charging past them. He intended to plunge straight through the building's broad opening and hurl the magicked dagger at Thoth-Amon before the Stygian could stop him. Failing that, he would see if his sword might deal a death-blow. Crom, a man could not cower forever in fear of the shadows of sorcery!

As he thundered past scores of sprawled remains, he spotted the huge battering ram lying before the crumbling ruins of a marble gate. Strange, that some of these warriors lay with their hands pinned beneath the ram.

He divined their purpose too late to check his headlong charge.

Four skeletons jerked suddenly to their feet and set the spike end of the battering ram's head to meet Conan's charge. He took the only way out—by leaping from the saddle.

The iron point grazed his side as he pitched from his saddle and thumped to the hard-packed sand. Startled, his horse veered away and missed impalement by a handsbreadth. Frantically trotting away, the beast crushed two skeletons beneath its hooves.

Scores of other skeletons rose like puppets on strings, jerking suddenly to their feet, swords and shields at ready.

"Crom's teeth!" Conan bellowed, forcing his bruised limbs to stand. He eyed the menacing horde warily, searching for the thinnest group. There would he strike in hopes of breaking through their mass.

187

Slowly they shuffled toward him, clumsy but minacious. Conan could hew them down by the dozens, but he reasoned that it would be harder work than a battle against foes of flesh and blood. He would have to behead them, and possibly cripple them as well. Were there but a few score of them, he would attempt it. But two hundred or so would wear him down; he would bleed and tire eventually while they hacked mindlessly.

Like well-drilled soldiers, they advanced in a formation, flanking him, offering no weak point to attack.

"Erlik blast your foul soul, Stygian!" Conan shouted. "Send a thousand of your mindless minions against me, and I'll still spit on your bloodied corpse ere the sun rises!"

With that, he filled the desert air with the hair-raising Cimmerian war-cry, and threw himself into the thick of the advancing army.

Stygian? Tevek raised an eyebrow. So this marauder must have known whom he followed into the ruins. Of course, that was of no consequence now. The necromancer gave his minions specific, if simple, orders and then entirely withdrew his vision from them. They would barricade the temple's doorway while surrounding the intruder. No mere swordsman could survive their onslaught. Without the smallest flicker of doubt, Tevek focused his attention entirely upon the overturned statue.

The Jackal lifted the curiously carved idol from the floor and hefted it. "Grrr—" came the scraping growl from the Acheronian's jawbone. "Urrrmmm. Rrreyg."

Tevek strode toward him and frowned. Speech—without necromantic aid? How could it be?

"Aaawd." The Jackal hoisted the god high above his shoulders, as if displaying a trophy. "Grrrimmm . . . Grrrey . . . God."

Through the broken roof, the deep hues of dusk cast dull, indigo shadows into the now-dim chamber. The necromancer unwound his gauzy blindfold and blinked, fascinated by the inexplicable sight before him.

"Grim Grrey God is . . . *mine!*" the Jackal grated.

Outside, the thin ribbon of the sun dipped below the horizon, further darkening the temple.

"The Grim Grey God is *mine!*"

"Incredible," mumbled Tevek as he gaped at the Jackal, who was no longer a thing of bone and sinew. Organs, muscle, and flesh now sheathed the huge frame, naked but for its breastplate and sword. His biceps rippled; in enormous hands he held the idol aloft. Ferocious, bloodshot eyes glowered from a ruddy, pockmarked face. Thick, brutish lips twisted into a hungry smile.

The necromancer cleared his throat. "Lay down the god and sleep," he said firmly.

The Jackal lowered the statue carefully to the floor, then rose to his full height and took a step toward Tevek.

"Sleep." Tevek repeated. "Sleep!" He then released the spectral cord that tied him to the dead one's spirit. He had not anticipated the strength of this one, the life-force that yet surged within those bones. Here was a rare phenomenon, one mentioned in only the most obscure and discredited of the ancient tomes. Of course! He had sensed that powerful aura when sweeping the sands and should have known it then—Blackblade was a *revenant*.

His spirit was possessed of such pure evil that it could, if disturbed or awakened, return for a time to its corporeal form and haunt the place of its death. The god-relic itself may have triggered the awakening, or it might have been Tevek's summons. He had sensed something powerful within this one, but the possibility that the Jackal might be a revenant had never occurred to him.

Tevek cursed his oversight. Revenants could be destroyed, but not controlled. Revenants crossed the border from death to life by sheer force of will—they regrew all the organs and flesh that they had possessed in life. Blackblade lived again.

Corded leg-muscles flexed, and knees bent. The giant Acheronian took another stride forward.

The necromancer swiftly gathered his will and let energy flow into him from the Black Ring. "Ereškigal, Lord of the Shadowrealm, take the soul of he who was named Dhurkhan—ahh!"

"Blackblade," croaked the deep, harsh voice. He gripped the hilt of his ponderous sword. Its point stood out an arm's length between the necromancer's shoulder blades. Thick, dark blood trickled down its dull length, spattering the floor with droplets and staining the scarred flesh of the huge hands.

Blackblade laughed, a sound like that of a rock-slide. Then he turned away from Tevek, as if the necromancer was unworthy of further attention. He kicked at the skull that had belonged to Solnarus, shattering it. Ivory shards scattered across the floor. "Where are your threats now, your cowardly tricks, your pitiful pleas to your frail and spineless god?" Another mocking laugh rang out across the chamber.

A moist wheeze issued from Tevek's throat, and he raised his hand to blast the Jackal with the Black Ring's full force. He channeled all the power he could muster, draining himself utterly, letting his ebbing life-force fill the ring.

Blackblade turned at the wheezing sound. He again drove his monstrous sword into Tevek, its edges scraping against Tevek's ribs. Then he jerked it free, stepped forward, and shoved the necromancer to the sand-covered floor.

Tevek fell with a solid, echoing thump. As he struck the floor, a long, trailing sigh escaped his lips, and he moved no more.

Conan held his formidable sword in a two-handed grip, swinging it as if he were a crazed woodcutter. Its keen edge sheared through brittle shields and awkward parries, through ribs and vertebrae. Twice he was nicked from behind, and he spun as he fought. It was as if he rode upon a madman's carousel of carnage, each slash threatening to upset his tenuous balance and hurl him to the ground, where the blades of his foes would sink into his vitals and send him howling to the pits of Hell.

A red mist swam in spiraling currents before him; the frenzy of battle boiled the blood in his veins and lent fury to his every stroke. For each spine he severed, he faced anew a slew of stabbing sword-points. He bled from a score of flesh wounds, the crimson flow mixing with the sweat that stung every cut, bringing pain that only further stoked the fire of his rage.

A warrior's blade slashed across his lower back, and he spun with a backhanded swing that scattered rib-bones and halved the assailant. The thing toppled backward, its arm chopping mindlessly into the air. Conan could only disable his skeletal foes; they never stopped twitching, and he took care where he stepped. Already his calves had taken the worst of it from downed opponents who simply kept hewing at him.

His backward swing spoiled his balance, and he twisted to recover, his knee bending sideways until he sprawled onto the hard iron of the battering ram's head.

He rose to his elbows, panting, shaking his head to clear the blood and sweat from his eyes.

A macabre scene spread out before him. Hundreds of spasming

skeletons, many still clenching swords, fumbled aimlessly in the sand and on the stone. Conan swallowed a lungful of air and dizzily stood, his heart pumping so violently that he thought it would burst.

Crom! That backstabbing soldier had been the last of them.

The Cimmerian paused to catch his breath and stretch his aching arms. He groped for the cloth sheath that held the Red Asp at his side, finding that it was still securely strapped there.

A grim smile creased his face.

He himself knew something of sorcery from past exploits, and he knew that spellcasters faced certain limits. Even Thoth-Amon must have expended considerable energy to coordinate that army. The Stygian might be in no better shape than Conan—perhaps he was fatigued enough to be vulnerable.

One throw. One good cast with the Red Asp was all he needed.

Conan rubbed his hands and the dagger's hilt with sand to clear them of slippery sweat and blood. Grim-faced, he proceeded into the near darkness of the corridor beyond the rubble of the marble door.

Tevek lay upon his back, his neck craned forward at a painful angle. He stared at the carmine blot that spread outward and soaked the breast of his dusty cloak. Time had slowed to a crawl; the Jackal seemed to move but a hair's breadth with the passing of every dozen labored beats of Tevek's slowing heart.

Then his heart pulsed once, weakly, and stopped.

A final exhalation escaped his lungs.

But his mind, though dark and cloudy, still lived.

I am slain, came the thought, moving slowly through mired awareness. All he could feel was the tingling of the Black Ring's energy within him, bound by the unspent willpower he had gathered before the Jackal's blade had pierced him.

He had the power within him, and he knew what to do.

Tevek Thul, I summon thee, his slurring spirit murmured to his motionless body.

His corpse obeyed; he explored it, able to command it as any other he had so often raised before. But he realized that he was blind and deaf. Further, his entire body lacked feeling; the sensation of touch had fled with death. He felt no pain from the gaping wound in his chest. At the same time, he realized that movement was more difficult without that feeling. He shook as if caught in the grip of a fever, and for a span he could do no more than twitch.

Soon, however, this awkward phase passed, and he attained a measure of control over his stiff muscles. His vision cleared somewhat, like the lifting of a fog, and he could see the slow-moving, hulking form of the Jackal a few paces distant.

Moments later, a strange exultation flooded through Tevek Thul's thoughts. He was dead; this much he knew, his body a lifeless chunk of flesh and inert organs. Decay would set in, leaving naught but the purity of bone. But his mind would endure; his essence, though perhaps dulled somewhat, would last forever, possessed of the same emotions he had felt before the Jackal had ended his physical life.

The prospect of immortality brought a renewed sense of purpose to him. He was now more capable than ever of enacting his plan of vengeance. There was much to consider, but he could see all sorts of possibilities. Unencumbered by the earthly bonds of flesh, he would be free to inflict centuries—*millennia*—of misery upon the mortals who writhed maggotlike in the world of the living.

Tevek's hearing began to return.

At first, only a discordant ringing filled his ears. Sounds were muted, as if they reached him from a great distance. Then, with sudden clarity, came fervent, almost inhuman, sounds.

The first three of the six words that comprised the true name of the relic had been spoken . . . by the Jackal!

Blackblade was summoning the Grim Grey God.

Jade's heart leapt into her throat when, in the distance, she saw Conan spring out of his saddle and narrowly avoid the iron spike leveled at him. She had been wrong to use the Cimmerian, but if she acted now, she might right that wrong. Steadying herself, she turned to pick up her sword and ride after the beset barbarian.

Jade gasped as she glanced at Toj's prone form, her hand flying to her face.

Toj—alive! His hand groped for something up his sleeve . . . but how? Between his fingers he held a thin, pointed piece of metal. She watched, frozen for a moment as his arm drew back.

The assassin sneered at her, flicking his wrist.

Before the blade left his fingers, there came a blinding flare of light from behind Jade. Its unbearable brilliance enveloped both thief and assassin.

The lethal missile furrowed Jade's throat, then soared past, its thrower's aim spoiled by the white flash.

Gurgling, Toj brought one hand to his eyes to shield them. His other hand took another *shaken* from his sleeve, and his arm was drawn back preparing to throw whenever his sight returned.

"You must not fail," tolled a voice behind Jade. There loomed the glowing apparition of Caranthes. From it radiated the unrelenting glare. "Let not the god's true name be spoken, or all is lost. I can project this image to Nithia, but all it can do is speak. Only you or Conan can bar the gates of Armageddon."

Jade cursed and lifted her thin-bladed sword.

Still blinded, the assassin hurled his *shaken* at the source of the oath. It clanged against the edge of her blade, striking sparks.

"Vermin," she hissed, muscles flexing as she swung her weapon like a headsman's ax. "May your foul soul sear in Hell with that of every wretch you ever murdered!"

Toj lifted his arm reflexively and tried desperately to roll away, but the icy grip of the Red Asp slowed him.

Jade's keen blade sheared through his forearm, lopping it off at the wrist. She drove the point downward with strength born of fury.

A howl of agony was torn from Toj's throat. His remaining hand seized the blade that transfixed his heart, but he did not feel its edge bite into his palm. All he knew was the pain of defeat, the pain of death that he had so often inflicted. None of his antidotes could save him.

His body convulsed once and was still.

"Hasten!" boomed the scintillating apparition. "Ride swiftly, for the true name is upon the lips of one who would speak it. You and Conan must silence the speaker. I cannot warn the Cimmerian, for the god radiates too strong an aura of Chaos for me to project my image inside the ruins. Go!"

Jade launched herself into the saddle, her fever forgotten. "Conan!" she cried, digging her boots into the flanks of her mount.

As she raced toward the marble walls, she saw that a swirling distortion had formed there, like the shadowy image of a cyclone, though no wind stirred the air. The sky itself seemed to tingle with dark energy that set her nerves on edge. Her horse dashed toward the heaps of splintered bone, toward the black maw of the temple into which Conan had disappeared.

"Now let the rest of the name be spoken." Blackblade's voice hammered the air, each syllable striking a deafening blow in the spacious temple. With his immane sword in one hand and the idol in the other, he poised statuelike in the temple, as if the work of a demented sculptor. *"Skaoa . . . Utlagi . . . Iolagi,"* he growled, his tongue stumbling over syllables no human throat was ever meant to utter again—the names Xaltotun had ripped from the throat of a tortured priest of Ibis, so long ago.

"Stay your sorcery, Thoth—Crom!" bellowed Conan as he burst into the inner sanctum. His eyes swept the scene. At his feet lay a crumpled, berobed shape, facedown on the floor. Before him stood a giant—a juggernaut in armor—who held aloft an incredible statue, a masterpiece of iridescent pearl. Whence came this titan . . . had he slain the great Thoth-Amon? Momentarily disoriented, Conan stood speechless, rooted in place.

"Eh?" Blackblade swiveled his red-rimmed eyes to stare with fury at he who had dared to interrupt him. Already, a strange swirl of darkness emanated from the statue, rising up and expanding as it surged through the broken roof. "You dare face *me*? Leave now or die, crushed like an insect beneath the heel of Dhurkhan Blackblade, mightiest warrior ever born!" He set down the pearl idol and charged forward, blade extended.

A chilling laugh rose from Conan's throat, and he lifted his sword in his right hand. "Many have made that claim, braggart. Join them all in Hell!" He gripped the Red Asp in his left hand and cocked it for a throw.

The crumpled form stirred at his feet, reaching forward, mumbling. Thoth-Amon—alive?

Conan saw the familiar copper ring, coiled around the finger of that groping hand. Not dead, it seemed. The Cimmerian could not risk a throw of the Asp. He plunged it into the back of the prone robed figure and bounded aside, out of the path of the onrushing giant.

Blackblade's first blow landed with a deafening clangor.

Conan nearly dropped his sword. The impact traveled through his arm to his shoulder and snapped his head backward. His blade snapped in half, the tempered steel slashing his face as it flew past him.

Recognizing that Blackblade relied entirely upon brute strength, Conan instantly changed tactics. He made a desperate parry, then lunged under the Acheronian's guard, prepared for Blackblade's savage riposte.

When the warlord's sword bore down on him, Conan threw himself to the floor. He felt a rush of air from the huge blade. His legs scissored out, knocking Blackblade off balance. The giant swayed; his knees buckled, but he managed to swing his sword as he toppled.

Conan grasped his hilt and tipped the blade's jagged end skyward, clinging to the grip with all his strength.

Blackblade fell full onto it, his own bulk punching it past his armor and driving it through his midriff. He grunted and sank to his knees, pinning Conan to the floor.

The Cimmerian twisted his blade and tried to rip it upward, but Blackblade let go of his sword and seized Conan's hands, pulling them from the hilt of the broken blade.

The huge Acheronian leered at Conan and yanked the length of steel from his own guts, laughing at the blood that sloshed onto his armor. He shifted his grip on the hilt and lifted the sword high, his arms rippling with layers of muscle, red foam flying from his lips. "So the flea can bite," he chuckled.

His arms came down.

Conan twisted aside and shot out his hands, grasping Blackblade's thick wrists. The jagged, blood-smeared blade-tip stopped a handspan from his eye.

Blackblade sneered and spat. He flexed biceps at thick as Conan's thighs and drove the sharp steel downward, slowly, pushing back the Cimmerian's arms.

Nineteen
Blood and Bone

Thoth-Amon felt the tremors of energy that emanated from within the ruined temple of Ibis. Like wrinkles in the very fabric of existence, they bespoke the awakening of the Chaos-God, imprisoned for eons, but stirring now to wakefulness. Had the true name been spoken already? Would the Grim Grey God appear and swallow this place in its voidlike maw? Not yet, he decided. But the key had been fitted in the lock of the god's prison, waiting only for someone to turn it. Tevek would doom them all, unless Thoth-Amon stopped him.

Slaying Tevek would not do—not yet. First he would recover his Black Ring from the necromancer. Then he would see if Tevek had learned the true name somehow, and if so, determine the means by which he had discovered it. When he knew what Tevek knew, he would finish the fool by abruptly snuffing the Taper of Death. Unfortunately, the translocation had drained his reserves of magical energy even more than he would have guessed. He could not risk a direct assault upon Tevek, not when the necromancer might turn the

Black Ring against him. Without his Black Ring, Thoth-Amon's options were limited.

The Stygian stooped upon the roof of the temple. His coal-black pupils scanned it briefly before he looked down, inside the building, to behold the scene within. The floor was too far away for him to jump. He peered at the berobed form crumpled upon the floor.

Tevek Thul! Unexpected was the sight of the necromancer lying still upon his belly, but more surprising still were the warriors who struggled, locked in combat, not three paces from the pearl idol.

The idol would not be easy to seize. He weighed the risk and decided he would first see if only these two brutes were present. If so, he could defeat them and take the stone. He peered at the larger of the two warriors, and a sudden shock of recognition paled his dusky face.

It was no ordinary warrior who fought within—neither of them were, he realized. The struggling duo were none other than Conan of Cimmeria, whose path—and purposes—had crossed his own more than once. The man had the devil's own luck. But more of a shock was the realization that Conan fought with a warrior who had been high of rank in the long-dead army of Acheron. There could be no mistaking the symbols emblazoned upon the backpiece of his armor—they were of the House of Ixion, father of Acheron's most insidious mage.

This was the warrior spoken of by Set—the warrior who possessed the full name of the Grim Grey God! Thoth-Amon knew then that he must destroy that warrior immediately. More than ever, he needed his Black Ring.

Thoth-Amon focused his thoughts inward and mumbled sibilant words in a rhythmic dirge. The spell would turn his physical form from solid flesh-and-bone into spectre. He would float through the hole in the roof, down to the floor, return to his corporeal form, and seize the ring.

Then he would blast the Acheronian warlord into oblivion and seize the pearl statue. Set would again be pleased with his chosen one.

When the last words of his chant faded, and he had completed his spectral transformation, a painfully bright glow lit the roof nearby. Thoth-Amon squinted into it, a bleak smile spreading across his thin lips.

"Caranthes, tender of bleating fools who debase themselves

before the lowest of long-vanquished deities. You are in water too deep for one who cannot swim, Caranthes!"

"You'll not have the god," replied the radiant apparition, no trace of fear in its dulcet voice. "You'll not unleash Chaos, degenerate one!"

"Drooling dotard! Father Set seeks order for the world, not Chaos."

"Spare me your lies." The apparition shook its head. "Only those of my priesthood know the god's name."

"Impotent Ibis-worshiper! The god has six names, only half of which are known to you. You were a fool to spiritwalk here, and leave your soul vulnerable to me. With the dark power granted me by Father Set, I shall seize the idol . . . and forever banish your essence into the blackest void!" As he spoke, Thoth-Amon stepped forward and extended his hands toward Caranthes, his fingers clenched like claws. From the palms sprang thin strands of green fire, like the fibers of a net.

Moments later, Caranthes' apparition was encircled by the strands. They squeezed inward, compressing the white aura.

Caranthes' image collapsed upon itself and winked out, to reappear a few paces away. "Your magic cannot deter me, Stygian," he said. "This time you have stuck out your scaly neck too far . . . feel now the holy fire of Ibis as it burns away your rancid soul!" The apparition's aura stretched and suddenly lashed out, like a tongue of white flame.

Thoth-Amon gestured hastily. A translucent green disc appeared in midair before him, barely deflecting the assault.

The duel raged on, while the strange, swirling effect expanded slowly outward, drawing nearer to the High Priest of Ibis and the Stygian Prince of Sorcerers.

Conan's muscles heaved until the tendons stood out ropelike on his massive biceps. In his fists he gripped Blackblade's thick forearms. Sweat and blood from the black-mailed behemoth dripped onto him as Blackblade shoved the broken sword closer and closer to Conan's face.

The Acheronian warlord laughed triumphantly. "Weak worm of a Northlander—I'll split your skull with your own blade ere I send you screaming to Gehanna!"

Reeling, blood coursing through his body like the rapids of a raging river, the Cimmerian shoved upward. He pitted his knotted thews against hie foeman's inhuman strength. From his bloodied lips came the Cimmerian war-cry, and with it, a burst of might welled from deep within him.

Blackblade's elbows bent backward, the snap of bone audible above his anguished yell.

Jade rushed into the chamber as the broken sword spun away. Several paces from her, Tevek was reaching around to tug the Red Asp from where it lodged in his back. "Conan—behind you!" she gasped.

The Cimmerian twisted his head around. "Crom!" He flailed with his fist at the lunging necromancer.

Blackblade picked up his huge sword and swung it.

The three combatants met at once, Conan's fist knocking Tevek's arm aside, into the path of the Acheronian's sword. Steel met flesh, slicing off half of the necromancer's hand, leaving only the thumb-stump attached. The detached chunk of flesh hit the floor, the Black Ring clinking against the marble.

Tevek, abruptly separated from the ring, felt his power diminish. His vision grew dark, his hearing faded. He groped for the severed member.

Conan saw the movement from the corner of his eye and kicked the hand away.

The necromancer trembled with a chill that seized every pore of his dead flesh, penetrating to the very marrow in his bones. He shook, losing control of his limbs, slumping to the marble but not seeing, hearing, or feeling the impact. *Death is so cold,* was his final thought, *so cold.*

Blackblade rose slowly to his feet, blood oozing from the hole in his midriff and spattering the floor in thick droplets. He limped toward the idol and cradled it in his dangling arms, swaying unsteadily.

Flashes of green and white, originating from the hole in the roof, illuminated the chamber.

"Thoth-Amon," growled Conan, staring upward.

"And Caranthes," panted Jade.

The Acheronian warlord chuckled, ignoring the spectacle.

The priest's apparition looked down upon them. "Nay! Take the god away from him, lest he utter more—" He stopped, winking out as green tendrils surrounded his alabaster aura.

"Crom and Mitra!" Conan grabbed Blackblade's sword, grunting with its weight, seemingly equal to that of a blacksmith's anvil. Wincing as he willed his strained, aching muscles to lift the immense blade, Conan heaved it into the air and managed a clumsy swing.

It bit into Blackblade's side, crunching through the breastplate. Red-slimed innards spilled onto the marble floor, and the Acheronian staggered. Stubbornly, he held onto the god and opened his mouth.

Conan forced his arms to lift the sword again, but they moved slowly, too slowly.

Swirls of shadow rose from the idol in whirling spirals, spinning outward and upward.

The Cimmerian felt invisible hands tug gently at him, as if trying to draw him into that spectral cyclone.

Above, Caranthes' apparition reappeared, this time less distinct and more ivory than white. "Flee!" he wailed. "Run for your lives, both of you!" He turned away from them and stared at the Stygian. "Thoth-Amon—we must destroy the idol together! Say the three names known to you, in reverse. Then I shall say mine!"

Thoth-Amon's clawlike fingers fired another burst of green strands. Thin and stunted, they traveled slowly through the shadow-filled air, clutching feebly at the ivory aura. But this time they slid away. "Speak your names first," he replied. "Then I shall say all six and destroy the god once and for all."

Conan struck again with Blackblade's sword. The giant's words turned to a grunt; he tottered but tenaciously clung to the idol.

The invisible pull became stronger, dragging Conan toward it and forcing him to drop the sword.

"Nay, you first, Stygian viper—" began Caranthes.

"Slack-witted sheep of Ibis—"

"Speak the name!" Jade shrieked. "Now!" She struggled to step away from the spinning disturbance that surrounded the pearl statue.

"Say it, by Crom!" Conan thundered.

"*Dreifa,*" Thoth-Amon muttered.

Conan wrenched his body from the air's binding grasp and dashed toward the temple's entrance.

Jade took hold of his brawny arm, running after him.

"*Avitun, Nauoga,*" continued the Stygian.

Conan and Jade ran through the corridor and out the crumbling door.

"Iolagi . . . "

Down the steps and past the heaps of bone, both into the saddle of Jade's steed.

"Utlagi . . . "

Galloping hooves, frustratingly slow-going even on the hard-packed sand.

"Skaoa!"

A low rumble shook the ground. The apparition of Caranthes flickered once and was gone.

Thoth-Amon's eyes narrowed. He floated down to the floor, toward the gory hand that lay there. He transformed again to flesh and blood, then tugged the Black Ring free. With a cry of exultation, he slid it around his finger. Thoth-Amon spared a final glance in the direction the Cimmerian had fled. "One day we shall meet again, dog!" he laughed. He would have given chase, but he had only just enough energy and time left to float to the roof and transport himself away. The barbarian was unimportant now anyway.

Moments later, Thoth-Amon disappeared in a flare of green fire.

Far away, from atop their horses, Conan and Jade watched in awe as the brass spire, the marble tower, the high walls—all bent inward, like wax melting in the hot sun. They swirled, mixing with the shadowy mist, which suddenly collapsed upon itself.

Of the temple, the tower, the spire and its occupants, naught remained but a chunk of white rock, nestled in the still sands of the Nithian desert.

Tevek's mind cleared. He knew instantly that he was no longer in the ruined temple. He had awakened in an unbearably bright place, and immediately he tried to close his eyes—but he could not. Lifting his good hand to shield his face, he saw that all of his flesh had fallen from him; only bone remained. He felt his head and realized that he had no eyelids—nor eyes. Only hollow sockets.

Human forms moved nearby in the searing whiteness, their somber faces somehow familiar. Yes, the people of the village—Kaetta. They clustered around him, pressing inward, trapping his arms, more and more of them, all those who had died in the massacre.

The brightness intensified as increasing numbers of his victims surrounded him.

He could not move, nor lift a hand to shield his eyes from the agonizing white fire that burned him, sending waves of wracking agony that crowded out any other awareness.

Tevek longed for the pain to diminish, but he knew it would not. A thing of bone and spirit was he, imprisoned in a Hell built by his necromancy.

Immortal.

Soundlessly, Tevek Thul screamed . . . and screamed.

And screamed.

Epilogue:
The Hawk

A warm tropical breeze stirred Conan's mane as he stared across the shimmering blue waters. "Crom, Rulvio, but it's good to be back among the dogs, with the wind at our back and the *Hawk* more seaworthy than ever."

"Aye, by Dagon's guts," Rulvio nodded, slamming his palm against Conan's broad, sun-bronzed back. He winked. "That be some treasure ye fetched up in the desert. Mayhap the lads would go afoot, were such bounty not so rare."

Sivitri had accepted Conan's offer to join him, for a time, aboard the *Hawk*. She stood at the rail, her generous charms revealed in her low-cut tunic and short breeks. A thin scimitar hung from her belt. She turned and shot a scolding look at Rulvio, tossing her hair back in defiance.

Conan grinned, rubbing his hands together. The stain from the Golden Lotus juice still lingered on his and Sivitri's fingers, where they had dipped into the last of the dead assassin's bladder of the precious nectar to rid themselves of the Nithian desert's wasting disease before its effects had begun to show. That same wondrous substance had also banished Toj's poisons from Sivitri's body.

"I see why you like the oceangoing life," mused the woman to Conan. " 'Tis freedom with not too steep a price."

The Cimmerian eyed her wolfishly. They had argued all the way from the Nithian desert to Saridis. There, they learned that Narsur had disappeared mysteriously, and with him had vanished the roomful of gold.

Sivitri had instead given Conan the huge amethysts from the door, appeasing his ire at the loss of the gold and softening his mood enough for another night in the citadel's baths. Conan grinned at the memory of the baths, and the nights they had enjoyed since then.

Wizards and bedeviled relics be damned! Better an honest rogue's life for him—fine wine in the hold, able-bodied lads in good spirits, cargo-laden merchant ships ripe for the plucking. At his side, a woman with beauty matched only by her passion, and adventure aplenty waiting in the waters ahead. Conan threw an arm around Sivitri and laughed gustily, watching the sun break across the ocean in a thousand dazzling hues.

TOR
BOOKS The Best in Fantasy

TOR
BOOKS The Best in Fantasy

TOR
fantasy

LORD OF CHAOS • Robert Jordan
Book Six of *The Wheel of Time*. "For those who like to keep themselves in a fantasy world, it's hard to beat the complex, detailed world created here....A great read."—*Locus*

WIZARD'S FIRST RULE • Terry Goodkind
"A wonderfully creative, seamless, and stirring epic fantasy debut."—*Kirkus Reviews*

SPEAR OF HEAVEN • Judith Tarr
"The kind of accomplished fantasy—featuring sound characterization, superior world-building, and more than competent prose—that has won Tarr a large audience."—*Booklist*

MEMORY AND DREAM • Charles de Lint
A major novel of art, magic, and transformation, by the modern master of urban fantasy.

NEVERNEVER • Will Shetterly
The sequel to *Elsewhere*. "With a single book, Will Shetterly has redrawn the boundaries of young adult fantasy. This is a remarkable work."—Bruce Coville

TALES FROM THE GREAT TURTLE • Edited by Piers Anthony and Richard Gilliam
"A tribute to the wealth of pre-Columbian history and lore."—*Library Journal*